DARK WINGS DARING

Dwain Cassady

Dwain Cassady: www.DwainWrites.com

Cover image by Brandi Doane McCann.
Author photo by Becky Frank.

This is a work of fiction. All names, characters, places, and companies are purely a product of the author's imagination or are used fictitiously. Any resemblance to any actual person, place, business, or event is purely coincidental with the exception that most of the places in Sitka, AK do exist. Please enjoy the read.

ISBN: Paperback: 978-1-7361395-2-3
      eBook: 978-1-7361395-3-0

ACKNOWLEDGMENTS

I am grateful to everyone who encouraged me along the way on this novel. While several people prodded me to write a sequel to Dark Wings Rising, Yvette Summerour planted the seed for the ending of the story. She along with Merilyn Guerry, B J Myers-Bradley, and Bob Thomason read through the manuscript and provided feedback that made it a better book. I appreciate all that you folks did! Merilyn's attention to detail and command of grammar amaze me. I would also like to thank Brandi Doane McCann for the cover design and Becky Hill Franks for the author photo. Their artistic skills and creativity are wonderful!

While the people and story are totally a product of my imagination, most of the buildings, street names, and locations are actual places in Sitka.

There are several websites that were essential to creating this story. I would be remiss not to mention them. First of all, you can find an account of the Tlingit creation story at www.indigenouspeople.net/creatlingit.htm. Below are some of the other sites I used:

www.sealaskaheritage.org/
www.everyculture.com/multi/Sr-Z/Tlingit.html
www.google.com/maps/place/Sitka,+AK
https://www.sitka.com/porky/porky.htm

Last, and most of all, I am grateful to you, the reader, for letting me share this story with you. If you would, please leave a review when you are done.

DARK WINGS DARING

CHAPTER 1

S unrise is supposed to bring peace and inspiration. Viviana stood on the rock outcropping just outside her cave, ran her fingers through her black hair, and watched the dark October sky turn a subtle pink, beginning to brighten. It would take more than a sunrise to quell the worry she was feeling today.

"You look tense," David McCutcheon said as he walked up to Viviana and put his arm around her shoulder. He could see the dawn reflecting in her raven eyes.

David's closeness did more to ease Viviana's stress than the sunrise. She leaned into him. "I don't see how we are going to make it," she sighed.

"What do you mean?"

"I don't think I can feed four people."

"You don't have to do it by yourself," David replied.

It had been only three weeks since David along with Sam and Evie Hanson had escaped from the MC2 compound, the headquarters of the giant energy conglomerate, with Viviana's help and the assistance of some crafty birds. Arnie Johnson and Christie Templeton had appeared that same day, having parachuted from a helicopter as the head of the militia made his exit from the compound. They had managed to expose how Mitch Carter, the owner of MC2, had been piling nuclear waste in an old coal mine in West Virginia.

Trained in survival by her dad when she was a child, Viviana had been living alone on the mountain for years, caring for herself successfully. Having so many mouths to feed weighed on her spirit.

Sam had managed to contact Christie's sister with his computer's satellite connection. They had hiked eight miles to rendezvous on a country road so Christie, Arnie, and baby Brittany could go with the sister and have more resources for caring for a one-year-old.

"I know everyone is willing to help, but it really all falls on me to figure out what to do. I'm not sure this area can sustain the four of us... At least the acorns are starting to fall," Viviana said with a sigh.

"You have a backpack on. Where are you going?" David asked.

"Actually, I'm back."

"What? What have you been up to?"

"I picked greens this morning."

"What do you mean you picked greens?"

Viviana removed her backpack and opened the zipper, showing David the pack stuffed with turnip greens.

"You went to the compound!" he nearly shouted.

A wave of crow calls came from the south. Rey, Viviana's self-appointed crow friend, cawed loudly and flew into the cave. Viviana and David raced right behind, pulling back a rhododendron branch to enter. Inside the narrow entrance, they stopped and listened. The soft whir of a drone passed by.

"A drone? What is a drone doing up here?" David asked.

"They are probably still hunting you! Will they ever give up?" Viviana said, even more exasperated.

"I guess a man like Mitch Carter doesn't give up easily. I wonder if they are still scouring the compound, too!" David said with a chuckle.

Viviana smacked him on the chest. "This is serious! They will kill us if the drone finds us. It is only a matter of time until one comes by when we are out gathering food or water."

Viviana led David on through the narrow entry way into the main part of the cave, a large vault that served as the common area.

Viviana had assigned bedrooms in different sections of the cave. "Grab the radio so we can hear the news." She looked over to see David rubbing his arm and trying to shoo Canto, the wren who had befriended him, away from twittering around his head. "What's wrong?"

"Nothing. Canto, behave yourself!"

"Canto says you are lying! What is wrong?"

"OK, I think the place where Evie cut out my ID chip has gotten infected. I didn't want to say anything."

Viviana ran over, "Let me see... Good grief! We need white oak bark," she muttered and headed toward the back of the cave. "Start a fire," she called back over her shoulder.

David had learned to obey when Viviana spoke. She definitely knew what she was doing in the forest. So instead of grabbing the hand-cranked radio, he laid the fire, using the magnesium that Viviana stored nearby to ignite it.

"What are you going to do with bark?" he asked when Viviana returned and began breaking the bark into her only cooking pot.

Viviana reached over and touched David's forehead. "You feel hot. First you are going to drink it, then we will use it as a poultice over the wound."

"I'm drinking bark?" David's brown eyes widened.

"I'll make a tea with it, Wordman," she said, using the nickname she had assigned to David after they met at a stream where he was always working on sermons. She ruffled his brown hair then poured water into the cooking pot. "Well?"

"Well, what?" David asked.

"The radio. I want to hear the news."

David retrieved and cranked the radio to charge it. The announcer's crackly voice came through.

"In today's top story, the Nuclear Regulatory Commission continues to monitor the Salty Ford nuclear dump site allegedly created by MC2. The NRC reported that they are continuing to weigh options for securing the site and for the cleanup procedure. The NRC cautions that an explosion is still possible, so the area remains closed. Mitch Carter, owner of MC2, continues to be unreachable and has neither admitted culpability nor offered to pay for the cleanup."

"I know where Carter is!" David piped up. "In the basement of his mansion he has tons of supplies, a satellite communication room, and I bet a lead lined room in the event of a nuclear explosion. He has been planning for the possibility that his storage site might blow up for who knows how long."

"Carter sounds like a fine piece of work!" Viviana said. She let the bark boil in the water for a while, then used a piece of cloth to filter the tea. "Here. Drink this," she said handing David the cup.

Viviana dumped the bark off the edge of the rock outcropping and returned to find David making an awful face.

"This is terrible! I'm sure one sip cured me."

"No. You have to drink all of it," she commanded and began breaking more bark into the pot.

"More?" David sounded terrified.

"This is for the poultice," she explained.

While Viviana was setting the pot on the fire, Evie and Sam emerged from their alcove in the cave.

"Good morning!" Evie chirped, her green eyes beaming as she smoothed her fiery red hair.

"What is that smell? I hope it's not breakfast!" Sam added, his black almond-shaped eyes searching for the source.

"It's my bark tea," David explained.

Sam ran fingers through his black hair and asked, "What did you do to deserve that?"

"David has an infection in his arm," Viviana said.

"A spoon full of sugar helps the medicine go down," Evie added. "It's a shame we don't have any sugar."

"Maybe this will help," Viviana said and planted a kiss on David's lips.

"Yep! That definitely helps," he said with a big grin.

Viviana pulled the pot from the fire and pulverized the bark. After it was cool enough to handle, she applied it right over the wound and wrapped it with a cloth to hold it in place. "Stay still while we fix breakfast," she ordered.

Viviana gathered what remained of last year's acorns and put Sam and Evie to work peeling off the cap and outer skin.

"I might as well get this over with," David said and gulped his tea. "Pass me some acorns."

"No, you have to keep your arm still," Viviana ordered as she brought a handful of huckleberries and put them to soak in water. Soon they would have breakfast.

CHAPTER 2

A loud snarl burst from the phone. "What do you mean, you lost them!" Mitch Carter yelled.

It was Wednesday evening, and Daniella Morrison, Chief of Security for MC2, had been dreading making this call. It had been an eventful day, culminating with her losing her cool and ordering the helicopter pilot to strafe the church with bullets in an attempt to bring an end to the hunt for Sam, Evie, and David. It was not a proud moment for Daniella.

She still could not believe she had lost three people, none of whom had any training in that type of operation, as far as she knew. She wasn't accustomed to losing, and she did not like it.

Gathering her gumption, Daniella responded to Carter's outburst. "We are continuing to search the compound and have drones patrolling the perimeter. I am confident we will locate them, sir."

"Daniella, you have security cameras all over the compound and razor wire fences surrounding it. How can you possibly not be able to locate these traitors?"

Daniella bristled at the controlled rage she sensed just under his words. "It appears that a huge flock of crows decided to sit on our security cameras right at the time the pursuit was happening. All of the cameras were blocked."

"Crows! You are blaming this on crows! Daniella, I thought more highly of you when I hired you. It looks like I will need to have a discussion with Zeke Starke about your future. Is he back yet?

"I haven't heard from him, sir."

"When you do, tell him I want to speak with him immediately. I'm not happy with his disappearing at such a critical time, either. And just in case they did get out of the compound, expand the drone search to the surrounding area."

"Yes, sir. We won't rest until they are apprehended," Daniella said, hoping the conversation was about over. Carter hung up without another word.

Daniella's anger rose to the surface, and she slammed her hand on the desk. She wasn't sure if she was angrier at Carter or at herself. She gave herself only a few seconds to vent, then called John, her second in command.

"John, I need you to deploy the armed drones in a search grid over a ten-mile radius from the compound."

"What if we locate them?"

"Engage immediately. We're not giving them any second chances," Daniella commanded with fury.

CHAPTER 3

Viviana handed off the two backpacks David had brought to her earlier and grabbed her bow and arrows. She looked up at Rey, "Help keep an eye out for danger, mi amigo."

"Why are you taking your arrows if we are just gathering acorns?" David asked.

"Insurance and opportunity," Viviana said.

Rey squawked and led the other birds, a bluebird, a tufted titmouse, and Canto out of the cave. Each bird had befriended one of the people and had helped in the escape from the compound. The four people followed the birds, and Viviana led them to a white oak grove. Viviana picked up a few acorns.

"These are the white oak acorns," she said, showing them a medium sized one. "These are the only ones we want because they are the least bitter. Make sure you leave at least half of the acorns in the area for the animals."

The four of them spread out and began gathering. David noticed that Viviana kept stopping and standing still, as though she were listening for something. Rey flew down and landed on her shoulder. Viviana glided silently away.

Wondering what she was doing, David resumed gathering acorns. Soon he heard the thwack of an arrow. Now, he was really curious. Following the direction Viviana had gone, he topped the hill to find her kneeling with her hand on the head of a dead deer. She seemed to be praying, her raven hair flowing over the deer's antlers. He stood silently, moved by the sight.

David was even more moved when Viviana looked up with tears streaming down her face. He rushed to her side. "What's wrong? Why are you crying?"

"He was an old deer with a broken leg. It always hurts to kill, though."

David couldn't help counting the points on the deer's rack: twelve. "But if he had a broken leg, you were putting him out of his misery. That was a kind thing."

David shuddered at the look Viviana gave him.

"It still hurts to take a life," she said. "This is one of God's creations."

David's heart did a flip. He had hunted deer and had always felt elation, a sense of power, at his kills. He saw in Viviana a connection to life that was deeper than anything he had ever imagined. Awe and inadequacy blocked any words, and he stood in silence.

"How did you know it was here?" David finally managed.

"You did not hear it?"

"No."

"Rey let me know that it needed…" Viviana stopped.

Following Viviana's eyes, David looked up to see Sam and Evie coming over the hill.

"What are you two…," Sam stopped when he saw the deer. "I see! Wow, that's a huge deer!" Sam and Evie hurried over. "It looks like we will be eating good tonight!" Sam added. "What can we do to help?"

"You three can go back to gathering acorns. I will dress the deer. I am very particular about how it is done," Viviana stated.

David started to argue that he had experience but stopped when he saw the resolute expression on Viviana's face. "OK, just let us know if you need anything," he said and resumed hunting acorns.

"Come. Let's get this to the cave," Viviana soon called.

David hurried over with Evie and Sam not far behind. Viviana had the meat laid out neatly on the skin.

"Now we can help! Can't we?" David said pleadingly.

Wiping her hunting knife with leaves and sheathing it, Viviana said, "Yes. You and Sam carry the deer. We go to a different cave to smoke the meat. Let's move before a drone comes."

They had walked about a quarter of a mile when David heard crow calls to the west. He cringed and looked to Viviana. She was scanning the area.

"This way!" Viviana commanded as she began to run.

David saw the rock overhang toward which she ran. He and Sam fell behind with the weight they carried, and the crow calls got closer and closer.

"Drop the deer!" Viviana shouted.

They obeyed and ran as fast as they could, getting to the overhang just as they heard the whir of the drone. David started to speak, but Viviana had her finger to her lips.

Instead of going on its way, the drone looped to the north and circled back around.

"Don't move," Viviana whispered. The drone came back and passed directly overhead. Then it moved on.

"Do you think they saw us?" Evie asked.

"I hope not!" Sam said.

"I think if they had seen us, the drone would have stayed in the area. Maybe it picked up the heat of the dear meat," Viviana offered.

"That was a bit too close for my taste!" David said.

When it seemed the drone wasn't coming back, Viviana said, "Let's try to get to the smoking cave."

As his eyes adjusted to the darkness of the tiny cave, David began to see small logs about two inches in diameter running across the cave at head height. To the side, there were huge piles of wood.

"We need green limbs about this big around," Viviana said making a circle about an inch in diameter. "And they need to have a fork in them." She found an example and showed it to the others. "We'll need fourteen of these," she said as she deftly broke the limb and finished hacking it off with her knife. She produced a y-shaped stick.

They quickly gathered the needed branches, and Viviana showed them how to bend and lash the tops of the y to make hooks on which to hang the meat. Choosing pieces of similar weight, Viviana hooked one to each end of the branch and hung it over the sapling logs at the top of the cave, which were slightly charred from previous fires.

"Do they ever catch on fire?" Evie asked.

"Sometimes the vines we lashed them with do. Every now and then a piece falls into the fire. It is smoked enough by then that I can wipe it off," Viviana explained.

"How did you learn to do all of this?" Sam asked.

"My dad taught me a lot. I worked out this smoking technique on my own."

David realized his heart was swelling with emotion. "You are one amazing woman!" he said and grabbed Viviana in a long hug.

"Hmm, hmm," Sam finally said. "I think we have work to do."

"You're right. This will be an all-nighter," Viviana said, pulling herself away.

CHAPTER 4

Viviana awoke feeling nervous. She could tell by the faint light entering the cave that dawn had arrived. She got up quickly to go check on Sam and the smoking process, taking her bow and arrows in case a bear came snooping and got aggressive.

The night before, Viviana had started smoking the deer meat as soon as it got dark in order to avoid any watchful eyes. They had enjoyed a feast straight off of the spit, and she had taught Sam how to manage the fire. David had volunteered, but she insisted he have more white oak tea and sleep because of his infection.

Walking toward the smoking cave, Viviana hoped Sam had succeeded. Their lives depended on having that meat. She arrived to find Sam asleep under a deer skin about thirty feet from the cave entrance. Viviana's panic quelled when she saw smoke seeping from the thatched door covering the entrance.

"Wake up sleepy head!" Viviana chirped, and Rey echoed with a caw. Wingston, the tufted titmouse, landed on Sam's chest and scolded like an angry squirrel.

"Gee thanks, Wingston! I was finally asleep."

"How did it go last night?"

"I kept the fire going just like you told me," Sam said.

"Great! The meat should be ready then," Viviana said as she pulled back the door of lashed limbs. Let's get it back home and have some breakfast!"

Viviana unrolled the deer skin and laid it out. Ducking into the cave, she brought out the branches and slid the meat onto the skin. Sam was up and helped. She rolled the deer skin up and tied off the two ends with the leg pieces.

"It looks like a big piece of candy!" Sam remarked.

Viviana hefted the hide into her arms and started for home.

"Let me help with that." Taking the hide Sam was surprised. "It's a lot lighter than yesterday!"

About halfway home, an unwelcome wave of crow calls began to flow up the mountain. "Oh no! There is no place to hide!" Viviana said. "Run to that big oak tree!"

Sam and Viviana ran to the tree and got on the side opposite the crow caws. Almost as soon as they were positioned, they heard the whir of a drone.

"This one is louder. It must be larger," Viviana whispered. She nudged Sam around the trunk of the tree, trying to keep the trunk directly between them and the drone. Almost as soon as the drone had passed, it began a loop and circled back.

"Keep going around the tree," Viviana whispered.

As the drone approached again, a gun began firing. Viviana grabbed Sam's arm. "Don't move!" The bullets blasted the ground and tree trunk as the drone flew slowly overhead. As soon as the bullets passed where they were standing, Viviana stepped out, nocked an arrow, and released. The arrow clipped a blade and sent the drone into a wild spin. It crashed into a tree and fell down the mountainside.

"They found us!" Viviana said, shaken.

"That was an amazing shot!" Sam replied. Viviana could see both fear and wonder in his eyes.

Wasting no time, Viviana ordered, "You take the deer, and I'll cover our tracks." They made their way back to the cave as quickly as they could.

Evie had a fire going and was brewing more white oak bark for David when Rey and Wingston burst into the cave just ahead of Sam and Viviana.

"You look like you've seen a ghost," Evie said to Sam.

"I almost was a ghost!" he replied.

"Oh no! What happened?"

"I lost an arrow," Viviana groaned.

"We were on our way back with the meat when a drone found us and fired on us. Viviana shot it down!" Sam explained.

"We have about an hour before they can get a search party up here. I imagine there are more drones already on their way. We have to get that fire out. Spread out the wood and cover it with dirt," Viviana ordered. She poured the tea for David and set the bark to cool.

"I can't wait," David said taking the tea from Viviana. This being his third dose, he just let it cool and then chugged it down to get it over with.

"I covered our tracks on the way. I think our best option is to stay put in the cave. If anyone needs to use the bathroom, you had better hurry!" Viviana said. Sam and Evie hustled out and back.

An awkward silence fell over the group. Viviana finally spoke up, "Someone needs to ask the question: Now what?"

"I've been thinking. We need a plan," Sam said. "But before we come up with a plan, we need to generate some options." He looked around the cave.

"What are you looking for?" Evie asked.

"Something to write on," Sam said sheepishly. "If my computer's battery weren't dead, we could use it. I guess we'll just have to remember our options. Everyone, list out any possibilities you can think of for getting out of this mess."

"The obvious option is to just stay in the cave till the search is over," David offered.

"But if they have kept the drones searching for three weeks, how long will they keep looking now that they have discovered where we are?" Evie responded.

Viviana closed her eyes and listened to the banter as she searched her heart for a solution.

"You're right. We could be here for weeks." Sam added.

"How will we know when it is safe to go out of the cave?" David asked.

"We won't." Sam said. "We will just have to take our chances when the time seems right."

Sadness settled into Viviana's heart as she realized what had to happen. She tried to hide the tear that leaked out, wiping it quickly.

"What's wrong?" David asked, having caught her.

"You will have to leave. This place will never be safe again."

"Don't you mean 'we' will have to leave?" David asked, making air quotes.

"How can I leave my home? How can I leave the animals?"

Rey squawked as if understanding and flew down to Viviana's shoulder. She rubbed her hand over his head and scratched his neck. The other three birds flew and landed on their friends' shoulders.

Viviana saw a tear working down David's cheek. "It looks like tears are contagious."

David scooted close to Viviana and put his arm around her. "Whither thou goest, I will go; and whither thou lodgest, I will lodge."

Viviana was confused by David's strange English. She cocked her head, looked him in the eye, and said, "What?"

"I'm staying with you or going with you. Wherever you are, I will be."

Viviana grabbed David in a hug and didn't let go. Her heart was racing. She felt such a strong connection with him, something she had not had since her father died. In fact, she had never felt anything like this. Home, David, danger, stay, go all swirled in her heart and mind. Her world seemed to be falling apart and piecing itself back together in the same instant.

David pulled away from the hug and got on one knee. "I don't have a ring for the occasion, but I do know that I love you, Viviana. I have loved you from the moment I first saw you by the stream. Will you marry me?"

Viviana's heart split in two. One part longed to say, "Yes." The other part screamed, "No! No! No!" Time froze. She could bear the tension no longer and bolted to the back alcove of the cave.

David looked at Sam and Evie.

"I would have said, 'Yes' to that," Sam offered.

After a moment of silence, David got up and followed Viviana. He found her pacing and muttering in rapid-fire Spanish. David stood waiting.

She stopped, looked David in the eye, and said, "Yes."

"Yes? You mean you will marry me?" David said uncertainly.

"Yes."

"Are you sure?"

"I would not have said it if I wasn't sure. My heart says that is what I want to do. My head says, 'How can this happen?' I used to dream of my wedding day when I was a child in Mexico. But after losing my dad and coming out here, I put the idea away. After meeting you, I didn't dare let the dream come back."

David rushed to Viviana and held her close. Viviana felt his warmth, and her heart relaxed and began to piece itself back together.

Cozy in David's embrace, Viviana suddenly jumped.

"What is it?"

"A helicopter! Don't you hear it?"

CHAPTER 5

Viviana raced back to the main vault of the cave to find Sam and Evie wide-eyed. The sound of the helicopter gradually increased in volume but stayed a good distance away.

"Why would they send out a helicopter when they have drones," Sam wondered aloud, feeling a sense of dread. Everyone was silent. The answer that came to Sam spooked him even more.

"What if they suspect we are in a cave and have brought ground-penetrating radar?"

"She said, 'Yes!'" David said with a big grin.

"Yay!" Evie responded and jumped up to congratulate them. "I think you will make a great team!"

"Congratulations," Sam said. "But you may not get a chance to have a wedding if we don't come up with an exit strategy."

The foursome sat back down to ponder possibilities.

"I'm thinking that we need to get farther away than we can go by foot," Sam said.

"That is true, but I don't think our birds can carry us," David said.

"If only we could contact someone to pick us up like we did for Christie and Arnie," Evie added.

"Maybe we could sneak into the compound and steal a helicopter," David offered.

"I'm afraid not," Viviana replied. "They have gotten wise to the crows covering the surveillance cameras. They sent out a security team when the crows blocked their view yesterday morning. I had to leave in a hurry."

"You went to the compound!" Evie exclaimed.

"She picked turnip greens," David scolded.

"We needed some green vegetables," Viviana said defensively.

Sam's eyes moved around the cave while the others voiced possibilities. He spotted the hand-cranked radio. "Your radio doesn't transmit, does it?"

"No, it's just a receiver," Viviana answered.

A dejected silence hovered while Sam continued to stare at the radio. An idea formed, and he smiled. "That just might work!"

"What might work?" Evie asked, sounding a bit annoyed.

"What if I cut the cord coming from the power generator and hook it to my computer charger? We might get enough of a charge to contact someone," Sam said with hope building.

"And if not, my radio is ruined?" Viviana asked.

"Possibly," Sam replied.

"Whom could we call?" David asked.

"Arnie and Christie would probably come back for us," Evie offered.

Sam suddenly stood up, "What if we get even farther away? I could contact Dad, and he could pick us up in his plane!"

"Um, I don't think there are any landing strips nearby," David pointed out. "Except in the compound."

"That would be suicide," Evie said.

"You are right," Sam replied. "We will have to find another landing site."

Sam started toward the radio but stopped, "Are you OK with my destroying your radio?"

"I don't see any other choice," Viviana agreed.

Picking up the radio, Sam said, "While I tinker with this, someone needs to fix something to eat."

"You are always thinking of food," Evie scolded.

"We need to stay ahead of the hunger in case we find ourselves without food for a long time," Sam explained.

"He is right," Viviana said. "Let's have deer and greens."

Sam set about cutting and splicing wires while Viviana, David, and Evie tore the greens into a salad and carved up some of the smoked meat. With the wires spliced, Sam began cranking. He cranked and cranked while the others ate.

David finished quickly and came to relieve Sam. During the transfer, while the crank was quiet, Viviana said, "Wait," holding her hand up. "The helicopter is getting closer."

"I had better crank like a wild man!" David said and lit into his job.

Sam wolfed down his food, then went to see if the computer would boot up. Nerves tense, he pushed the power button. The screen lit, and the solid-state computer was up and ready in seconds.

"Wow! It worked!" Sam said, not believing his eyes. Sam unplugged the computer and went close to the entrance of the cave, making sure he couldn't be seen. He established a satellite connection and opened the email program. He decided to send the email to his dad, mother, and grandfather to increase the chances that it would be seen immediately.

Sam typed, "We are in trouble. The compound is closing in on us, and we need to get out of here. I will relay our current coordinates and be searching for a possible landing site. Would you please fly down and get us? Thanks, Sam."

Sam hit send, then pulled up the coordinates of his current location. He copied these into a new email and sent it. Finally, he began a search for possible landing sites.

Evie, David, and Viviana hovered to see the screen. Evie gasped when the "Low Battery" warning flashed.

"Great!" Sam said. "At least we are making progress." He went back into the cave, plugged in the computer, and resumed cranking.

"Sam, I hate to state the obvious, but why don't you move the radio to the cave entrance?" Evie said.

Sam's cheeks reddened. "Why didn't I think of that?"

David grabbed the radio and followed Sam to the entrance of the cave. With the thump of the helicopter in the background, Sam reconnected while David cranked.

Sam pulled up a satellite image of the area centered on the coordinates of their current location. All he could see was Crow

Mountain. He began to zoom out. The MC2 compound came into view along with other mountains and wilderness.

"The closest air strip is at the compound," David said.

"I don't think that's an option," Evie scolded.

Sam kept zooming out. He began to feel discouraged as he realized just how isolated they were. "I wonder if Carter built his compound in the middle of nowhere to keep anyone from seeing what he was doing with the radioactive waste," he groaned.

"This is getting us nowhere. Let me try this," Sam added, opening the search engine and typing "air strips near me." "How are you doing with the cranking, David?" he added.

"My hand is getting dizzy, but other than that OK."

"We can help when you get tired," Viviana pointed out.

Suddenly all four birds burst into the cave at full speed.

"Shhh," Viviana whispered. "Stop cranking."

Rey made a quiet caw. Viviana put her finger to her lips and motioned everyone to come away from the cave entrance. She crept silently back to the opening and lay prone to peek out. She could see an MC2 bonfire red cap moving about fifty yards down the mountain.

With the thump of the helicopter covering her sound, Viviana walked back to the others. "There is a security guard about fifty yards west of us. The search party is here already."

Rey, Azul, Canto, and Wingston flew silently out of the cave. Viviana got her bow, nocked an arrow, and sat facing the cave entrance.

"Now what?" David asked.

"We wait," Viviana said. "Wait and hope they don't find us."

"And pack," Evie added standing up. "We need to be ready to go in a hurry."

Sam and David stood to load backpacks.

"No, you crank, Sam. I'll pack," Evie ordered. He knew she was right and knelt by the radio, pouring his nervous energy into the activity.

CHAPTER 6

Time crawled, weighed down by the angst of waiting and wondering. Evie carefully loaded two backpacks with what she thought would be essentials, making sure to leave room for food and water. She counted the marks she had made on the wall of the cave since they had been there. Twenty-two.

"I have learned a lot in twenty-two days," she thought and reflected on what she now knew about the things she could and couldn't eat, how to build a fire, even things as simple as using the bathroom. "Life here is all about the things that matter: food, water, warmth. I was looking forward to Viviana teaching me how to make a deerskin dress." Living on the mountain suited her artistic spirit, and Evie had wished on more than one occasion that she had materials for painting. A shower might be nice, but an oppressive weight had left her spirit now that she was out of the compound.

She walked back into the main part of the cave and found that David had relieved Sam of cranking. She stopped in her tracks and said, "Listen. Do you hear that?"

"Hear what?" Sam asked.

"The helicopter is gone."

"You're right!"

"Wait, is that good news or bad news? Do you think they located us?" David said stopping the crank.

Viviana, who had stood to stretch her legs, held a finger to her lips. "We need to be quiet. The helicopter will no longer cover our voices," she whispered.

"I hope it has just gone back to refuel," David whispered, and Evie could hear his stress.

No one said anything for a while, and the silence increased Evie's angst. She began searching for something to do in her mind.

"Sam, why don't you try to find a landing site, again?" Evie whispered.

Everyone looked at Viviana, and she nodded her head, "Yes," then held up a hand for Sam to wait. She commando crawled to the entrance and peered out.

"I don't see anyone now. Just don't get too close to the entrance," she whispered, staying where she was.

Sam sat down far enough from the entrance not to be seen and woke up the computer. He saw an email notification from his dad.

Evie knelt beside him and peered at the screen. "Hi, Son. The plane is being fueled, and I will be ready to leave in a few minutes. Your grandfather will radio the details to me. My search showed the closest landing option to be the interstate, which is about fifteen miles west of you. It will take me about twenty hours to make the trip with refueling and a nap, making my ETA at 11:00am tomorrow. Here are my proposed landing coordinates."

Evie saw the string of numbers that followed. "He's going to land on the interstate! That's crazy!"

"You're right. Let me see if I can find a better option," Sam whispered and entered, "landing strips near me," into the search engine again. The MC2 jetport was the first on the list. Second was Lexington at twenty-five miles away.

Sam clicked on it. The website showed that it was closed due to disrepair.

"It looks like Dad did his research," Sam said. "Twenty hours. Does anyone know what time it is?"

"3:15," David whispered back.

"So, he did mean 11:00 our time," Sam whispered with his mind turning. "How long will it take us to walk fifteen miles? Seven or eight hours?"

Viviana nearly laughed and put her hand over her mouth to stifle it. "If it were a straight shot on a nice trail, we could do that. There is no telling how many detours we will have to take or how far we will actually have to walk."

"We can't leave now! It's too dangerous," Evie pointed out.

"Evie is right. I don't think we dare leave till night," Viviana added. "And traveling at night through mountains we don't know will take even longer."

Wingston gave a short scratchy chirp that sounded like a scold.

"I know we have you, my friends. And you are all valiant. But you don't know where we are going," Evie whispered.

Wingston flicked his wings and scolded again, so very quietly.

Evie threw up her hand and put a finger to her lips. Then they heard footsteps on the path just below. Evie froze and realized she was hardly breathing. Viviana silently nocked an arrow.

The footsteps continued past, and Evie took a deep breath. Everyone sat silently, and Evie could see shock on each face. The scare sent a shiver through her own heart, too. "That was way too close," she thought, but didn't dare speak. Evie was feeling trapped. The cave suddenly felt like a prison.

Evie noticed a subtle change in David's face out of the corner of her eye, and it drew her attention back to him. "Is he really smiling?" she thought. Looking more closely, she realized that David looked pleased.

Lost in wondering what David was thinking, Evie jumped when Rey suddenly flew out of the cave. A few seconds later she heard what sounded like someone climbing the cliff from the path below.

Viviana made a sign of drinking and eating, then putting it in a bag. Sam shut down the computer, and Evie, David, and Sam grabbed food and water and stuffed it into the backpacks as quietly as they could.

They heard a slip followed by curses. Evie stopped and listened while Sam put the computer in its bag. The climbing resumed. Evie could hear the man getting closer to the top. Viviana stood with her arrow aimed at the entrance of the cave.

An explosion of crow caws filled the air. Evie heard a scream and a thud. A moment later, Rey flew back in the cave cawing urgently. Viviana crawled to the entrance and peeked out. She crawled out of the cave far enough to see over the edge of the cliff, then silently came back in.

"The crows apparently knocked the security guard off the cliff. He looks unconscious. I think Rey says we have to leave."

"What is this?" David said bending down to pick up an electronic device. "It's the guard's radio! Way to go, Rey!"

"Report in, Mike," the radio suddenly squawked. David jumped and almost dropped it.

Viviana put her finger to her lips and pointed to the back of the cave, where she slept. David put the radio under her bedding.

Evie could see Viviana concentrating and waited as patiently as she could.

"There is another cave about a mile and a half east of here. I think that is our best bet. I just hope I can find it again," Viviana said. "Let's go. Keep silent and listen for drones."

"And watch the birds," Viviana added, amazed at their cleverness.

CHAPTER 7

Viviana looked around the cave while everyone donned backpacks. A wave of grief washed over her as she realized this might be the last time she ever saw her home. She wasn't even sure how many years she had lived here, but it was home. She stuffed a few herbs into her pack and stuffed her grief. She motioned for the other three to wait.

Viviana crawled out to the edge of the cliff to confirm that the guard was still unconscious. She looked around to make sure no other security guards were in sight then motioned for the others to come. Evie, Sam, and David scurried down the cliff, using rhododendron trunks as a ladder. Viviana followed.

On her way down, she noticed the guard's revolver wedged in a rhododendron branch and grabbed it. At the bottom, she handed it to David.

"We may need this," she said.

David checked the safety and wedged it into the back of his pants.

Viviana set a quick pace, heading south along the same trail by which they had arrived at her cave a little over three weeks ago. Viviana's nerves were taut. Knowing how vulnerable they were, she picked up the pace to a trot.

After about a quarter of a mile, Viviana led the crew off the trail to the east. She whipped out her knife and whacked a branch off a tree. Sending the others on, she carefully covered their tracks for about a hundred feet. Their four bird friends easily kept pace with them.

Viviana realized that David, Sam, and Evie made a lot of noise hustling through the forest. "There is nothing I can do about that now. I should have been training them for something like this," she thought with regret. Pushing on seemed better than stealth at this point, so Viviana kept her pace.

As they topped the ridge, Rey gave a warning caw and suddenly flew southwest. Viviana held up a hand to stop the group. After a few seconds they could hear the whir of a drone.

"Run!" Viviana commanded and took off at full speed. The sight she saw looking back over her shoulder caused her to stop dead in her tracks. In the distance, she could see Rey flying straight at the drone. He flipped and latched onto its underside. Viviana was mesmerized. The others couldn't take their eyes off Rey, either.

Finally, Viviana recovered and said, "Rey is blocking the drone's camera! Let's go!"

Resuming the run, Viviana led the way to where she thought the other cave would be. She stopped, feeling puzzled. Looking around, she did not see any signs of it.

"I need a minute to get my bearings," Viviana said. She studied the mountain, remembering that the cave was somewhere on this downhill slope. She remembered a stream nearby, which is one of the reasons she had considered it as a possible home. But she didn't see signs of a stream anywhere.

A shrill chirp pierced the air, and Viviana looked up to see Canto flicking his wings. As soon as she saw him, he flew off.

"Canto wants us to follow him," David said with certainty.

They ran with Canto flying from branch to branch ahead. He led them straight to a cave. It wasn't the one that Viviana had in mind, but it would certainly do. Wingston flew in right behind them.

They huffed and puffed to catch their breath. The cave was small compared to Viviana's home, but it was deep enough for them not to be seen from the entrance.

"I hope Rey is OK," Evie said.

"Me, too," Viviana replied.

"I can't believe he landed on the belly of that drone!" Sam said.

The crew became silent, and Viviana worried about Rey while she tried to plan their next move.

"We will need water soon," she noted. "If they find the cave, they will know we have fled. Then, they will widen the search. If they don't find the cave, I think we are safe here."

Rey fluttered into the cave just behind Azul, and everyone greeted the hero.

"Way to go, Rey!" David said and scratched behind his head.

When the excitement settled down, Evie said, "David, what were you grinning about before we left the cave?"

"I know how we can get to the interstate," David said, grinning again.

Viviana tried not to let her skepticism show when she asked, "And how is that?"

"We go down to the road leading from the compound tonight and hijack a truck in the morning."

"What?" all three said together.

"What truck driver could resist stopping for a beauty like Viviana or Evie who was wounded on the side of the road?"

"Are you crazy? We can't hijack a truck!" Sam said.

"Why not?" David replied. "They are already trying to kill us. Hijacking a truck will just inconvenience the driver for a few hours."

"And by the time they find the truck, we will be long gone," Evie said. "I think it might work!"

"But that is right back near the compound," Sam objected.

"They are concentrating their search near the cave. I don't think they will expect us to be on the road near the compound. It's like running toward the helicopter, Sam," David countered.

Viviana pondered David's idea while they argued back and forth, weighing the chance of succeeding with hijacking a truck against trying to hike in the dark in unknown territory. She noticed Sam's eyes light up when David mentioned running toward the helicopter.

"That did work out, didn't it," Sam said, remembering their escape from the compound.

"I think we have to chance it if we are going to meet up with your dad and get out of here," Evie replied.

Viviana realized they had stopped talking and were looking at her. The decision crystalized in her mind, and she said, "David's idea is better than trying to find our way there on foot in the dark. I just hope a truck comes along in time!"

CHAPTER 8

The darkness of the cave was soothing to Sam. Wrapped in the shroud of earth and rock, he felt safe from prying eyes. He could hear more than see David and Viviana sitting close and leaning into each other.

"I am glad you said, 'Yes,'" David whispered.

"Me, too," Viviana whispered back.

"I hope you won't miss the cave too much."

"I believe there are points in life when it is time to move on and go a different direction. I think this is one of those points for me. I am ready for a new future, as long as it includes you."

Sam found Evie's hand and squeezed it. She squeezed back, then Sam jumped.

"Oh! I have to email Grandpa!"

Sam fumbled the computer out of its bag and booted it up. Working as fast as he could to conserve what little power was left he typed, "We will be there. We may miss the coordinates a bit but will relay our exact location when we arrive. Powering down to conserve battery."

Sam closed the laptop and drifted off into thought, "This has been a tough couple of days. I'll be glad when we get to Sitka and can relax. I am not surprised any more at what these birds can do. They are really smart. The birds..."

"The birds!" Sam almost shouted, startling the others. "What about the birds?"

Viviana lifted her arm, and Rey flew over and landed on it. "My friend Rey will be fine. He can certainly take care of himself. But I will sorely miss you."

Rey squawked and turned his back.

"I'm afraid it will be time to say, 'Goodbye,' my friend. You have helped me so much. I will never forget you," Viviana said and wiped away a tear.

"These birds have saved our lives," Evie offered. She held up her arm, and Azul flew over.

"Let's not say, 'Goodbye,' too quickly. We may need them tomorrow," David said.

"Speaking of tomorrow, we need a plan," Sam said. "I wonder how long it will take us to get to the road?"

"We are on the eastern slope of the mountain," Viviana answered. "It's at least two hours, maybe two and a half, to get to the compound. We could get to the road east of the compound quicker."

"I think we should be at the road by sunrise. We may have to wait a while, but we could find a place to hide," Sam said.

"Oh! There is an old logging road that leads off the mountain. It's the one Zeke Starke used when bringing Brittany out to shoot her," Viviana remembered. "That will be an easier hike. I would still allow an hour and a half, though."

"OK. What do we do when a truck comes?" Sam asked.

"I think we have Evie or Viviana lying on the side of the road like she is dead or injured. When the driver stops to see what is wrong, we surprise him with the gun. Or her if the driver is a woman," David said.

"Then we hop in the truck and take off! I think it will work," Sam said.

"What about the driver?" Evie asked.

"Evie's right. If we leave the driver, he could call for help. If we take him with us, what will we do with him?" Viviana wondered.

"I think we have to take the driver with us," David said.

"I think we leave the driver on the side of the road with no phone or radio," Viviana said.

"But, he could just walk back to the compound and get help," David pointed out.

"If we take him with us, he will know where we have gone," Viviana observed. "We will be five or six miles from the compound. Getting back will take a while."

David started to object but realized she was right.

"With the head start, we should be able to get all the way to the interstate before the compound is alerted," Evie added.

Sam yawned and realized he was having trouble keeping his eyes open. "That sounds like a plan. I think I need some sleep."

The force of being up most of the night tending the meat and the stress of the day washed over Sam. The sun had sunk to twilight.

"I agree. We should sleep and get up to go around three," Viviana said.

"Let's eat a bite first," David suggested and pulled some deer meat out of his pack.

Viviana stood up, "Hand me your water bottles."

"Why?" David asked.

"I am going for water. We're about out," Viviana said.

"I'll go with you," David said.

"No. It's safer if just one goes. I can be quiet," Viviana said in a tone that left no room for protest. Viviana emptied her backpack and put only the empty water bottles in it. She held the last one up and said, "Rey?"

Rey led the way out of the cave, and Viviana followed.

Sam, David, and Evie anxiously chewed on deer meat while awaiting Viviana's return. Sam grew more and more sleepy while he ate. Finally, he lay down and drifted off.

"Sam. Sam, it's time to go. Wake up!"

Sam heard Evie's voice and slowly awoke. As it dawned on him where he was and what was about to happen, a jolt of adrenaline brought him fully awake.

"Wow! I was sleeping hard!" Sam said.

"We know," Viviana replied. "We kept hearing you mutter in your sleep."

"You were saying something about a storm coming," Evie explained.

"Oh yeah. I had a dream that we were at Viviana and David's wedding. We were on the beach, and I could see storm clouds building out over the ocean. They were menacing and kept getting closer. Nobody else at the wedding seemed to notice. The ceremony just kept going. Then you woke me up."

"Dream time is over," Viviana stated. "We have a hike to make. Backpacks on. David, keep the gun ready."

David pulled on his pack and pulled the Glock from his waistband.

Sam realized he was feeling excited rather than afraid, which surprised him.

"OK, everybody. I should have taught you this a long time ago. Listen to how to fox-walk in the woods. You put the outside of the ball of your foot down first, roll onto the ball of the foot, then come down with the heel. Try walking in place. Ready, set, go. Outside ball of the foot, roll onto the ball, then heel. Outside, ball, heel. Outside, ball, heel. We want to be as quiet as we can. They may have night search parties out," Viviana finished her short course.

CHAPTER 9

Viviana led them out into the cold October night. A full moon floated toward the west. Sam watched as Viviana eyed the sky before setting off toward the south. He saw the shadows of four birds heading in the same direction.

Sam tried to remember the fox walk. His first few steps were awkward. Then he seemed to find a rhythm with his knees a little bent. "I'm quieter than I thought I could be," he thought.

After a few minutes, the undergrowth became thick. Sam blocked his face with his arms and got caught on a few briars. He wanted to ask if Evie was doing OK but knew he couldn't risk it.

The undergrowth thinned out. Viviana stopped and held up her hand. Everyone stopped in their tracks. Sam almost didn't breathe. He could hear something moving down the mountain to their left.

"It's just a bear," Viviana whispered.

"Just a bear!" Sam thought as his heart quickened.

Viviana waited a bit then resumed the march.

After a few more battles with dense underbrush and a steep downhill walk, Sam's feet landed on something level and clear. Viviana turned right and followed this path, and Sam realized they were on the logging road. Since Viviana was making no sound, Sam continued his fox walk. "This is starting to feel natural," he thought.

Though the road was filled with ruts and large rocks, the walking was easier than in the woods. They made good time. "I wonder if they found the cave," Sam thought.

The moon hovered just over the horizon when Sam spotted the soft gleam of solar panels reflecting in the gray ribbon of asphalt. The road was just ahead. Viviana led them off to the right where there was a ring of rocks perfect for sitting. She stood still and appeared to be listening. Sam heard the flutter of bird wings, and Rey gave a calm caw.

Sam thought that meant that there were no security guards nearby but watched Viviana for confirmation. She sat down and whispered, "Rey says we are safe. I guess now we wait."

"Wait and finish our plan," Sam said. "We still don't know how we are going to stop the truck, or car, or whatever comes by."

"I think Evie should lie on the side of the road like she is injured," David said. "When the driver stops, I will sneak up on him with the gun, then we'll take the truck."

"You guys realize this is illegal, don't you," Viviana warned.

"Trying to kill us is illegal, too," Evie answered. "I don't have any problems with it."

"Me either," David said.

"If the pastor is OK with it, then I think we're good," Sam chuckled.

"But, we are wrong," Evie said. "It needs to be Viviana on the side of the road. And she needs the gun."

"Why? If she has her bow and I have the gun, the driver is more likely to surrender," David countered.

"If the driver recognizes me, he might call the compound before getting out of the truck."

"You are right," Viviana said. "Good thinking! Is anyone good with a bow?"

"I wouldn't say I'm good at it, but I took an archery class in college," Sam said.

"I used to bow hunt," David offered.

"Do you think you could shoot the driver if necessary?" Viviana asked.

David was quiet a minute. "No. I don't think I could."

"Sam?"

Sam's insides knotted up. He wanted to say, "Yes," but he pictured himself actually shooting the driver. He wasn't sure, so he said, "Maybe?"

"Great!" Viviana said.

"It won't come to that," Evie said.

Sam knew that tone. It was the one Evie used when she knew something, and she was always right.

"If Evie says that we won't have to shoot the driver, then I am sure she is right," Sam said. "I'm sure I can look menacing."

"How can you know that we won't have to shoot?" Viviana asked.

"Sometimes things just come to me, and I know," Evie tried to explain.

"All I can say is that I have learned to trust her," Sam said. "The first day we came to the compound, she said, 'This is a dark place,' while we pulled through the check point. She is always right."

Faint light began to peek in the east. "Let's look for a good place to pull off our hijack," Viviana said.

The four of them walked to the road, turned west, and looked up and down. Viviana scouted and found a mountain laurel thicket on the north side of the road. If she positioned herself a little east, then Sam would be shielded by the truck as he sneaked up on the guard, assuming the vehicle came from the direction of the compound.

Viviana led them up and behind the laurels.

"I wonder how long we will have to wait," David said.

"I don't know," Viviana said. "When the driver is on the other side of the truck and you can't see him, slip out and come around the back side, Sam. David and Evie, you wait until we signal you."

"OK," all three said at the same time.

Viviana went back to the road and east about a hundred feet. Sam watched as she sat down. "I wonder what the driver will think about a woman dressed in deerskin on the side of the road. You don't see that every day!"

Almost immediately, they heard a vehicle coming. Viviana started to lie down when all four birds came screaming with alarm calls. Viviana jumped up and ran into the woods.

An MC2 jeep with four security guards passed and turned up the old logging road. After it was out of sight, Viviana came back out and made a show of wiping her forehead and shaking off the sweat. David chuckled. Viviana sat back down and resumed the wait.

It was nearly an hour before they heard the tires of an electric truck coming. Sam's nerves tensed as he watched Viviana lie down. She sprawled on her stomach, facing the ditch with the gun underneath.

"She looks like she's been hit by a car," Sam thought. He nocked his arrow and got ready. A box truck came around the curve, and the brakes squealed as it began to slow.

"It's action time!" David whispered.

Sam's guts tightened even more. The truck came to a stop with Viviana still in front of it. Sam watched as the driver hesitated, seeming unsure of getting out. Finally the driver opened the door. He looked tense, and Sam thought the driver might be afraid he was going to find a dead body.

As soon as the driver was out of sight around the truck, Sam slipped out of the thicket as quietly as he could. He rounded the back of the truck with arrow drawn to find Viviana, gun pointed at the driver and receiving his phone. His revolver was lying on the ground.

"I'm sorry, but we are going to borrow your truck," Viviana was saying.

Sam motioned for the others to come. He opened the back of the truck since there was room for only two in the front. They had not discussed it, but David went to the driver's seat. Sam crawled up into the back.

"I think we have to bring him with us," Evie said. "There might be another security team on the way."

"You're the ones the security guards are looking for!" The driver said.

"Shut up and get in," Viviana commanded and handed the driver's revolver up to Sam. "Shoot him if he even thinks about resisting."

The driver climbed into the back of the truck. Sam noticed that he was wearing an MC2 militia uniform and seemed very calm. He was tall, fit, and appeared to be in his late forties. He had short curly black hair and deep brown eyes.

"Sit down," Sam said trying to sound menacing and pointing to a place on the bed near the cargo pallet.

The driver obeyed, saying, "You realize that you are heroes, don't you? Well, you're heroes to everyone but Mitch Carter and his cronies. The whole compound is talking about what you did. It's even on TV news."

"So far that hasn't helped us any," Sam said. "We are still running for our lives. What are you hauling today?"

"I have no idea. They told me it was secret and to just deliver it."

Sam flipped on the cargo light. A jolt hit his nerves when he saw the trefoil radioactive warning symbol. "Is this what I think it is?" Sam demanded pointing the gun at the driver.

"I told you, I don't know what is in there. They just told me to deliver it to this place in West Virginia."

"Guys, we have to go!" Evie urged.

Sam reached to pull down the door. A flurry of wings filled the doorway as Canto, Azul, Wingston, and Rey flew in.

"I guess they are coming along!" Sam said and pulled down the door. "I hope you enjoy the ride."

CHAPTER 10

The truck lurched forward, and Sam crashed to the floor, dropping the revolver. It slid right to the driver. Sam froze face down on his belly as fear flooded every cell in his body.

The driver slowly picked up the revolver. Sam eyed him as he pushed himself into a sitting position. "He looks too calm," Sam thought.

The driver looked the gun over, then slid it back to Sam. "I'm glad you have the safety on. You realize that we are all going to die if whatever is in that crate is not insulated well enough," he said. "By the way, I am James. James Carson."

Sam was stunned but picked up the gun. "Hey, James. I'm Sam. And this is Evie," he managed, shocked that James gave the gun back to him.

"I know. Your pictures are posted all over the compound."

Sam stared, speechless. He glanced over at Evie, and she was smiling. He looked back at James and then Evie. "What are you smiling about?"

"Don't you see? He is on our side."

"What?"

"So what do you plan to do with me?" James asked.

"To be honest, I have no idea," Sam said. "Why doesn't he seem worried?" he thought. Then, "Aren't you worried we might kill you?"

"Not you two. Now, that odd woman in the deerskin dress is another matter. Ex-Navy SEAL here. I know how to assess dangerous situations."

"What do you think we should do with you?" Evie chimed in.

"First, we need to get the driver's attention. Maybe there is a Geiger counter in the truck we can use to find out how much radiation we are being exposed to."

Sam still had trouble believing this surreal situation. In a fog, he got up, squeezed around the crate, and banged on the front wall of the truck. Nothing happened, so he banged harder. Sam leaned against the wall as the truck slowed.

Once it stopped, Sam squeezed back around the crate and waited for the door to open. Nothing happened. Sam looked at James, "Don't try to escape. I still have the gun."

"I wouldn't even consider it," James replied with a smile.

Sam tried to lift the door, but it was latched. Finally, he heard the latch open, and the door raised six inches.

"What is it?" David asked sounding leery.

"There is a crate of radioactive material back here," Sam said as he pulled the door open. No one was there. Puzzled, Sam looked at Evie and then James.

"They think I might have overpowered you and taken the gun. Hop out so they know it's OK," James said.

"That does make sense," Evie offered.

Sam hopped down from the truck. "It's OK. Everything is under control."

Viviana stepped from behind a tree, arrow nocked.

"There is something radioactive in the truck. James suggested we look for a Geiger counter to see if it is safe to be back here," Sam repeated.

Viviana closed the distance to the truck in a trot. "OK. David, check the cab for something to measure radiation," she said with her arrow trained on James.

"Look, lady, I'm on your side. Apparently I have been duped into hauling more of Carter's radioactive waste. Now that the delivery is botched, or at least I assume it is, I will be a liability. How do you think my future with MC2 looks?"

"You may be right, but I don't trust easily. You will have to earn it," Viviana replied not lowering her arrow.

"Do you think you could hit me if I ran?" James asked.

"Yes."

"I believe you. So I'm staying put. Just don't get any ideas that you need to kill me, OK?"

"We'll see," Viviana replied.

David came back with a box with buttons and dials. "Does anyone know how to work this thing?"

James held out a hand, "I'm detailed to the nuclear plant. Or at least I was."

He turned on the device and began studying the dial. "Looks good from here." Climbing into the truck, he held the Geiger counter directly over the crate, which had four birds sitting on it. Rey squawked a protest.

"Wow! They actually sealed this like they are supposed to. It is safe to be back here. What's with these birds?"

"It's a long story," Sam said, checking his watch. "It's 8:49. We have a little over two hours till rendezvous. I think it will only take us about forty-five minutes to get to the interstate. Any ideas how we kill that extra hour?"

"Please don't use the word 'kill,'" James said with a smile.

"It looks like we need to spend part of the time trying to figure out what to do with this guy," Viviana said.

"Oh, I'm James, by the way. It's nice to meet you."

"Viviana," she said, eyes squinted.

"And I'm David."

"Well, now that we are all introduced, what do we do next?" Evie asked. "James, what do you want us to do with you?"

"We're not far from the logging road. He could easily go back from here," Viviana pointed out.

"I think you should take me with you," James said.

"You are not in a position to be offering suggestions," Viviana snapped.

"Well, you are the ones that got me in this position. I will at best be fired from MC2. Possibly eliminated as a liability. I think you owe me something that gives me a fighting chance," James argued.

David shrugged his shoulders. Sam looked at Evie.

"He's right," Evie said. "We do owe him something. I sense that we can trust him."

"But we can't take him with us! We're going to," David was cut off in the middle with Viviana's hand over his mouth.

"We are trying to get away from this mess, not invite it to follow us!" Viviana scolded.

"We could drop you in a small town between here and the interstate," Sam offered.

"Then he could just call and let MC2 know where we are," Viviana observed.

"Speaking of calling, could I have my phone back?" James asked.

"It's in the woods on the side of the road," Viviana explained.

"That was smart. You're a crafty one!" James replied.

"I think we should put him out before we get to the next town. It will take him long enough to get to a place to call for help that we should be gone," Viviana offered.

"You'd just leave me on the side of the road to die of thirst and hunger," James asked.

"You look resourceful. You'd survive," Viviana replied.

"But I don't have anyone to call," James said looking concerned for the first time. "I don't have any family. My parents and brother died of hunger. I only escaped by joining the navy. My only friends are at MC2."

"I think we have to take him with us," David said. "We can't just leave him."

Sam looked at Evie, who nodded "Yes." He saw from the frown on Viviana's face that she still wasn't convinced.

"I think I agree with David and Evie," Sam said.

"I hope I don't have to say, 'I told you so,'" Viviana said.

"If James was going to West Virginia, then we need to go north on the interstate. I'm sure MC2 is tracking this truck. Do you think you can find it, David?" Sam asked.

"Sure. It's that way," David replied pointing west.

"So where are we going?" James asked.

"What do you think of Alaska?" Sam said.

CHAPTER 11

David turned onto Hwy. 501, following the old sign that said Buena Vista was to the right. After several miles, David noticed the beginnings of a small town.

"Buena Vista," he said reading the sign, which had let loose and was hanging sideways. Viviana seemed tense sitting across the truck.

"Are you OK?" he asked.

"I don't like having an extra person with us. Who knows what he might do? He might try to let MC2 know where we have gone."

"At least he doesn't have a cell phone anymore," David said.

"He was a Navy SEAL. He will be able to figure out a way to do what he needs to do."

"He might be of help to us then."

"Why would we need help? We will be in Alaska soon."

"You're right. Why would he want to go to Alaska?" David asked, beginning to understand Viviana's consternation.

They fell silent as the main part of town came into view. An old restaurant on the right that looked like a long brick house had a hole in the sign by the road, making it look like "ODD'S BARBECUE." A couple of the windows were broken out. A little girl, gaunt and dressed in rags, stared as they drove by.

David couldn't believe his eyes as they passed house after house and building after building that looked desolate. Occasionally a desperate looking person peeked out a broken door or stood in a weedy parking lot. There were several spots that had greens growing in yards.

Coming to a fork in the road, David went right.

"I think you should have gone left," Viviana said.

"Oops. You are probably right. But this is still going in the right general direction."

David spotted two or three dozen people gathered around an inviting three-story brick building. It appeared the doors had been painted green a long time ago and were barely hanging on their hinges. As he got closer, David noticed many of the people had books. A number of people meandered in the street, too, so David slowed down.

"I wonder what this is about?" David mused.

"They stare like they have never seen a truck before," Viviana observed.

The people in the road seemed to forget to move, and he stopped the truck.

"They all look so…"

"Haggard and hungry," David finished Viviana's sentence.

The people in the road finally inched to the side, and David pulled forward. At the corner just past the next building, David stopped.

"What are you doing?" Viviana asked.

"They are hungry, can't you see?"

"I see, but why do you stop? We need to go."

I am going to share our deer meat with them."

"What? We don't have enough to feed that crowd!"

"A little is better than nothing," David said, and opened the door.

"What if they mob us and take the truck?" Viviana scolded, getting out with her bow.

"What are you doing with your bow drawn?" David said as he met Viviana at the back of the truck.

"I don't trust James," she said. "Or these people."

David lifted the door.

"What's up?" Sam asked.

"Look at these people," David said and watched as Sam and Evie's mouths dropped open. James just looked sad.

"This looks just like where my family died. Just a different town," James said.

"I want to give them our deer meat," David said.

"You are right! They need it worse than we do," Evie responded.

Sam nodded, "Yes."

A woman walked toward the truck. Viviana spun her arrow from James toward the woman, who stopped.

"Relax! They aren't going to hurt us. Put your arrow down," David said.

"How do you know?" Viviana asked.

"Look at her face."

Viviana did, then lowered her arrow. The woman advanced and asked, "What do you want?"

"You look hungry. We don't have much but would like to give you what we have." David explained.

Sam began opening backpacks and pulling out smoked deer meat.

"So this is the town gathering place," David observed.

"It is the old library. We borrow the books for reading and teaching our children," she explained.

"Will this meat lead to fights?" James asked.

"No. We are all poor. We share. We don't have the energy to fight."

Several children came running up and a few more adults cautiously approached. David handed over the meat to the adults. David noticed the first woman counting.

"There are twenty-seven of us," she called out.

"Do you need water?" Evie asked.

"No, the river gives us plenty of water," she replied. "Thank you so much. You have saved some lives today, at least for a little while."

David choked up, but managed, "I wish we could do more."

"I hate to say it, but every stop this truck makes will look suspicious to MC2. I am sure Carter is having it tracked," James said.

"You are right. We need to get going," Sam said.

"No, we need to disable the tracking device," Viviana replied. She went to the front of the truck and opened the hood. Too short to see in, Viviana climbed up the bumper and onto the frame. Looking around the computer apparatus, she located the GPS tracking device.

As she reached to pull it off, Sam said, "Wait! How much time do we have?"

"It looks like an hour and fifteen minutes," David responded.

"Let's drive fifteen minutes in the opposite direction to throw them off track and then pull it off," Sam suggested.

"Brilliant," David added.

"That is a clever idea," James said. "But I would only go five minutes. If they discover I'm going the wrong way and can't reach me by phone, they will send out an Apache. I doubt they will bother stopping the truck to ask what happened."

David came to a large intersection and veered right, knowing the interstate was to the left. They passed the remains of a college campus and came to a bridge over a small river.

"Stop!" Viviana shouted.

David braked and pulled to the side of the road just past the bridge.

"Let's throw it into the river," Viviana said. "If it floats, maybe they will think you took a wrong turn and have turned around."

"That's part of why I love you," David said. "You are beautiful and brilliant!"

Viviana climbed back onto the truck and pulled out the tracker, unplugging its battery connection. David lifted the back gate as Viviana walked to the middle of the bridge.

"She's throwing it in the river?" James asked.

"Yep. If it floats, it will look like you are headed back in the right direction since the river sort of follows the road," David said.

"I wish we had a map," Sam said.

"I'm sure the interstate is that way," David said, pointing west.

"Why don't we pull over under a bridge where the interstate crosses until it's time," Evie suggested.

"Great idea!" Sam said.

"It might work better if we drive as far away as we can get," James said. "If they search, they will begin wherever the tracker ends up. We might be spotted when we get on the road." "He's right," Evie said when she was interrupted by a shrill chirp from Canto and a squawk by Rey.

Everyone looked at the birds, and Viviana said, "Helicopter! Everyone in the truck!"

CHAPTER 12

David pulled the truck onto the road. "Where do we go?" he said as he continued east.

"There!" Viviana said, pointing to a gravel road that turned off to the left.

"There?" David said as he slowed to make the turn.

"Yes. It goes under the cover of trees. With the leaves turning to their fall colors, maybe they won't notice this bright red truck."

The road led into the deep shade of a dense forest. David rolled down his window to listen for the helicopter. "I don't guess it has to be an MC2 chopper," he said.

"Yeah, right," Viviana countered.

The helicopter was noticeably closer. David stopped.

"It sounds like it is at the bridge," Viviana said.

"We just had to hijack an illegal shipment!" David said.

"Just listen," Viviana said.

The helicopter seemed to pause for a bit and then headed back west. David pushed the accelerator and zoomed down the road.

"At least we seem to be going in the right direction," he said as the road bumped along in a generally northwest direction. "I bet they're having fun in the back!"

"Maybe you should slow down," Viviana suggested.

David tried to hit the brakes for a series of rough ruts. Too late. He hit the first one too fast. The truck bounced and careened to the left, right into a tree.

David looked at Viviana, whose eyes were wide.

"Can you back up?" she asked.

David put it in reverse, but the wheels spun. "We're stuck."

"We'd better check on Evie and Sam," Viviana said and flew out of the truck. David followed.

As Viviana slung the door up, David could hear the chatter of birds. Canto flew right in his face, wings fluttering, and chirping shrilly. Then he landed on David's head.

"What are you doing?" David asked.

"I don't think he likes your driving!" Sam said. "I can't say I'm a big fan right now, either."

"I was ambushed by a rut," David started to explain. All four birds sounded alarm calls and flew down the road.

"The helicopter is coming back," Viviana said. "We need to hide. Grab the packs and run!"

Viviana took off in the direction the birds had flown. About a tenth of a mile down the road, Rey cawed from the top of a rhododendron thicket. Viviana motioned for everyone to climb in underneath the dense cover. David was the last one in and could hear the helicopter coming nearer.

It seemed to be following the road down which they had driven. It passed directly overhead and circled back.

"I think the pilot spotted the truck," David said as it seemed to hover in that location. As soon as David got his words out, the truck exploded. A rush of wind and heat knocked him from his squatting position.

"Wow! We're lucky you wrecked!" James said.

"They just blew up radioactive waste! We had better get out of here in a hurry!" Sam said.

He started to move out of the thicket, but Viviana grabbed him. "Wait. Let the helicopter leave first."

"Are the birds OK?" Evie asked.

All four landed on the road in front of the thicket as if to say, "Present and accounted for."

The helicopter flew south in the direction of MC2.

"It looks like the pilot decided the mission was accomplished," James said.

"Apparently Carter considers you expendable. Let's go," Sam said as he crawled out of the thicket.

"This road seems to be headed in the right direction," David said. "Maybe we should follow it." David looked at his watch, "We have forty-five minutes to get there. I hope we can make it." He noticed Viviana studying the sky.

"Get where?" James asked.

"Let's move!" Viviana said and set off at trot.

David was surprised by her sudden move, but quickly followed. The other three joined the pace.

"This is really nice," David said as he jogged beside Viviana, almost forgetting that he was running for his life. The hardwood trees with the beginnings of fall coloring shaded the road with patches of deep shadow and stretches of dappled sunlight. The birds flew from branch to branch just ahead.

"Does anyone care to explain what the plan is?" James asked. "Inquiring minds need to know!"

"My dad is picking us up on the interstate," Sam said. We are supposed to meet him at 11:00. I need to relay our coordinates to him, so he knows exactly where we are."

"Thanks," James said. "Now I know why we're in such a hurry."

After about twenty-five minutes, David was huffing and puffing. Viviana stopped and pointed ahead. The trees stopped at an intersection where the road they were on ended. Past it was a steep bank.

"Could that be it?" Evie asked.

Sam leaned over and grabbed his knees, trying to breathe. "Why aren't you out of breath?" he asked Evie.

"That was just a walk in the park," she said.

Evie pointed to where she could see the top of a truck going by. "We made it. Now what?"

Careful not to come out from under the trees, Sam looked around. To the right the new road went uphill until it was nearly level with the interstate.

"I say we go right, get under that tree by the interstate, and let Dad know where we are," Sam said.

Sam led the way up road. Near the top of the hill, he turned toward the interstate, climbed the fence, scrambled up a six-foot bank, and knelt under a large oak tree. He booted up the computer and eyed the battery: 19%.

"Guys, I hate to say it, but that looks like an MC2 truck coming," James said. "Nothing else could be that bright red!"

David saw the sun reflecting off of the truck down the road.

"Back down the bank!" Viviana ordered, and everyone scampered back toward the fence and crouched.

Sam rushed his fingers to find the GPS coordinates and emailed them to his grandfather. "Mission accomplished!" he said as the battery warning light flashed at fifteen per cent.

"Maybe we should just wait down here, out of sight," Evie offered.

"That's a good idea," David said.

"What if we miss him when he drives by?" James asked.

"There is no way we will miss him," Sam replied.

"I hear a plane," Evie said, scanning the sky. "Could that be him?" she said, pointing to the west.

"He's picking us up in a plane! Are you crazy?" James said.

"It was Dad's idea," Sam said as he climbed back up the bank. The others followed.

"This is going to be so cool!" David said. "I wish I had my phone so I could video it."

As the plane approached, the fivesome began to wave their arms to attract his attention. The plane flew right at them, dipped a wing in greeting, and then banked south.

"I'm glad there is not much traffic out," Sam said.

"The interstate is mostly used for truck traffic now." James said. "Hardly anyone travels by car anymore. But I have read that the interstates used to be packed with cars."

David noticed Viviana looking nervous. "You have been awfully quiet. What's wrong?"

"I can't believe this is really happening," she said.

"I know! It's going to be amazing to see a plane land on the expressway."

"No, I can't believe I am really leaving,"

"Oh. I'm sorry. I promise I will take care of you," David said.

Viviana leaned into him for a hug. "I've never been on a plane before, either."

"It will be fun! You'll love it!" David replied.

They both watched as the sky-blue plane lined up with the interstate and came in for a landing. It stopped right in front of them, and Sam ran forward to open the door.

"Anyone need a taxi?" Kat Hanson, Sam's dad, called. Kat was built somewhat like a grizzly bear, thick and strong. His long black hair, pulled back into a traditional ponytail, was greying around the temples.

"You are a sight for sore eyes!" Sam said as he stood back to usher the others in. Evie climbed in followed by Viviana. Then the cabin flooded with fluttering wings, caws, and chirps.

"What the! Hey! Get out of here!" Kat yelled.

"It's OK. These are our bird friends. They have saved our lives numerous times," Evie explained.

"I see. I'll have to charge you double for the extra passengers," he said with a smile.

"EAGLE VIEW TOURS," David read aloud, noticing the side of the plane painted with mountains, clouds, and a lone eagle soaring.

"Better hurry," James said. "Here comes a truck."

David hopped in, James followed, then Sam hustled in. The Cassio Ultra single prop was quiet as it idled on the expressway. When Kat throttled up, the hybrid engine came alive, and the plane surged forward, throwing Sam into Viviana's lap.

"Quit that! David is watching!" Sam teased as he pulled himself up and sat by Evie.

David craned his neck to try to see behind the plane.

"Don't worry, the truck will slow down," Kat said. "It's not every day you come upon a plane taking off on the interstate!"

The plane lifted off the ground and climbed skyward.

"I think you're cutting off my circulation," David said once he noticed the vice grip Viviana had on his arm. Looking over, he saw her eyes were closed.

"I didn't think you were afraid of anything!" David said. "Look out the window. This is the best part!"

Viviana took a peek and relaxed her grip. David watched her face more than the scene below. A wonderful, deep warmth flooded his heart.

CHAPTER 13

Once Kat leveled the plane at its cruising altitude, Sam moved up front next to him.

"What's with these birds?" Kat asked.

"To be honest, I have no idea. They just showed up and adopted us. They helped us escape the compound and get here. It appears they intend to stick with us no matter what."

"I was expecting just you and Evie. You have picked up quite a crew."

"It's a long story," Sam said and went on to tell him the events of the last few weeks.

* * *

Kat piloted the plane up the coastline, and the inviting town of Sitka came into view at about two o'clock Saturday afternoon. Something large and white gleamed at the pier.

"Wow!" Sam said as he caught a glimpse of the huge yacht docked at Crescent Bay.

"It looks like money has come to Sitka," Kat said. "I hope they are looking for a sightseeing tour."

Sam poked Evie, who had nodded off, "Look at this yacht!"

"Talk about ostentatious!" Evie replied.

"That thing must be over a hundred feet long!" David said.

"Gawking time is over. Seat belts on for the landing," Kat ordered.

As Kat lined up with the runway, Evie pointed, "See the green onion dome, David? That's St. Michael's Cathedral."

"Wow! It's pretty!" David replied.

With the plane safely on the ground and taxiing toward the hangar, Sam said, "James, you have been awfully quiet."

"I'm trying to sort out my options. I'm in Alaska with winter coming and nothing but a light jacket. As far as anyone knows, I am dead. I have no place to stay and no way to earn money. It seems like a predicament."

"Well, I can put your mind at ease for the time being. Everyone will stay with us. Between our house and Grandpa's, we will find room. If you know anything about boats, you can always fish for a living. But I must say, lately catches haven't been what they used to be," Kat said.

"Why is that, Dad?" Sam asked.

"I have no idea. Since July, the fish just haven't seemed to be there. The catches have gotten smaller and smaller. People are struggling to make ends meet."

"That's odd. Last year you said there was a record catch. Do you think people are overfishing?"

"Not that I'm aware of. The Fish and Game Department keeps a close check on that."

Kat pulled the plane into the hangar, and everyone got out. Sandra, Sam's mother, came around the corner with her blue eyes beaming and ran to Sam, grabbing him in a hug.

"I am so glad to see you! You shouldn't worry your mother like that! And you're growing a beard?" she said moving from Sam to Evie and finally Kat. "We have a few extras, I see."

"This is David, Viviana, and James," Sam said.

"It's nice to meet you," Sandra said, smoothing her long blond hair against the wind and shaking each hand warmly. When she came to Viviana, she paused. "My, that is an interesting dress! You are quite fashion forward, I guess. Um, Kat, there are birds on the plane. And it looks like they are watching us."

"It's a long story, Mom. These are our bird friends, Wingston, Rey, Azul, and Canto." Wingston flew and landed on Sam's shoulder.

"My goodness!" Sandra jumped. "I'm glad you told me to drive the Suburban," she said. "Shall we go to the house?"

Sandra led them to the vehicle. Sam noticed that she kept a wary eye on the birds as they flew along.

"Prepare yourself, Mom. The birds will fly into the Suburban. It's OK."

They put the four backpacks, Viviana's bow and arrows, and Kat's duffle bag in the back. The four birds landed on a backpack each, and Sam pulled down the hatch. The tires hummed as Sandra drove the electric Suburban across O'Connell Bridge. Sam looked back to his right to catch a glimpse of Mount Edgecumbe, the dormant volcano on Krusof Island to the west. Seeing the mountain sparked a memory.

"Have you heard the story of the April Fool's joke?" Sam asked.

"This sounds interesting," David said. "Please tell!"

"Someone set a bunch of tires on fire in the crater of the volcano before sunrise one April Fool's Day. People thought the volcano was getting ready to erupt until they noticed 'April Fools' painted in huge letters around the rim." Sam said.

"Now that's creative!" David said, laughing. "Hey! There is that yacht we saw from the air! I would love to spend some time sailing on her!"

Everyone was tired and lapsed into silence. As the Suburban rolled along, Sam watched the familiar sites of his hometown pass by. An uneasy feeling began to grow.

"I wonder what the future holds," he thought. "I did everything I could to escape this place, and now I'm back. I wonder if I'm stuck here."

Sam shook his head. "Good grief! It was fourteen years ago when I left. How can it still bother me? I just need to put that behind me," Sam thought as he remembered his unpleasant teenage years that were filled with taunting and bullying just because he was half Tlingit and half Caucasian.

Evie's head slumped over onto Sam's shoulder. She was asleep. He looked down the top of her head, eyelashes, and the line of her nose. The uneasiness fled at the flood of joy filling his heart. Somehow, seeing Evie peacefully sleeping had always moved Sam.

"With you by my side, any place is home," he thought. And smiled.

CHAPTER 14

I haven't been inside a house in years and years," Viviana whispered to David as Sandra parked the Suburban in the garage.

David squeezed her hand, "I'll protect you," he said.

Viviana smacked him on the chest. "That's not what I meant. I think I'm nervous about being cooped up." Realizing that she said that a little too loudly, Viviana blushed and caught Sandra eyeing her in the rearview mirror.

"It will be OK," Sam said. "If you feel too cooped up, we can set up a tent."

"Sam, we'll not have her sleeping outside," Sandra corrected.

"We'll fill you in on the whole story when we get inside," Kat said. "We have two extra bedrooms and some blowup mattresses left over from Sam's sleepover days. We might be able to just let everyone sleep here."

"OK," Sandra replied. "I think showers will be the first order of business."

"Mom!" Sam protested.

"What? I was just stating the obvious," she said.

"We've been living in Viviana's cave for the last three weeks. That's why we're a bit scraggly," Sam said.

"This is going to be an interesting story!" Sandra said.

Kat opened the hatch, and the birds flew out. He grabbed two of the backpacks and handed Viviana her bow. "You folks travel light!" he said.

Kat held the door, and everyone filed in. Viviana was the last. Rey landed on the door and squawked. He looked at the other birds, who were sitting in a tree in the front yard and squawked again.

Viviana held up her arm and Rey landed. "It's OK, mi amigo. You can wait with the others." He flew to the tree.

"Wow! How did you do that?" Kat asked.

"Crows are very smart. We have been together a long time. Rey understands me."

Viviana hesitated, looked over at Rey, then went through the door. The house was a two-story colonial style home with the master bedroom on the first level and two bedrooms, a bathroom, and study upstairs.

"David and Viviana can have the guest room, and James can use the study with a blowup mattress. Is that OK?"

Sam noticed David's anxious look. Finally, David said, "Viviana and I aren't married, at least not yet."

"Oops!" Kat said. "The study is too small for two people. I guess we will have to send at least one of you over to Dad's house."

"I can do that," James volunteered.

"Who's first for the showers?" Sandra asked after everyone had placed their backpacks in the appropriate rooms.

"I'm good," James said, holding up his hands. I just showered yesterday.

"You two go ahead," Sam said to David and Viviana. "I'll fill Mom in on the details."

"Do you need help turning on the shower?" David asked Viviana, which earned him another smack in the chest.

"I remember how to do that."

Kat put on some coffee while Sam, Evie, James, and Sandra sat at the kitchen table. With the steady breeze and humidity, it felt cold outside at forty-eight degrees, and a hot drink sounded good.

"I want to hear every detail of what happened!" Sandra said.

"After Evie mailed Grandpa the thumb drive, we tried to rescue Arnie, my predecessor, who was being held by Mitch Carter," Sam began and went through the whole search, all the setbacks, and how they finally escaped the compound.

"You mean Viviana has been living in that cave all by herself for years!"

"Well, she had Rey, the crow."

"And that dress she is wearing is some kind of animal skin?"

"Yes, she made it out of deer skin."

"Wow! OK, where does James come in? He's not as rough looking as the rest of you," Sandra asked.

Sam went on to relay how the drones had found them and how they had escaped by hijacking the truck. After telling her about the truck being blown up, Sam said, "That reminds me! I need to let the Nuclear Regulatory Commission know about the truck. Dad, can I use your computer?"

"Sure, as long as you don't think it will cause any trouble. I don't want those people coming after you!"

Sam hustled up to the study and sent an email to the NRC informing them of the location of the truck and its nuclear waste.

He came back down and warmed his coffee in the microwave. David appeared dressed in his same clothes.

"Oh dear," Sandra said. "You are too tall for any of Sam's old clothes and too thin for Kat's. Let's get you a bathrobe while we wash what you are wearing."

Kat didn't own such a thing as a bathrobe, so Sandra brought out her fuzzy pink one.

David was sitting in the kitchen with the others when Viviana came downstairs. She saw David and burst out laughing.

"I'm sorry! I couldn't help it. The sight was quite a shock!"

Sandra sidled up to Viviana. She was a bit taller but still had a trim figure. "I think you could wear some of my clothes," she said. "What do you think of that?"

Viviana paused and looked down at her dress. "This is all I have worn for years. But I guess I would fit in better with normal clothes."

"Let's go have a look," Sandra said.

Kat's phone rang. "It's Grandpa," he explained as he answered. "Hey, Dad! How are you?..... We just got in, and they are fine, a bit scraggly but fine."

Kat listened, and Sam watched his eyes squint with a serious expression. "Tonight?" Kat said with exasperation. "7:30. OK, I'll be there. Hey, why don't you come and have supper with us about six?"

"What was that about?" Sam asked.

"The yacht we saw is owned by none other than Holmes Harrison, the owner of Global Food Source. He is requesting a town meeting tonight at 7:30. I have no idea what it is about, but it can't be good."

Viviana returned in jeans and a sweater.

"Wow! Look at you!" David said.

"Kat, you look so serious," Sandra said.

"It looks like the yacht might have brought in a storm," he answered.

CHAPTER 15

As Sam finished his dinner, he felt torn. He was worn out but knew that he ought to go to the meeting with his dad and grandfather.

"I hate to eat and run, but I guess we ought to get moving if we are going to get there on time," Kat said. "Are you ready, Dad?"

"Let me finish my pie, Son. This guy can't be as important as pecan pie."

"Sandra, are you going? Anyone else for that matter is welcome, but I know you must be tired."

"I think I'll stay with our company," Sandra said. "I'm sure they are more interesting than a rich windbag."

"I think I'll go with you," Sam said. "I'm too curious to stay home."

Skauty swallowed his last bite of pie and pushed back his plate. "I have a bad feeling about this. Why would this guy rent out Harrigan Centennial Hall and invite the whole town?"

"There is only one way to find out. Let's go," Kat said.

They loaded up into Kat's brand-new Tesla SUV. He entered Harrigan Centennial Hall as their destination, and the vehicle drove itself, even finding an empty parking space.

"I still don't trust these things," Skauty said. "I would rather drive myself."

As they walked toward the hall, Sam heard a buzz of people wondering what was going on. Six men in dark suits were lined up at the door, guns obvious below their coats.

"I guess the welcoming committee is intended to scare us," Kat said.

"They don't realize that just about everyone here will have a gun," Skauty added.

Sam greeted a number of people he knew with handshakes as they made their way to the auditorium. Six more dark suits were positioned around the room.

"I believe you were right about the storm," Sam whispered to his dad as they found their seats.

People continued to file into the room. Seven-thirty came and went. There was a loud murmur in the room when suddenly confetti popped everywhere, and Holmes Harrison came flying in on a Segway. He hopped off and ran onto the stage. A short, balding man with greying hair and round glasses, Harrison exuded energy and confidence.

With a big smile, Harrison surveyed the audience. "Didn't you love the confetti? Wait, you look so somber. Today is a momentous day for Sitka! I bring you good news of great joy! Tomorrow will be a new day with wonderful possibilities! But, before we get to the good news, let's back up and look at what brought us to this point."

Harrison clicked and some slides and graphs appeared on the large displays behind him and to the sides.

"He's way too perky for me," Skauty said. "I think he's trying to grease us up before he cooks us."

Sam chuckled and returned his attention to Harrison.

Using a laser pointer, Harrison highlighted the graphs that showed a decline in fishing over the last four months.

"You see, I am aware of how you are struggling. The last few months have seen a decline in your catch, which means a decline in the money in your pockets. Many of you have spent your lives on the sea fishing. Not just you, but for generations past you have taken to the sea to earn your living. It is a hard life. But it is an honest life, and you help feed the world.

"I have heard your worries that you may not be able to continue doing what you love. Giving up fishing would be a devastating blow to so many of you. What would Sitka be without its fisheries?

"That's where I come in and why I asked you to come tonight. The mission of Global Food Source is the same as yours. We want to provide wholesome food for the world. I have the resources to help you weather downturns in the market and seasons, like this one when your catches are down. I can help you continue the life you love whether it is a record season or one like you have had this year. If we come together, we can keep Sitka a thriving place! And I can promise that the fishing will improve."

With a flourish, Harrison brought up new images, a different one on every screen. Brand-new fishing boats, an architect's rendering of housing complexes, shiny office buildings, and wonderful greenspaces marched across the screens.

"This is your future! What I am proposing is that Global Food Source come in and set up each of you in a new fishing boat with all the modern equipment. We will provide housing, security, health care, a salary, everything you need! The only thing you will have to worry about is doing what you love: fishing!

"I told you a new day is dawning for Sitka! Your wonderful future begins tomorrow! Global Food Source representatives will be right here at eight o'clock tomorrow morning to answer your questions and get you signed up to be a part of the Global Food Source Village."

Hundreds of balloons began to fall from the ceiling, each with a card showing a smiling Harrison and "Welcome to the new Sitka!" Harrison hopped onto his Segway and rode out.

Rage coursed through Sam's veins. He grabbed a balloon, popped it, and wadded up the card. The murmur in the crowd was a mixture of elation and anger. Skauty had his head propped in his hands, shaking it slowly. Kat stared blankly ahead.

"He can't just waltz in and take over a whole town!" Sam said.

"Apparently he thinks he can," Kat said. "But I'm afraid he is tangling with the wrong people."

"The Tlingit will be no man's servant. We are part of the land and sea, and the land and sea are a part of us. No one can separate us," Skauty said.

The crowd began to exit the auditorium. Sam heard some people expressing outrage that this foreigner had dared come in and propose taking over the city. Others were high fiving each other and talking about how nice it would be to have a new fishing boat. Two men squared off and were about to come to blows.

Skauty walked up. "We are neighbors. Don't let this stranger drive a wedge in a life-long relationship. Most of the time if something seems too good to be true, it is. I fear this man's proposal is barbed with poison. Let's join together and check it out before we turn on each other."

"Thank you, Chief," both men said and shook hands with Skauty. Then they shook hands with each other.

"What do you want us to do?" one asked.

"Let's go home and see if we can find out what this man has done in other places. Tomorrow I will ask for a meeting on behalf of the Tlingit people. We will see if he is open to respecting our rights," Skauty responded.

Pride welled up inside as Sam watched his grandfather handle the situation so deftly. At eighty years old and after a heart attack, Skauty still had a forceful presence that elicited respect. He had been chief of the clan, which currently included everyone who identified as Tlingit in the Sitka area, for forty-three years.

Sam noticed that a crowd had begun to gather around. They were looking to Skauty for direction.

"What do we do, Chief?" one rugged fisherman asked.

"I think this man proposes to buy us for himself," Skauty said. "I know he is offering some fine trinkets, but I fear he has not fully laid out the consequences of accepting his offer. As Tlingit, we belong to no man. Before any Tlingit signs on to this, I want to talk with Harrison to get the whole story. The first thing in the morning, I will request that he meet with me and explain exactly what this will mean for us."

"I think we have to take his offer," one man said. "We haven't been bringing in enough fish to keep going. It's either accept or go broke."

Several others voiced their agreement while one woman spoke over the din. "I don't want to be his servant, and I'm not living in his fancy buildings! I would rather starve!"

Others chimed in agreement with her.

"It is hard to make a decision when we don't know all of the facts. Let's wait till we talk with this Mr. Harrison and get the full details. Then we can make an informed decision. I know life has been hard the last several months and so many of our lives are tied to the ocean. But we can't make a decision on something when we don't know how it will actually affect us. We need to be patient and learn more," Skauty answered.

Sam observed the somber looks on people's faces. The celebration had been replaced with worry. Sam felt the tension in the room. Suddenly he remembered his dream of the storm clouds coming.

CHAPTER 16

On the way home Sam mostly listened as Skauty and Kat fumed about this stranger coming in to disrupt the way of life in Sitka.

"How dare he presume that any one of us would want to work for him rather than ourselves!" Kat said.

"I agree," Skauty said. "But word on the street is that people have caught nearly nothing the last week. It's like the fish just up and left for a vacation."

"I don't know if it means anything, but the night before you picked us up, I had a dream that we were at David and Viviana's wedding. It was on the beach, and storm clouds were gathering just off the coast," Sam said.

"It looks like your dream is coming true," Skauty said as the Tesla parked itself in the garage.

Sam followed Skauty into the house with Kat right behind. They found Sandra and Evie talking in the kitchen. David and James were on each end of the couch with Viviana curled up between them, her head on a pillow in David's lap. All three were asleep.

"What was that all about?" Sandra asked.

"The owner of Global Food Source wants to take over our fishing industry," Kat said. "He's offering new fishing boats, housing, and a guaranteed income if we sign up for his program."

"That sounds too good to be true," Sandra said.

"That's what I said," Skauty added.

"It's a bad offer," Evie said. "It will be a compound just like MC2. He will own the people."

"I don't think it will be..." Sam started to say when his heart skipped a beat and he caught himself. "You are probably right, Evie.

We need to find out what he has done in other places. Dad, do you have an extra computer charger?"

"There's one that went with my old computer somewhere around here," Kat replied. "I think it's in the closet in the study."

Sam scrounged around in the closet till he found the old laptop on the floor. He was trying to pull the cord out from under a box when David came in and asked, "How was the meeting?"

Sam jumped and nearly fell face-first into the closet. He recovered and said, "Not so good. It looks like Global Food Source wants to establish a compound here in Sitka."

"Here? Why would anyone want to set up a compound here?"

"Sitka is a prime fishing area. I guess they want to control all food sources." Sam replied.

"I hope we didn't jump out of the frying pan and into the fire!" David said. "I'm beat. I'm going to bed as soon as you are finished rummaging around."

"I want to see if Global Food Source has been setting up MC2-like compounds anywhere else. Then I'll go to bed, too."

"When is this going to happen?"

"The owner wants people to start signing up tomorrow."

"That's brash! But what else would you expect from these ultra-rich folks?" David said and yawned.

"I get the hint!" Sam said and left the room.

He went to his old room, plugged in the computer, and booted it up. Sam smiled as he looked at the computers he had collected and displayed on a corner shelf that reached floor to ceiling. The bottom one was an old desktop dated back to the 1990s. It boasted 16KB of RAM. "I still can't believe that thing actually worked," Sam thought as he brought up his search engine and entered Global Food Source.

Except for adding a queen-sized bed after Sam and Evie married, his parents had not changed his room. Sam looked around at his mementos and felt an odd sensation. "This is the first time I have ever been back home without somewhere to go when the visit is over," he thought. He had spent so much time trying to get away as a teenager that it felt strange not to have plans to leave now.

Sam refocused on the computer and pulled up the website for Global Food Source. He found the usual corporate rah-rah about how great the company was and its mission. He clicked and found a map that listed all of Global Food Source's farmland. He kept searching but never found anything resembling a compound. He also noted there was nothing about seafood locations.

"Maybe this is his first jump into the seafood industry," Sam thought. With a yawn, he closed the computer and started to go downstairs. Coming softly from the guest bedroom he heard, "Rey. Rey."

Sam knocked on the door and heard a window close before a guilty-looking Viviana opened the door.

"I guess you heard me," she said.

"Did he come in?"

The flutter of crow wings that preceded Rey's landing on Viviana's shoulder was his answer.

Sam almost laughed, but stifled it, "It's OK. Just don't let Mom know."

"We haven't slept apart in years," Viviana explained. "I was worried."

"What about the other birds?"

Viviana opened the door a little wider, and Sam could see them all lined up on the head of the bed.

"It's a good thing Mom sleeps downstairs!" Sam smiled.

Sam made his way downstairs and to the kitchen. Sandra and Evie were still chatting away and Skauty was pecking something into his phone, lost in concentration.

"I've changed my mind," Skauty announced. "I'm going to call our people together before I talk to Harrison. I want to hear their questions and concerns first. I called a meeting for 8:30 in the morning at the high school gym. You should get the notice on your Tlingit app."

"Oh no! We left our phones in the cave," Sam said.

"No, we didn't," Evie responded. "They are in one of the backpacks. Of course, we don't have chargers."

"You're a genius! We can use Mom and Dad's charging pads," Sam said as he gave Evie a hug and started to go hunt their phones. "Wait! We can't turn them on or Harrison could locate us. It won't hurt to charge them, though."

Skauty stood and stretched as Sam came back with the two phones.

"I need to get to bed. It's late for an old man."

"Do you mind if James stays with you?" Kat asked.

"That's fine, if you can wake him up," Skauty said.

"Hey, James!" Kat called.

James stretched and came to the kitchen. "Sorry. I think I fell asleep."

"I'm afraid you are stuck with me," Skauty said. "Let's head to the house. Kat, could you meet me at eight at the gym?"

"Sure. See you in the morning."

CHAPTER 17

Kat and Sam walked into the gym precisely at eight o'clock. Sandra and the others were coming closer to eight-thirty.

"This place brings back bad memories," Sam said.

"At least we don't have to worry about your being sent home for fighting anymore," Kat teased.

"Funny, Dad," Sam replied. Sam remembered some of the fights from high school. He had lost his temper plenty of times when being bullied. "Did you ever realize I was not the one who started the fights?"

"Of course! Why do you think we didn't punish you?" Kat asked.

"You know, I had never thought of that. I always assumed you believed the school when they blamed it on me."

"I know the kids were hard on you, and I'm sorry. I wish there were something I could have done. But that was a battle you had to fight on your own. It looks like you succeeded, too!"

Sam was floored by the discovery that his parents knew what was going on and realized that he had overcome such an obstacle. "Thank you," he said.

Opening the doors to the basketball court, Sam saw James helping Skauty hook up a speaker system.

"Good morning," Skauty called. "I guess you could have waited to come later. James is proficient at this set up business."

"Hey, James," Sam said. "What can I do to help?"

"We need this drop cord run to a power outlet," James said.

"Did you and Grandpa get along OK?"

"Oh yeah. He makes a wonderful breakfast!"

James was still testing the PA system when people started drifting in around eight-fifteen. Sam noticed that most people had somber expressions. A few seemed lighthearted. Then the crowds started pouring in. By the time Skauty stepped up to the microphone, there must have been nearly five hundred people present.

"Good morning, my fellow Tlingit souls. It is good to see each of you today. I am sure all of you are aware that we were presented with an unsettling offer last night. The offer seems to have both barbs and blossoms, like a rose. This man, Harrison, is offering security and the chance to continue our lives in fishing. But what is the cost?

"We know that all over the country, businesses have set up compounds in which their workers live. In the lower states, you are either a part of the compound or you suffer. It appears that Harrison is proposing to install one of these compounds here in Sitka. My grandson and his friends, who are here today, have just escaped from one of these compounds and have bad reports about the integrity of the operation.

"We have tough decisions to make. I know that the fishing has not been good the last few months. But we have weathered lean times before. Let's not make our decision based on the recent downturn. I asked you to come today to share your thoughts and feelings. I want to know what you are thinking about this offer. I also want to know your questions and concerns. I think we need more information before we decide, and I plan to take our questions and concerns to Harrison, himself. We are Tlingit and have a right to know what we would be getting into."

Jeffery Troutman, a grizzled mountain of a man, stood and said, "The last couple of weeks, I haven't caught enough fish to cover my fuel, much less make a living. I have never seen it this bad. I can't imagine why this man would want to buy up our fishing industry now."

Cheryl Singer, one of the pharmacists in the village, was next, "I want to know why he can't take over the industry but let us live in our own homes and have our own schools."

"Here! Here!" rang around the auditorium.

"I don't see any other option. I think we have to take his offer. What else can we do? If we refuse, we will have no way to make a living," Roger Oakton said.

"Personally, I can't wait to get my hands on a brand-new boat! My 'Salmon's Revenge' is on her last leg," William Sebring said.

The meeting went back and forth with expressions of concern and doom countered with optimism and hope. Skauty wrote down all of the questions and concerns that people mentioned.

"I think it would be helpful if we had Sam to come and tell us more about the compound he was in. Sam," Skauty held out his hand in a gesture inviting Sam to the microphone.

Sam's nerves zinged. He froze for a moment then began to head toward his grandfather.

"I wish you had warned me about this," Sam whispered as he approached.

Skauty patted him on the shoulder, "The thought just occurred to me."

"Grandfather said the offer is like a rose; there is good and bad. In the compound, we made a living and had a place to live, pretty much everything we needed. Everything but our freedom, that is. They placed chips in our arms so that they could track our every move. We had to get permission to leave the compound even just to go hiking. The corporation provided a lot but dictated everything we did. Evie likened it to a feudal system where we gave our allegiance and service to the great lord in exchange for protection. I imagine Harrison has the same system in mind."

"Thank you, Sam," Skauty said, coming back to the microphone. "I will go directly from here to Harrison and request a meeting. I will send the answers I get on the Tlingit app as soon as I have them. I advise everyone to wait until we have answers before signing his offer. Thank you so much for coming today."

The crowd hummed loudly as people discussed the predicament on their way out.

"Why do I get the feeling you are against this offer?" Kat said with a grin as he walked up to Skauty.

"Was it that obvious?" Skauty replied.

"Closing with Sam's dire description was just a small hint," Kat replied.

"Tlingit were created to be free, like the raven. I, for one, will live in no man's compound."

CHAPTER 18

Skauty worked to squelch his anger as he strode into Harrigan Hall. He was pleased to see only a few people lined up at the tables to sign up for Harrison's offer. Waiting his turn, Skauty stepped up to talk to the company representative, who appeared to be one of the men in the black suits stationed around the room last night.

"I'm Skauty Hanson, Chief of the Tlingit clan in this area. I represent over five thousand Tlingit. We have some questions I would like to discuss with Mr. Harrison before we can decide on this offer."

"Hello, Mr. Hanson. I'm Raymond Sands. It's nice to meet you. Mr. Harrison normally does not meet with individual people, but in your case he might make an exception. We know your people are important to this venture. I will relay your request to him. Is there a way I can contact you with his answer?"

"I will be happy to leave my phone number," Skauty replied, and Raymond took it down.

Skauty drove to Kat and Sandra's, where lunch had been promised. When he stepped in the door, Evie rushed up and embraced him.

"Great speech, Grandpa!"

"Thanks, Evie," he said.

"How did it go at Harrigan Hall?" Sam asked.

"Either very well, or I got a polite brush off. I guess we'll just have to wait and see."

"I bet he will be willing to talk with you. Whether or not he'll give any concessions is another question," Sandra said.

"I think our best option is for Harrison to go away and leave us alone," Kat said. "But I have a feeling he has already invested too much to consider that."

"I am hoping for a compromise in which we remain in our own homes but work for him," Skauty said. "I'm afraid that is the best we can do in this situation."

"Harrison hasn't set up compounds in his farming business, so maybe he will be open to that. It would save him a lot of money," Sam pointed out.

"What do the farming businesses look like?" Evie asked.

"Let me show you," Sam said and opened his computer. He pulled up an aerial shot of one of Global Food Source's farms. Zooming in, he showed them the farmland surrounded by a razor wire fence.

"The fence looks just like MC2's," Evie said.

Sam dragged the map and showed them a row of houses, "This is where the farmers live. You can see the storage barns, too."

"What is that long building?" Evie asked.

Sam zoomed in a little farther. "It looks like a motel," Sam said puzzled.

"I bet that's for migrant workers at harvest time," James offered.

"Sam! This is a compound! It's just on a smaller scale. See the security booth at the entrance?"

"I think the day just got a little darker," Skauty said.

Sandra had put on chili in a crockpot, and James was helping with the cornbread when Skauty's phone rang.

"Hello," Skauty said and listened. "That will be fine. Thank you very much." He hung up. "Harrison will meet me at 1:30 on his yacht."

"That was quick. Maybe it's a good sign," Kat said.

"I think we need to start generating options in case he says no," Sam said.

"It's hard to plan a way out when you don't know the box you're in," Skauty said. "Let's try to enjoy this family reunion and a nice bowl of chili. Then we can find out what we are facing."

*   *   *

At 1:15, Skauty walked up to the gangplank leading to Harrison's yacht. Two guards were posted, and the taller one said, "Mr. Hanson, I presume."

"Yes."

"We will need to frisk you before letting you onto the yacht."

Skauty rolled his eyes as he lifted his hands. The shorter guard patted him down and nodded to the other.

"Right this way," he said and led Skauty onto the yacht and into a conference room. "Mr. Harrison will be right with you," he said and left.

Skauty looked around at the opulent room with a mahogany table, plush chairs, and prominent bar. Skauty turned inward and started rehearsing what he would say. He was lost in thought and jumped when Harrison threw open the door.

"Welcome, Mr. Hanson! I am sorry to keep you waiting. I was finishing up a phone call."

"Thank you for seeing me," Skauty replied.

"What will you have to drink? I have quite an assortment on board."

"Water would be nice," Skauty replied. "I just finished a spicy bowl of chili."

"Water it is!" Harrison snapped his fingers and sat down across from Skauty. Almost as soon as Harrison's fanny hit the seat, a woman appeared with a glass of ice water and what appeared to be a mimosa.

"I am glad to have the chance to talk with you. Your people have been a part of this land for eons, and it would not be right for them not to have a part in its future. I can assure you that there will be no discrimination in this new community we are creating. That simply won't be tolerated. I am even considering naming the compound, 'Tlingit Bay.' Now, what questions can I answer for you?"

Skauty noted the polish with which Harrison presented himself. He also discerned an underlying resolve in the set of his eyes. "Like a hunter eyeing his prey," Skauty thought.

"As you said, the Tlingit have been here for eons. We are a part of the land, and the land is a part of us. We appreciate your generosity in coming to our aid just when the fishing seems to be drying up. It is important to my people that we be able to keep our Tlingit customs and ways of life."

"Yes, yes. That is important. I can assure you that in the community your ways of life will be respected and allowed to continue. You will be free to do your pot lunches and everything."

Skauty swallowed his resentment at Harrison's ignorance and tried to speak with an even tone, "The gatherings are called potlatches. What is important to us is to be free. We would like for you to consider taking over the fishing industry without building the community, as you call it. Allow us to live in our own homes and be free. We will work for you as you have described. It will also save you a lot of money."

"I have considered that option, Mr. Hanson. But the numbers just don't work. Since the industry is currently on a downturn, the only way I can afford to take care of you and your people is if I can control the cost of housing, energy, food, and et cetera. I agree that the startup cost is greater, but in the long run, this community I propose will sustain us through down times like this."

"I see," Skauty said, trying to think of another argument. "Why would you want to take over the industry right now when it looks so dire?"

"Mr. Hanson, you know as well as I do that this will turn around. These waters have been fished by your people for centuries. A few bad months is no reason to turn my back on them. I am simply seizing the opportunity of motivation. People who are struggling are more motivated to find a way out."

"You are correct that the fishing should rebound. But you are wrong about motivation. Freedom is more important to the Tlingit than money and security. We have battled the whimsical sea for centuries and plan to continue doing so. What if you didn't guarantee an income and just paid us by the catch? That should help the numbers."

"My people have been over this carefully. We concluded that the best option is to build a self-contained community out of which to operate the fishing industry. Your people will simply have to be willing to try something new."

"So your answer is no?"

"No, my answer is yes. I answer yes to a new future of security and the ongoing battle of that whimsical sea. I answer yes to the opportunity for Tlingit people to carry on their customs within this new community. I answer yes to having you and your people provide input into what you need to make that happen. My answer is yes! I trust that your answer will be yes, too!" Harrison finished with a flourish and left the room.

Skauty shook his head, and immediately a man and a woman in sharp business attire entered.

"Good afternoon, Mr. Hanson! My name is Anne Solomon, Vice President of Development for Global Food Source. This is Hal Anderson, our head of Community Design. It is a pleasure to meet you."

"Good afternoon," Skauty said coolly.

Solomon laid a notepad on the table. "Mr. Harrison wanted us to meet with you to discuss what the Tlingit people will require for the new community."

"We would also like to give you the opportunity to be the first Tlingit to sign on to this wonderful offer," Anderson added, pushing a contract toward Skauty.

Skauty sat silently for a moment. "I am afraid you have put out your oars before the boat is in the water. I will have to discuss Mr. Harrison's refusal to entertain our proposal with my people first." Skauty walked out of the room without looking back.

Anger seared his gut as he walked down the gangplank and across the parking lot to his Cherokee, totally ignoring the two security guards. He slammed the door shut and rubbed his hands on his knees, trying to decide his next move.

Nothing came, so he banged the steering wheel, cranked the SUV, and drove. He found himself pulling into Totem Park, where he parked the car and went to sit on a bench facing the harbor. A breeze chilled the air. The sky was dreary with clouds. It seemed to match his mood.

Skauty thought about how the street the park is on was named after the same warrior for whom he had named his son.

"Legacies," he thought. "What kind of legacy am I leaving for my son and grandson? Locking them up in this man's prison just so they will have food to eat? That is not the legacy I want to leave. What has my life come to?"

Skauty could see Mount Edgecumbe to the west. "I wish you would come alive and swallow this man up!" Skauty said aloud. Then the realization of what he had to do crystalized in his soul. He drove back to Kat and Sandra's house invigorated with purpose.

CHAPTER 19

Skauty burst into the house.

"What's the verdict? Did he go for the idea?" Kat asked.

"No. He seemed too smitten with his own plans to entertain any other option."

"That's ridiculous! Why wouldn't he go for an idea that saves him money? It seems money is his main interest," Sandra said.

"I bet money ceased to be an issue for him long ago. Maybe he is seeking power and control," Sam wondered.

"If that's the case, then trying to reason with him will be useless," Kat said. "What do we do next?"

"I think we have to try reasoning with him," Skauty said. "But I need more leverage. I have to be sure the entire clan is united on this. I'm going to see if we can use the gym in the morning."

"School will be in session," Sandra cautioned.

"This is an urgent matter. I think Terri will allow it." Skauty pulled out his phone and paused. "Everyone try to come up with ideas as to how we can stop this man. It is time to fight."

Sam rubbed his neck and felt knots in the muscles. His world was spinning. A month ago, he had an ideal job, a nice apartment, and thought he had achieved his dreams. "Now I have none of that. I'm back in the place I vowed to escape and am facing a battle that I can't imagine winning," he thought.

Sam noticed that Evie had caught him lost in thought. She gave him a smile, and he smiled back. Despite the fact that his world was tumbling, Sam felt happy.

As Skauty walked into the kitchen to call Terri about using the gym, Sam said, "OK, let's have some ideas. We have a foe to defeat!"

"It appears he only has twelve men as his security guards, based on what we saw at the first meeting," Kat said. "We easily out number them if it comes to a fight."

"That's true. But I bet he has a militia and could have plenty of people here in a hurry," Sam said making a note to check Global Food Source for a militia and where it is stationed.

"The fact that he was willing to meet with Grandpa tells me he really wants this venture to work. Why is that?" Evie asked.

"It's the path of least resistance?" James asked.

"I know! He needs the Tlingit because we already know how to fish these waters. He could round up people by the thousands and bring them in, but they wouldn't know the first thing about fishing," Sam said excitedly. "If he needs us, then we are in a stronger negotiating position!"

Skauty came back into the den, "It's set. We can meet in the morning at 8:30. What are you smiling about?"

"I think Harrison needs us," Sam said. "He can't run a fishing industry without people who know how to fish. That means we have more bargaining power than we thought."

"I hadn't thought of that," Skauty mused. "You may be right. If we can go back with a united front, maybe he will reconsider. I will put that in the meeting announcement."

Sam opened his computer, which was never far away, and searched for Global Food Source's militia. "It doesn't mention a militia anywhere that I can find."

"Well, I wouldn't think you would broadcast to the world where your defenses are," Evie answered. "Check MC2 and see if the website mentions their militia.."

Sam pulled up the MC2 site. "Each compound is strongly defended with its own militia," Sam read aloud.

"Could Harrison be new enough at this game that he doesn't have one yet?" Sandra asked.

"I'm betting not," Sam answered.

"He has so many farm sites that he couldn't stock each one with a militia, could he?" Evie asked.

"You're right! Maybe he didn't mention it so no one would know where they are stationed. That would create less risk of someone causing trouble on any particular property."

"I think we have to assume reinforcements will come if we try to take Harrison by force," Kat added.

"What's this, 'Take Harrison by force' business?" Skauty asked.

"Earlier I pointed out that Harrison appears to have only twelve men on his security team. It wouldn't be hard for us to outgun them if needed."

"Let's hope it doesn't come to anything like that," Skauty said. "I'm liking Sam's idea that we have more negotiating power than we realized."

The door opened, and David and Viviana popped in, holding hands.

"We've been walking the birds!" David said. "We took them down to the river. Is that a glimmer of hope I see on your face, Sam? Did Harrison accept the proposal?"

"No, but we came to the realization that he needs the Tlingit in order to succeed with his fishing industry. If you're going to fish, it helps to know how," Sam answered.

"Good point! You should tell that to Harrison."

"That's the plan. Grandpa is going to try to get the Tlingit united behind the idea of not agreeing to fish for Harrison unless he grants us the right to live in our own homes and continue to be free."

"It sounds like a fool-proof plan. I don't see what Harrison has to lose!" David said.

* * *

People poured into the gym on Monday morning. The crowd was larger than yesterday and ended up being standing room only. Skauty took the microphone.

"Thank you for coming today to address this future-altering decision. As you know, Harrison rejected our first request to continue our current living situation and work for him. In fact, his assistants presented me with a contract and asked that I be the first to sign on."

Sam heard a collective intake of breath.

"I didn't sign it. I don't intend to ever sign it."

Cheers erupted in various places, but Sam noticed it certainly wasn't everywhere.

"Sam made the observation that Harrison cannot run his fishing industry without people who know how to fish. Without our knowledge of the sea, he will not succeed. I told Harrison that I needed to talk with you about his rejection before I made a decision.

"What I want to take back to him is a united front that none of us will agree to his terms. He either chooses our proposal or pushes ahead without our knowledge and expertise. Can we come together as a people and resist this assault on our way of life?"

Sam estimated about two-thirds of the crowd applauded. When the applause slowed someone shouted, "We are going to suffer this winter if we do not accept this man's offer."

"We know the fishing will improve. It always has," Skauty said. "Think about how you will feel if you sign your soul away and the fish return a month later. Could you live with that?"

"I couldn't live with that decision," Jeffery Troutman bellowed. "In fact, I couldn't live with that decision even if the fish never return. I will live free. I will never sign this man's contract. If you are the Tlingit I know you are, you will not give in to this man's quest to control you, either."

Silence fell over the gym after Troutman spoke.

"Jeffery speaks the truth," Skauty said. "As Tlingit, we do not belong to a man. We belong to the land and sea. Let us fight together to keep it that way. If we are divided, Harrison will pick us off one by one. If we are united we can defeat him."

This time the applause seemed to come from every person in the crowd. Sam noticed a smile grow on his grandfather's face. Someone started chanting, "Freedom! Freedom! Freedom!" Soon the auditorium shook with the chant.

Skauty waved his hands to quiet the crowd. "Remember, they are trying to hold school today. I will present our request as an ultimatum this time. Harrison will have no option. We either continue living as we have, or he has no one to fish."

The applause was deafening. Finally people began to exit. Many tried to get to Skauty to shake his hand and to thank him. Sam's heart swelled with pride as he watched the respect people showered on his grandfather.

Sam rode with Skauty to Harrigan Hall. He smiled when they entered and found only the three men in their black suits. No one was signing up.

"I need to see Mr. Harrison again," Skauty said.

"He just called and said you would probably show up. He said to send you on over if you are available to meet now."

"OK. Thanks," Skauty replied.

Sam noted irritation on his grandfather's face as he turned to head out of Harrigan Hall. When they were out of the gym, Skauty said, "I guess Harrison knew about our meeting today."

"I think he is keeping eyes on you," Sam said. "I wonder if he had one of his people in the meeting?"

"I didn't notice any strangers, but I wouldn't be surprised."

"Well, let's see what he has to say this time," Sam said.

"Oh, are you going with me? That will be good," Skauty replied.

They approached the two guards at the gangplank, went through the frisking process, and were ushered into the same conference room. Harrison came in all smiles and handshakes.

"And who might this be?" Harrison asked as he shook Sam's hand.

"This is Sam, my grandson."

"Very nice to meet you, Sam. So what was the verdict? Did your people see the light and agree that my community is the best way forward?" Harrison asked.

"No. Exactly the opposite. We will agree to fish for Global Food Source only if we are allowed to remain in our own homes and continue our way of life."

Sam saw the smile and congeniality slide off Harrison's face. It was replaced with cold steel.

"That is not an option, Mr. Hanson."

"I believe it is an option, Mr. Harrison," Skauty returned with equal firmness. "You need our fishing expertise to succeed with this venture. You could bring in people and try to train them, but it would take years to build the capacity that we can bring from day one. Mr. Harrison, you need us."

Harrison slammed his hand on the table, stood up, and stalked around the room. Finally he stopped and glared at Skauty, "You are the chief of these people. I assume you have their best interest at heart, as I do. I will give you until next Sunday to convince them that my community is the way to go."

With that, Harrison stomped out of the room.

"He is not a man to listen," Skauty said.

"That's for sure," Sam replied.

"I guess that's that. We might as well go."

*   *   *

Harrison led Anne Solomon and Hal Anderson onto the bow of the yacht. He watched as Skauty and Sam walked past Harrigan Hall toward their car.

"These people are going to cause trouble," Harrison said. "Doesn't it say somewhere in the Bible that it is expedient for one to die for many?"

"I believe you are right," Solomon answered.

"I wonder if that is the case here," Harrison said.

CHAPTER 20

I f he's not a man to listen, maybe he is a man who sees," Skauty said as Sam drove back to the house.

"What do you mean?" Sam asked.

"What if we organize a picket line in front of his yacht?"

"I don't think he would be very impressed," Sam said.

"Do you have any better ideas?"

"Well, no."

"It would keep the people engaged, too. We can't afford for people to get spooked and start signing over their rights. I need to keep the clan united."

"Maybe you are right. That could be the best thing to do. It appears there is not much point in taking the boats out fishing right now."

"Try to think up slogans for the signs," Skauty said and leaned his head back on the headrest.

Sam and Skauty joined Sandra, Evie, and James at the kitchen table. Kat poured coffee for everyone.

"Harrison just walked out of the room. He was unwilling even to listen," Skauty reported.

"So, now what?" Kat asked.

"We start a picket line in front of his yacht. Maybe he'll get the message," Skauty replied.

Kat laughed, "A picket line? Really? I don't think he will be impressed."

"Can you think of any better ideas?" Skauty snapped.

"What if we just ignore him? Pretend that he is not here?" Evie asked.

Everyone looked at Evie, and Sam grinned.

"Now that would get under his skin," Sam said. "No more meetings. Just go on about life as if he doesn't exist."

"Do you think that could work?" Skauty asked.

"He has been in the driver's seat so far," James pointed out. "If you ignore him, then he would have to come to you with a proposal. It does take some of his power away."

"What do I tell the people?" Skauty asked.

"Tell everyone that Harrison refused the offer, so we are just going to carry on as we always have. We will fish and live our lives no matter what Harrison does," Sandra said.

"OK," Skauty said. "The deal is off. Unless Harrison comes around and offers what we want, we just ignore him. I will send that out to the people."

"Wait, what about fishing. People are antsy since there are no fish to catch," Kat pointed out.

"What if we try going north," Skauty said. "Let's send the boats up around Glacier Bay National Park. They could fish those waters, and we could ferry supplies back and forth."

"Brilliant!" Sandra said. "Why haven't we thought of that before?"

"People are prone to keep doing the same thing until there is a sharp enough pain," Skauty answered.

"I would love to see the look on Harrison's face when he sees the boats pulling out," Sam said feeling encouraged.

"That reminds me, apparently someone is informing Harrison about what we are doing. He seemed to know about our meeting this morning. He was expecting me when we got to Harrigan Hall," Skauty said.

"Even if he knows, what can he do? Follow the fishing boats in his yacht?" Kat said. "I say let's go for it. Having a good catch will give people hope. Being gone will get their minds off Harrison."

"OK," Skauty said. "I'll send out the word."

As Skauty stood to go to the den to compose his notice, the door opened and Viviana and David popped in.

"Where have you two been?" Evie asked.

"Back to the river," David said. "There were some bears out fishing today."

"They used to be hibernating by now, but with the warmer weather they stay out till the end of November," Kat said.

"Those are big bears! They make Virginia's black bears look like puppies," David said. "Guess what, we've been making wedding plans!"

Sam noticed Viviana blush.

"We're thinking three weeks from last Saturday. That is, if this thing with Harrison is resolved. Just a simple ceremony by the water if the weather is OK. Of course, we will have to find someone to perform the ceremony."

"That sounds wonderful!" Evie said.

"How did the meeting with Harrison go? Did he see the light this time?" David asked.

"No, he just walked out of the room," Sam said.

"What are we going to do now?" David asked.

"Grandpa is sending the fishing boats north to see if they have better luck. We are just going to ignore Harrison and hope he goes away."

"That sounds like a plan!" David said. "These rich folks don't seem to like not getting their way."

"I doubt he will just go away, though," Evie said.

"There is no time for just sitting here," Skauty said. "People have agreed that going north is the thing to do. We need to help get the boats stocked."

The village moved at a frantic pace all afternoon with people coming and going from stores to boats. It was a whole town affair. By late afternoon, the boats were stocked with enough food and supplies to be out for a week.

* * *

Tuesday morning, before light began to show over the eastern mountains, Skauty was up and getting dressed. James dragged himself out of bed to see what was going on.

"I'm going down to see the boats off. They will leave at dawn," Skauty explained. "You can go back to bed."

"Do you mind if I come with you? I always enjoy seeing boats off. It reminds me of my SEAL days."

"You are welcome to come," Skauty said as he pulled a wooden hat from the top of the closet.

"Wow! What a hat! What is that?" James asked.

"It is the hat of our clan," Skauty said handing it over for James to see.

James rubbed his hands over the intricately carved red cedar. "That is amazing!" he said. When he looked up to hand the hat back, Skauty was holding a Chilkat blanket.

"OK, that is just too cool! What is that?"

"This is the clan leader's blanket. I wear these for ceremonial occasions. I want to wear them as the boats embark to send them off with good fortune," Skauty explained. "Come, we must go."

They arrived at the harbor just as a pink glow showed over the mountains. Skauty shook hands with the crews as they put the final provisions onto their boats. He walked to the end of the pier and stood erect and still as the boats filed out of the harbor.

As Skauty and James walked back to the car, James asked, "What is that doing here?"

Skauty looked out to see a cargo ship in the distance.

CHAPTER 21

Holmes Harrison smiled after Dirk Donegan, his head of security, finished his report regarding the stocking of the boats and their embarking this morning.

"I have always enjoyed a worthy opponent," Harrison said. "It makes the take-over so much more satisfying."

He dismissed Donegan and took a sip of his coffee. Leaning back in his chair and propping his feet on the desk, Harrison remembered some of his more hostile take-overs. He smiled as he thought of the nastiest one he had ever done. It ended with the CEO committing suicide over the deal.

"That was unfortunate," he said to himself and smiled again. Consolidating his control of America's food production had been a long process. And he wasn't through. He still needed to gain control of the seafood industry. That was his final challenge, and it began with this venture in Sitka.

Harrison had married young, right out of college, but his wife left him before they had any children. He was such a driven man that he had no time for her. After she left, he realized that his real love was business and had never even considered marriage again. He had clawed his way to being a member of the A-30, the group of thirty ultra-rich people who controlled America's business and ran the country.

"These silly people," he thought as he stood to look out the window into town. "You think you can outmaneuver me. I'm afraid you are sorely mistaken, Mr. Hanson."

While Harrison stared at the green onion dome on St. Michael's, a plan formed in his mind. "If I grab a snake by the throat, it is under my control."

* * *

Skauty and James drove to Kat's house, arriving just in time for breakfast: pancakes and bacon.

"I see my timing is still good," Skauty said, smelling the bacon.

"You nailed it," Sandra said as he and James joined the others at the table. David and Viviana were sitting at the bar since the table held only six.

"The boats are off. I hope it is a success," Skauty said.

"Don't you think it odd that Harrison showed up right as the fishing tanked?" Evie asked.

"He does seem to have impeccable timing," Kat said.

"But do you really think it's a coincidence? I think something is fishy here. I mean, is there any way he could have caused the decline?" Evie asked.

Evie's words struck Sam. He wondered if this could be one of her insights as he half listened to Kat saying, "If Harrison had killed off the fish, there would be dead fish everywhere. He could run a sound generating device that emits a frequency the fish don't like, but a boat would have to be out there all the time. Someone would have seen it."

"Evie, do you feel that could be true?" Sam asked.

"Yes, I do," Evie said.

"I think a hacking session is in line after breakfast," Sam said.

Settling down with a second mug of coffee, Sam opened his computer to see if he could find a way into Global Food Source's network. After an hour and a half, Sam found himself muttering in frustration, "This guy is serious about his security!" He kept trying till he finally found a way in.

Sam searched through the system and found files about Sitka. Pulling those up, he saw mostly what had been on the screen during Harrison's initial speech.

"Look at this," Sam said calling Evie over. "He has a detailed design for the compound he plans to build. It looks like he is planning to raze everything east of Crescent Bay and below Baranof

Street for his compound. At least he is leaving the National Historical Park mostly intact."

"What about the people that live in that area?" Evie asked.

"I guess they are just out of luck until the compound is built," Sam answered.

"Have you found anything about fish?"

"Not yet. I just have gotten in."

"Well, keep looking."

Sam kept hunting, and a half hour later he felt puzzled. "I don't see anything related to the fishing industry other than the compound. You'd think he would have notes for the business aspect of his plan."

"You said he was serious about security. Maybe he is keeping those plans on a different computer," James offered.

"Bingo!" Sam said and began looking for other computers logged onto the system. Sam located four computers currently active.

"Here is a computer named, 'Master Ship!' I wonder whose that is," Sam said with a facetious smile.

As soon as Sam attempted to find a way into that computer, it disconnected and was gone.

"Uh oh!" Sam said.

"What's wrong?" Evie asked.

"Master Ship disappeared. I wonder if he realized I was trying to hack in," Sam said. "I'm pulling out, just in case. I'll try again later."

Skauty and Kat had been busy planning a supply run for the fisherman. Kat would take a boat with fuel and food north tomorrow. After lunch, Skauty said he needed to go home and catch up on chores. He insisted that James stay and visit and left him there.

Kat and the younger folks spent the afternoon loading supplies onto the boat he would take tomorrow. After supper, Sam drove James to Skauty's house. They found him in the den reading.

"How are you doing, Grandpa?" Sam asked.

"I'm fine! Sometimes an old man just needs some down time."

"Are you coming for breakfast in the morning?"

"I wouldn't miss it. We have to send you off in style," Skauty replied.

"Send me off?" Sam asked.

You don't think Kat can make that run on his own, do you? He will need some help."

"Oh. I hadn't thought of that."

"I'd be happy to go, too," James volunteered.

"I was hoping so. You should know your way around a boat," Skauty teased.

"Great! I'll see you in the morning," Sam said in parting. As he left rain began to fall, and the wind howled.

* * *

James heard a loud bang in the middle of the night. Then he heard the floor creak. He got up to make sure Skauty was OK and heard, "Come on old man. You are going with us."

Peeking out the door, James saw four armed men pulling Skauty toward the front door.

"At least let me get clothes and a jacket," Skauty said rather loudly.

"OK, but hurry," one of the men said.

James thought quickly, grabbed his coat, and slipped out the window. He hurried to the front door and leaned against the wall just to the side of it. The wind-driven rain was cold.

When the door opened, Skauty walked out first. Next, James saw a revolver. He grabbed the man's arm, slammed it against the door frame, and wrenched the gun from his hand. The man screamed with pain, and James pushed him backward into the other three. He yanked the door closed.

"Get next to the house," he whispered and Skauty stepped off of the porch and crouched next to the house.

"Now what?" Skauty asked.

"We make a run for it," James said.

"Son, I'm eighty. I don't run."

"Do you have your keys?"

"Of course, I have my keys," Skauty said.

The door opened, and one of the men put his gun out. James grabbed his arm, slammed it against the door frame, and took the gun. The man pulled back and slammed the door.

"They are slow learners," James said.

"Now it's two against two," Skauty said as James handed him the second revolver.

"They are probably watching out the window. I'm going to fire into the window, and we'll try to get to the Cherokee," James said.

"Do you have to mess up my house?"

"Do you have a better idea?"

"We could wait for them to surrender," Skauty said.

"They're warm and dry. We're cold and wet. I don't see that working out in our favor," James replied.

"OK," Skauty agreed. "I'll move as fast as I can."

James fired into the window, and the glass exploded. He fired two more shots as he raced to the vehicle. Skauty cranked it and flew out of the driveway. James fired twice more to make sure they didn't get a shot off.

"It would have to be raining," Skauty said. "I hope the wind doesn't blow in too much water."

James couldn't believe his ears. "Someone tried to kill you, and you're worried about rain getting into the house?"

"It's my house. I have lived there a long time. Now what?"

"I guess we go to Kat and Sandra's, unless you have a better idea."

"We could pay a visit to Harrison and repay the hospitality," Skauty said.

James looked at the old man wide-eyed, "I don't think we should push our luck tonight. We made it with two against four. I don't like the odds of two against however many they have on that yacht."

"I guess you're right. But he is not getting away with this," Skauty said.

A sleepy Kat answered the door. "What in the world are you doing here this time of night?"

"We had visitors. They were obnoxious, so we came here," Skauty grumped.

"What are you talking about?" Sam said as he came down the stairs.

"Four men broke in and tried to abduct Skauty," James explained. "We got away."

"He shot out the front window," Skauty complained.

"Who shot out the front window?"

"James."

"I was covering us so we could get to the Cherokee."

"I think you had better come in," Kat said. "Then you can tell me the story in a way that makes sense."

By then, Sandra was up to check out the commotion. Skauty explained what had happened and how James had saved the day.

"I guess that was Harrison's response to our fishing expedition," Kat said.

"He must have thought if he had Skauty in custody the rest of the clan would surrender," Sandra said.

"How are we going to keep you safe?" Kat asked.

"Why don't you leave on the supply boat?" James asked. "They won't be able to find you, then."

"That will at least buy us a day or two," Kat said.

"Harrison thinks he can go ahead with his plans no matter what we do," Sam said, fully awake now. "He is going to ram this compound down our throats. He is a powerful man, and if we are going to stop him we will need powerful leverage."

Kat, Sam, James, and Skauty slipped onto the boat and pulled out of the harbor before dawn, leaving Harrison in their wake.

CHAPTER 22

Sitting at the desk on his yacht, Holmes Harrison squelched the growing rage that gnawed in his throat. "Please explain to me how four armed security guards could let an eighty-year-old man get away, Mr. Donegan."

"We were under the impression that the old man lived alone. Apparently, we were wrong. Someone surprised the men as they exited the front door, taking two of their guns and breaking Vandiver's wrist. They were pinned down with gunfire as they escaped," Donegan explained.

"Your detail didn't think it worthwhile to follow him?" Harrison said, fixing cold eyes on Donegan.

"I apologize for failing, sir. The men chose to get medical attention for Vandiver rather than pursue Hanson."

"Donegan, we have tipped our hand with no results. That puts me in a bad position. I expect you not to fail me again."

"Yes, sir."

After an awkward silence, Donegan left. Harrison chewed some antacids and pondered his next move.

* * *

Gray dawn oozed in the cloudy east as Kat piloted the boat north. Sam, James, Skauty, and Wingston were in the cabin with Kat.

"We need a plan," Sam said.

"It's hard to make a plan when we don't know what we are fighting against," Kat said.

"It looks like Harrison thought he could kidnap Skauty and hold him to force the rest of the Tlingit to comply with his wishes," James offered.

"What would it take for Harrison to go away and leave Sitka alone?" Sam mused.

"If he wants to control all food industries, then I don't think anything short of his death would stop him," Kat replied.

"I think I like that idea," Skauty said.

"We can't kill the man," Sam said. "That's just wrong."

"I don't consider trying to take me from my house by force exactly right," Skauty said. "Besides, my window is broken."

"Sam, before we're too far out, call Mom and tell her to send Larry out to fix that window."

"OK, I'm on it," Sam said taking Kat's phone.

"I need to warn people about what Harrison was up to last night," Skauty said. He pulled out his phone and sent a message via the Tlingit app. Skauty ended the message with, "Be vigilant. We don't know what this man will do next."

Sam stared out to sea. Random thoughts popped into his mind as he tried to focus on forming a plan. "That's about how far Evie runs when she does a 5K," he thought as he eyed the horizon. He shook his head and tried to drive his mind back to the problem at hand.

"What will it take for Harrison to give up on this venture? He wants control of the seafood industry. He wants to control the people that work for him."

"He wants total control," Sam said aloud, not realizing he spoke.

"Well, that's obvious," Kat said. "The question is what can we do about it?"

"Obviously, we have to make the situation one that he can't control. We have to make Sitka such an irritating and vexing place that he decides to set up his compound elsewhere," Sam replied.

"But how?" Skauty, James, and Kat said at the same time.

"I'm still working on that," Sam said feeling the enormity of the task weighing on him.

"Winter is coming. If we can stall for a few weeks, he may give up at least till spring," Sam said.

"That's right! If he doesn't start building soon, he will need to wait out the winter. That's why he only gave us a week to comply. He intends to start building next Monday." Kat replied.

"And that's why the cargo ship is here! It's probably filled with building supplies and equipment!" Sam said.

"Do you think he will start building even if people haven't signed on?" James asked.

"I don't know," Sam said. "He doesn't seem to be one who is easily deterred. But if we can bring home a good catch and show him that we can continue fishing even in the down times, he might reconsider our original proposal."

"Maybe you should just move and let him have the place," James said.

Skauty, Kat, and Sam looked at him as if he had lost his mind.

"Sitka is our home," Skauty said. "Our people have lived here some ten thousand years. How could we leave?"

"I certainly hope it doesn't come to that," Sam said hoping to diffuse the shock.

Silence fell on the group. The sound of the boat's engine filled the void. Sam looked to the eastern horizon as he weighed the implications of James' statement. Sam had grown up resenting Sitka and the clan because of the bullying he experienced. Leaving Sitka had been one of his life's objectives. But he realized that the rest of the clan did not feel that way.

"They are anchored to this piece of earth," Sam thought. "What James said makes sense. If there is a good catch, why not just move the clan north and walk away from Harrison? That seems logical," he thought.

But something was souring that thought. Sam realized that it wasn't his mind but his heart that tugged at the idea of leaving. It dawned on Sam for the first time in his life that he, too, was anchored to the piece of earth called Sitka. The realization landed like an earthquake.

"Sitka is our home. We can't leave," Sam said out loud.

"You are right, Sam," Skauty said putting an arm around his grandson. "We have to fight for our place in this world. If we don't do that, we can't be who we were created to be."

Sam felt the earthquake again in his heart. He hugged his grandfather back.

The trip north took about four hours. Kat made radio contact with the fleet of fishing boats, and they gave him their coordinates. Kat located the first fishing boat and tied up with it.

"How is it going?" Skauty called out as James finished tying the boats together.

"The fishing's great!" Jeffery Troutman called back in his booming voice. "We will be totally full by early tomorrow and will have to head back."

"That's great!" Kat answered. "Harrison's mouth will drop open when he sees what you have!"

Skauty and Jeffery talked fishing while Sam, James, and Kat moved fuel and food supplies, including homemade apple pies, to Jeffery's boat, "The Bear's Mouth."

They completed the same routine with the other boats till the mountain of fuel containers was gone. James took the helm while Sam pulled out lunch for everyone.

After lunch, Skauty yawned, "I think this old man needs a nap."

"I think I'll join you," Kat said, and they went to the sleeping berth.

"Your grandfather is an amazing man," James said when Kat and Skauty were gone.

"Yes, he is," Sam agreed.

"To tell you the truth, I am glad that you folks hijacked my truck. Sitka is such a wonderful place. I hope I can find a way to stay here. I can't imagine why you ever left."

"It's a long story," Sam said.

"We have four hours," James prodded.

"OK, but don't fall asleep at the wheel!" Sam said. "It started when my father met my mother. Grandpa was already the clan leader and was very much into tradition. Mom was a journalist from Chicago and obviously not Tlingit. My grandparents initially refused to accept them when they married against their wishes and against Tlingit tradition. Obviously, my grandparents eventually came around.

"But I was born a half-breed. From the time I can remember, the other kids called me names. It got worse in high school, and I ended up fighting a lot. I can't remember when, but at some point I decided that I didn't want any part of Sitka.

"I left for college, got my PhD, and never considered returning for more than a visit."

As Sam was telling his story, he found himself thinking that it sounded petty. "Why would I let teenage problems drive me from my home?" he wondered.

Sam jumped when he realized James was talking, "I certainly can understand that. It sounds like life was miserable for you."

"Thanks," Sam said. "It all seems so long ago, now. I will probably be stuck here with no options because of how I left MC2."

"I see what you mean. I have heard that the A-30 will blacklist people. If we can't stop Harrison, you may have no options here, either."

"Now that's an encouraging thought!" Sam replied.

"Sorry," James said. "I guess we will just have to make sure we stop him."

Sam drifted off into thought, and James piloted the boat on south toward Sitka. James marveled at the beauty of the mountains rising to the east. It was six pm when they neared the harbor, where a very unwelcome sight greeted them.

CHAPTER 23

Skauty and Kat had long since come back to the cabin from their naps. As soon as they were in range, both cell phones began chirping out notifications. The messages all said the same thing: "A cargo ship has docked at the cruise ship site north of town."

"I see Harrison has decided to move forward with his plan," Kat said as he watched the onboard crane offload a bulldozer and set it next to two others on the concrete.

"Surely that's just a scare tactic. He wouldn't start building before he has people committed to moving in, would he?" Sam asked.

"I wouldn't put it past him," Skauty said. "Having unlimited funds tends to lead to unlimited drive. Not getting his way is not an option for him."

"So, if he is going to do whatever it takes to build this compound, where does that leave us?" Kat asked.

"I think we're in the proverbial pickle," James said.

Sam hadn't noticed Wingston fly off the boat, but he noticed when the bird came back chirping a scratchy warning.

"What's up with Wingston?" James asked.

"I think he is warning us that something is wrong," Sam answered. He picked up the binoculars and looked toward the harbor. "I see three of the black-suit guys walking around. They are watching our boat. I have a hunch they are looking for Grandpa," Sam said as his gut tightened.

"Dad, how would you feel about another nap?" Kat asked.

"Sounds better than going for a walk with those goons," Skauty said and made his way down to the berth.

Kat moored the boat at the dock. Sam kept his eye on the three black suits and Wingston as he worked to tie down the boat. They finished preparing the boat and gathered their supplies. Sam, Kat, and James got off, leaving Skauty below.

One of the black suits approached, "Mr. Harrison would like to speak with Skauty Hanson. Have you seen him?"

"We've been out on the boat all day. Didn't catch a thing," Kat responded. "If I see him I will be sure to relay your message."

Sam noticed Wingston was sitting quietly on top of the cabin and felt relieved. A bald eagle landed on the other corner of the cabin with a screech. Sam looked the bird in the eye and wondered.

One of the black suits pointed to the eagle, "Look at that!"

Kat said, "If you will excuse us, it has been a long day," and started to walk off. Sam and James followed. Sam struggled not to look back, thinking it might create suspicion.

When Sam heard the eagle screech and one of the men yelp, he couldn't help it. Looking back, he saw the man stepping onto the boat with his hands covering his face. The eagle circled around and dived at him. The man flailed his arms and ran.

Kat and James had noticed the commotion, too. Kat walked back to the two men who were still standing near the boat. "Don't even think of getting on that boat. You have no business there."

The men glared at each other. Kat stood his ground until they walked away. Kat, Sam, and James waited until the men were out of sight. Kat called Skauty on the phone, "It will be dark in about an hour. I think you had better just stay put until we come back for you." Hanging up, Kat went back and locked the cabin door, something no one ever had to do in Sitka.

They spent a tense hour waiting for the twilight to sink into darkness. Sam relayed how Wingston had warned them and how the eagle had attacked.

"Your grandfather has an eagle friend," Viviana said. "That makes sense."

"Do you think so?" Sam asked.

"Why else would it attack?" Viviana answered.

"Wait a minute," Kat said. "Are you trying to tell me that somehow this eagle knew Dad was on the boat and was trying to protect him?"

"You saw what Wingston did," Viviana said in reply.

"Well, yes. But…" He fell silent, unable to find another explanation. Viviana slipped up the stairs.

"I wonder if Grandpa knows about the eagle," Evie said as she paced the kitchen.

"Evie, could you sit down? You're making me even more nervous than I already am!" Sam said trying to will the darkness to come faster.

"I can't. They are going to get to Grandpa before we do," she replied.

Sam recognized the tone in Evie's voice. "We have to go now!" he said standing up.

Viviana came trotting down the stairs, bow in hand and quiver on her back. Everyone looked.

"What?" she said. "There may be trouble."

Kat, Sam, James, David, and Viviana piled out the door and rushed down the pier. Viviana broke into a run, and the others followed. Sam could see something large moving on the pier.

Coming up behind Viviana, Sam saw that it was an eagle. Viviana had stopped, knelt, and was looking the eagle in the eye. Wasting no time, Sam turned to the boat. The cabin door was standing open. Sam bolted inside calling, "Grandpa!"

No answer. Rushing into the berth, Sam felt himself go numb when he confirmed what he already suspected. "He's not here!" Sam called in a panic. Sam ran back to the deck and found everyone silent with shock.

Viviana was looking under the eagle's left wing. "She's been shot," Viviana said. "It looks like the bullet went through. I think I can save her."

Sam had trouble processing Viviana's words because he was reeling from the discovery that his grandfather was gone.

"Do you think he just left and went home?" Sam asked weakly, already knowing the answer.

"I don't think so, Son," Kat said.

The eagle gave a soft call, and Sam looked over, amazed to see that it was actually letting Viviana pick it up.

"How can she do that?" James asked.

"She just has a way with animals," David answered.

No one asked what Viviana planned to do with the eagle. They knew it would be riding home with them. Sam didn't want to leave, though.

"Maybe he went for a walk. Look around the pier," Sam said.

"Sam," Kat said sternly. "The eagle would not be shot if he were just out for a walk. Take Viviana and the eagle back to the house. I'll wait here for the police."

"We should have just taken him with us after the men walked off," Sam said as a wave of guilt rolled in. "I should have stayed with him." Sam's mind roiled with similar thoughts on the long walk back to the car. He kicked himself with thoughts of what he could have done differently.

James and David crawled into the very back seat of the Suburban, leaving the middle seat for Viviana and the eagle. Sam slammed his door, and a tear rolled down his cheek.

"What are we going to do? We have to get him back," Sam said.

It was a silent ride home. The eagle seemed content to be held by Viviana. They walked into the house to find intense faces on Sandra and Evie. Sam shook his head, and Evie burst into tears.

"I knew it!" she said.

Viviana carried in the eagle.

"What in the world?" Sandra gasped.

"They shot her when they abducted Skauty," Viviana said. "This is his eagle friend. I need honey for her wound." Viviana took the eagle up to her room. Sandra recovered from the shock and went for honey.

"All I have is manuka honey," Sandra said as she came into the room.

"That's perfect!" Viviana responded. She settled the eagle on the floor and looked over the wound. "It grazed her breast and went through the wing. I think she will heal up just fine."

Viviana took the honey and began rubbing it into the wound.

"Why isn't it biting you or something?" Sandra asked.

"Birds are very smart. She knows I am trying to help. I will need a sheet."

Viviana folded the sheet into a twelve-inch width and swaddled the bird so that its wings were bound.

"I'll get safety pins," Sandra offered.

Meanwhile, Sam went back and picked up his dad. His mind was reeling, and he couldn't concentrate to generate any logical thoughts. He kept muttering as he drove to the house, "What are we going to do?"

Kat sat quietly, "First of all, if you don't stop muttering, neither of us will be able to think! What do you think they hope to gain by abducting him?"

"It has to be that they think they can coerce the Tlingit to sign onto their plan."

"You always talk about Tlingit people as if they are someone else. You are Tlingit, too. Remember?"

"Sorry, Dad. I guess I spent so much of my life resenting the bullying I got and wanting to get out of here that I don't really consider myself part of the clan."

"I see," Kat said.

Sam didn't want to get into any of the old arguments with his dad, so he said, "We need a plan."

"I guess we either negotiate or gather a group of people and try to get him back by force," Kat offered.

"I don't think the by force option would work. All they need is one person with a gun aimed at Grandpa, and then what could we do?"

They arrived at the house and sat down at the kitchen table with Evie, David, and James. Kat's phone chimed. "It's the Tlingit app. It says, 'I have reconsidered Mr. Harrison's offer. It has so many positive possibilities that I think it would be a mistake not to accept it. I, for one, am gladly signing on today. Skauty.'"

"That sounds like Harrison rather than Dad," Kat said.

"Obviously," Evie said. "They think they can lie their way into this deal. Grandpa would never willingly go against what he said."

"I'm going to let everyone know what has happened and that this statement is a lie," Kat said and started tapping on his phone.

"Wait!" Sam said. "Don't send anything. If you do, Harrison will know that everyone is aware of what he has done. Let me see the phone. Maybe I can remove Grandpa from the list of recipients. It would be better to leave Harrison wondering why no one is rushing to sign up."

Sam was able to copy the list of recipients and start a new thread minus Skauty. "OK, any ideas on how to word this?"

"Just tell them what happened and that we are trying to come up with a plan," Kat said.

Sam began typing in the message.

"And tell them that any ideas would be appreciated," Kat added.

CHAPTER 24

Before Sam could get the message entered and sent, responses were pouring in on the original message. They ran the gamut from accusing Skauty of being a traitor to thanking him for finally seeing the light.

Sam read out what he had composed, "The message you received stating that we should sign up for Harrison's plan was fake. Harrison abducted Skauty within the last two hours. We are sure that it was Harrison who sent the message using Skauty's phone. We are trying to come up with a plan to get Skauty released. Any ideas are welcomed. Also, please do not mention anything about Skauty's abduction on the original message. I have removed him from this thread so that Harrison can't see our discussion. Thanks, Kat."

Sam looked around, and everyone nodded, "Yes." He hit send. Before Sam slid the phone back to Kat, the chimes started.

Kat started reading through the responses, but they were coming in faster than he could read. "It looks like most people are ready to storm the boat and put an end to Harrison in a variety of ways. Oh, here's a new idea. Jeffery says we should ram the yacht with his fishing boat and then storm it."

"We need an idea that doesn't get Grandpa killed in the process," Evie said. "In fact, we need an idea that gets Grandpa released and scuttles this whole compound business at the same time."

Sam, Kat, and James looked at Evie. "Well, I don't know what it is, but that's what we need," she said.

"Kat!" Sandra called down the stairs. "We need Sagu's kennel for this eagle."

"I'll bring it right up," Kat said. "I sure do miss that dog. She certainly lived up to her name and brought us a lot of joy," referring to their Malamute who had died last summer.

"I need a piece of paper," Sam said and went to the printer. Returning, Sam made two columns with the headings, "Rescue Grandpa" and "Stop Compound."

Sam paused, then drew an arrow from "Rescue Grandpa" to "Stop Compound" and put a question mark above it. "If we rescue Grandpa, will that stop the compound?" he asked.

"It will certainly fortify the resistance," Evie said.

"OK, what do we need to know before we come up with a plan?" Sam asked.

"Where are they holding him?" James offered.

"Good point. I just assumed they had him on the yacht," Sam said.

"The most likely places are the yacht or the cargo ship," James said.

"Yacht or cargo ship?" Sam wrote. "What else?"

"Would Harrison kill him?" James said.

"What?" Sam asked, shaken at the thought.

"If Harrison is the type of man who would really kill someone to further his plans, then we are in a desperate situation. If he is like you when you kidnapped me, then we don't have much to worry about," James explained.

"Will he kill?" Sam wrote. Sam reflected on the previous meeting with Harrison. "Is he the type that would stop at nothing to get what he wants?" he thought. "He certainly seems unpredictable," Sam said out loud without realizing it.

"That's not good," James said, and a heaviness settled over the room.

"I don't know how she did it, but Viviana has that eagle swaddled like a baby," Kat said as he came back. "What did I miss?"

Three sets of somber eyes looked back. "Harrison may actually be willing to kill Grandpa to get what he wants," Sam said.

"We have to pray and trust that won't happen. Pray, trust, and come up with a plan, that is," Kat said as he pulled his chair up to the table.

Sam felt paralyzed. His mind flooded with images of his grandfather dying at the hands of Harrison. Fear, sadness, and rage swirled into a tornado in his heart. He saw images of his hands around Harrison's throat, and it felt good. Slowly Sam slipped back out of himself and realized everyone was staring at him.

"What?" he asked.

"You left us," Evie said.

"I was imagining choking Harrison," Sam replied.

"I think we would all like a turn at that," Kat said. "How are we going to get to him?"

Sam's mind re-engaged, and he looked at his paper. Seeing things written had always helped organize his thinking.

"First, we need to know where they are holding Grandpa. Without that, it is hard to plan," Sam said.

"If we assume it was Harrison who sent the message, I'd say he is on the yacht. Harrison doesn't seem the type to hang out on a cargo ship," Kat said.

Sam circled yacht.

Sandra passed through the kitchen and grabbed her purse. "Get Skauty saved. I'm going to the store for shavings and fish," she said as she went out the door.

"I know," David said. "We could sneak onto the boat and get Skauty off."

"That is a possibility, except for the guys in the black suits who, I am sure, are trained security guards," James pointed out.

"What if the guards weren't on board?" David asked.

"Why wouldn't they be on board?" Sam responded.

"Because we create a diversion that draws them off the yacht," David said.

"If they are a trained detail, then there will always be two guarding the prisoner," James said.

"Two is better than twelve," Sam offered.

"I have another idea," Evie said. "What if we just keep ignoring Harrison? What would happen if we did nothing, if no one signed up for his program, no one called to discuss what could be done? We just keep pretending that Harrison isn't here and go about business as usual."

"That is probably the opposite of what Harrison expects us to do," Sam said.

"Harrison expects us to capitulate to his demands, to come crawling to him with our tails between our legs," Kat said. "But if we do nothing then he just continues to move forward with the compound."

"Oooh! I have another idea! Aren't there laws that protect Native American lands? Shouldn't forcing people off of their land and into the compound be illegal?" Evie asked.

"There are laws, but they don't mean much. The government has always found a way to work around them if it suits them," Kat said.

"But Harrison is not government. Maybe we could at least slow him down with a lawsuit," David said.

Sam wrote, "Lawsuit re: Native American Land" on his paper. "Do we know an attorney who might do this?" he asked.

"There is an attorney in the clan who has always assisted with legal matters. I could give her a call," Kat said.

Sam put a "1" by lawsuit. "I think that should be our first step. Could you call her tonight?"

"I'm on it," Kat said and began searching for her number in his phone. He dialed and put the phone on speaker. A woman answered and Kat said, "May I speak with Tamarack Woods?"

"This is Tamara," she replied.

"Hey, Tamara. This is Kat Hanson."

"Hey, Kat. I was devastated to hear about Skauty being abducted. Is there anything I can do to help?"

"That's why I'm calling. I have you on speaker so we can all hear what you are saying. We were wondering if there are any laws about Native American property that would stop this compound from going forward?"

"I'm actually ahead of you on that one. I looked into it, and since Harrison is purchasing the land and offering market value, there is nothing we can do."

"I see," Kat said.

"What about Skauty? Did you call the police?"

"Yes. They said they would question Harrison, but they couldn't search his boats since they don't have any evidence that Skauty was abducted much less that Harrison did it. I haven't heard back yet."

"Let's just hope that Harrison doesn't pull his boat out of the harbor. He will be out of their jurisdiction."

"Uh oh. I hadn't thought of that," Kat said.

Sam felt a jolt as it dawned on him that Harrison could sail away where they couldn't get to him. "What are we going to do?" flashed through his mind yet again.

CHAPTER 25

Sam kissed Evie goodnight and tried to go to sleep. After an hour and a half of trying to force his body to be still when it wanted to toss as much as his mind, he went downstairs to the den. He paced in the dark hoping to avoid waking his parents. He tried to generate solutions, but his mind couldn't focus. Finally feeling exhausted, Sam lay down on the couch.

Somewhere in the night he fell asleep and dreamed. As dawn began to lighten the darkness, Sam awoke with energy and began cooking breakfast for everyone.

With the smell of bacon drifting in the air, people began to filter into the kitchen. Sam was whistling and began taking orders for eggs.

Evie was the last to come down. "Sam, you are entirely too happy this morning. What's up?"

"I had a dream last night."

"It must have been a doozie," Sandra said.

"It was," Sam said. "It started out just like the dream I had when we were leaving the mountain. Do you remember the one about the storm rolling in on David and Viviana's wedding?"

"Yes," Evie said.

"This time the storm came on shore, and the rain poured in torrents. Then it started raining fish. One fish came up to me and began talking. It said, 'Come with me, and I will show you the way.' It held out a fin. I took hold of it, and we began walking into the ocean."

"And that's why you are so happy this morning?" David asked.

"Yes. Don't you see? The fish are the solution. If we can get the fish back, that will restore confidence to our people. They will be willing to fight off Harrison's compound. When the compound is defeated, Harrison will have no reason to hold Grandpa. We have to focus on getting the fish back instead of rescuing Grandpa."

"You mean just leave him in Harrison's hands?" Sandra said.

"Well, for now, I guess," Sam answered, suddenly feeling less certain.

"I think you are right!" Evie said. "It's like dominoes. If we get the fish back, everything else starts falling, too."

"I think we need to keep working on ways to get Dad out of Harrison's clutches, though," Kat said. "We still don't know what he might do."

Kat's phone chimed with a message on the Tlingit app. Kat read, "The sign-up center is now open for your convenience. Please stop by and register to be a part of this wonderful new community. -Skauty."

Icy water crashed on Sam's optimism.

"It's OK, Sam. We can't expect Harrison just to fold his hands and do nothing until we foil his plans," Evie said.

"You're right. We need to tell everyone to hold tight and be patient while we figure this out.

Kat opened the thread that did not include Skauty's phone and sent out the message, ending with, "For now, let's just not respond at all. Thanks, Kat."

Jeffery responded, "Are you sure you don't want me to ram the yacht?"

"Not yet, but hold that thought," Kat responded.

Sam pushed his plate away and flipped over the paper he had begun last night, writing "Fish" at the top. "We need to think of all the ways that Harrison could have driven the fish away."

"We already mentioned sonar and poison," David said. "Are there any other possibilities?"

"Since we haven't seen a bunch of dead fish, it couldn't be poison. And we haven't noticed a strange ship that would be canvassing the area with sonar," Kat said.

"What if Harrison hired someone in the community to do it? They could be sailing around, and we wouldn't notice," Sandra said.

The crew went silent. "That's a scary thought," Kat said. "The boats should be back today. Since they have a good catch, it will probably be a few days before they go back out."

"I don't think I can stand to wait three more days before we do anything!" Sam said.

"Did anyone stay behind?" Evie asked.

"Why?" Sam responded.

"If someone was on Harrison's payroll, they might not feel the need to go off for a few days. They might even have continued running the sonar to keep the fish away!" Evie answered.

"Brilliant, Evie! Let's check to see if any fishing boats went out while the rest of the fleet was away," Sam said adding a note to his page.

"I could fly out over the sound and see if I spot any boats that look as if they might be doing something suspicious," Kat said.

"Another great idea!" Sam said, hope beginning to rise again.

"What are we going to do if we find someone is using sonar to scare off the fish?" David asked.

Another moment of silence.

"If it is one of us, I hope community pressure will be enough to get them to stop," Kat offered.

"If not, maybe Jeffery could ram their boat," James said.

Everyone looked at James like he was mad, then Kat burst out laughing. "That would be quite a sight!" he said.

Everyone joined in the laugh, and the tension lifted.

"But we still have no idea what to do if we find a boat doing that," Sam pointed out.

"How is the eagle this morning?" David asked.

"She seems content in her cage," Viviana answered.

"We should name her," David said.

"No. It is for Skauty to name her," Viviana replied.

Kat pulled his phone back out and called the airport to schedule his flight.

"I'd be happy to go with you," James offered.

"Thanks, James. I'd appreciate the company."

Sam pondered over his paper, which had only three lines. "It just seems like there should be more to do," he muttered to himself.

"I'm going to check in with the police before we go," Kat said and dialed the station.

"Well, that's not good news. Thanks for letting me know," Kat said as he hung up. "Congress has granted the dirtbag diplomatic immunity. The police said they can't even question Harrison."

"So, we are on our own for this," Sam said feeling another jolt to his optimism.

* * *

Kat taxied the sky-blue plane onto the runway and accelerated for takeoff. Flying out over the sound, James scanned the ocean with binoculars.

"After a few minutes, Kat asked, "Tell me about yourself, James. What sort of work have you done?"

"I grew up in a small town that was devastated by one of the A-30 compounds. We scraped and scrounged, trying to survive. My father, mother, and brother all died from diseases brought on by starvation. I turned eighteen a week after my mother died and signed up for the Navy. It saved my life. I had the opportunity to become a SEAL. After I retired from the Navy, I went to work for MC2 as a security guard."

"How did you like that?"

"It never really set well with me. I felt like I was working for the very ones who took my family's lives. To be honest, I was relieved when Sam hijacked my truck. It gave me the way out I had been looking for. How about you? What sort of work have you done over the years?"

"I started out fishing and decided that was too much like work. So I got into charter fishing tours. After about ten years there was so much competition, I moved into air tours. And that's what I've been doing since. The cruise ships have kept my business going. Of course, as the number of A-30 compounds has increased, there are fewer people able to travel. It is mostly the upper management of the companies now. But they can afford to pay a nice fee."

Kat continued flying west over the southern end of the sound. "So far I see nothing suspicious. Do you?"

"Not a thing," James replied. "Whoa! Look at that pod of dolphins! There must be forty or fifty of them."

Kat turned the plane so he could see the silver backs and fins breaching the surface. "Those are Pacific white-sides. I don't believe I have ever seen a pod that large."

Kat turned the plane and resumed heading out over the sound.

"That's a big ship!" James said pointing to the south. Training the binoculars on it he said, "It could be an old navy frigate."

"Let's take a look," Kat said and turned the plane south.

"It is a frigate! The navy decommissioned those a long time ago."

"What is it doing out here then?" Kat asked.

"I have no idea. Don't get too close, though. They have antiaircraft guns."

"Roger that! I think I'll turn around now," Kat said.

"Well get a little closer so we can see what it is up to," James replied.

"OK, but if we get shot down, I'm going to haunt you for eternity!" Kat replied with a bit of nervousness.

"Who could have gotten their hands on an old navy ship?" James asked.

"I know one scallywag in particular who could afford to buy one. Do you think it could have anything to do with Harrison?"

"I suppose it could. It could also be Russians or any number of terrorist groups. It looks like it is just sitting there. I wonder if it is dead in the water."

"Can we turn around yet?"

"Yep. Let's veer away so they know we aren't coming any closer. I think we need to report this to the Coast Guard when we get back."

Kat gladly turned the plane and headed back toward Sitka on the northern side of the sound.

CHAPTER 26

When Kat pulled into the driveway, he saw a strange car. "I wonder who is here," he muttered. Walking into the kitchen, they found Tamara, the lawyer.

"I wanted to come by and let you know I am thinking of you and am willing to do anything I can to help get Skauty back," she said.

"She brought pie," Sam said, pointing to the chocolate pies on the table.

Tamara was tall, thin, fortyish, and had long black hair gathered with a scrunchy at her neck. Wearing a long, flowing earth tone skirt and blouse and no makeup, she presented an earthy demeanor. Her dark almond eyes were bright with a natural joy.

Sam noticed that James was staring as Tamara gave Kat a hug and introduced herself.

"Hi, I'm Tamarack Woods, but everyone calls me Tamara."

"It's a pleasure to meet you. I'm James," he said shaking her hand.

"Is it too early for pie?" Kat asked.

"Not if we have coffee with it," Sandra said as she put plates and forks on the table.

"What did you see in the sound?" Sam asked.

"Nothing but an old Navy frigate about ten to fifteen miles out," Kat said.

"And a huge pod of dolphins," James added.

"What is a frigate doing out there?" Sam asked.

"I don't know, but I'm going to make sure the Coast Guard knows about it," Kat said pulling out his phone to make the call.

Sam got out mugs, creamer, and sugar. He started to cut the pie, but Evie said, "You'd better let me do that,"

Sam's cheeks reddened a bit, and he said, "I know. I can't cut straight," and handed the pie cutter to Evie.

Sam sat down, pulled out the sheet from earlier in the morning and added, "Frigate?"

"Do you think he means to bring the frigate up and shell the city if we don't sign up for his program?" Sam asked.

"That's pretty drastic," Evie said.

"But a couple of missile attacks might scare people into compliance," Sam pointed out.

"They could actually fire the missiles from where they are now," James pointed out.

"That's comforting," Sam said feeling his neck muscles tighten. "So Sitka could explode at any moment."

"From what we have seen of Harrison, I think he will give an ultimatum first," James said. "And he would probably pull the frigate into sight for effect."

Kat came back in smiling, "We can relax about the frigate. The Coast Guard said it is registered to a French oceanic research company that is doing mappings of the ocean floor to search for fault lines."

"With a frigate?" Sam said.

"Maybe they got a good deal on it. It would hold all their equipment," Kat offered.

"I hope the Navy removed the ammunition before selling it," James said. "Let's get back to Skauty. Tamara, is there anything we can do legally to get Harrison to let him go?"

"We could file a lawsuit to request an exception so that his yacht could be searched. But I'm sure his lawyers would make that drag out a long time. I'm also not sure we have enough evidence to get the exception if it proceeded. No one saw Skauty being abducted, did they?"

"No. We left him hiding in the boat hoping Harrison's thugs would think he wasn't with us. When we went back after him, the cabin door stood open, and he was gone," Sam said.

"It sounds like we either have to convince Harrison to let Skauty go or go get him ourselves," James said.

"Go get him?" Sam asked.

"Maybe. I have been thinking more about a rescue mission. I think Viviana and I could slip on board at night and rescue Skauty," James said.

Viviana looked up from her pie and raised one eyebrow.

"That sounds too dangerous," Sandra said.

"I agree," David said. "If anyone goes with you, it will be me. I don't want Viviana to be at such great risk."

"Now that WOULD be dangerous!" James said.

"What do you mean?" David asked.

"I mean Viviana knows what she is doing. She and I would have a much better chance than you and I. Sorry." James replied.

"No. No. There are way too many guards to try that," Evie said.

"If we go in the middle of the night, most of them will be sleeping," James said.

"Do you really think you can do it?" Sam asked, hopeful.

"We would need some equipment and need to do some research on that yacht. Does Skauty swim?" James asked.

"He used to, but he hasn't been in the water for a long time," Kat said.

"Has he ever scuba dived?"

"Not that I'm aware of," Kat answered.

Viviana had raised both eyebrows. At first Sam thought he saw fear on her face, then he realized she appeared more curious than afraid. The room went silent, and Sam realized everyone was looking at Viviana.

"What?" she asked.

"What do you about James' proposal?" Sam asked.

"I have never scuba dived, but I'm sure I could learn. I don't like the close quarters of the yacht. A lot of things could go wrong. But that is to their disadvantage, too. If we could find a time when a number of the guards were off the boat, it might be doable. In the middle of the night, one call for help would have us terribly out numbered."

"I see your point," James said.

"Maybe we should reconsider David's idea of a diversion," Viviana said. "If we are going to do this, we want the odds in our favor."

"Um, you do realize there are legal consequences to breaking into someone's yacht," Tamara said. "In fact, I don't think I need to be hearing any of this conversation. You are probably going to need me later."

"There has to be a better solution," Evie said.

Sam's heart sank again. "I just want Grandpa out of that man's hands before he does something terrible to him. I was just starting to get my hopes up."

"I think we need to think long-game strategy. If we did get Skauty off the boat, then what?" We would still be in the same situation with regard to the compound," Tamara said. "Let's focus on how we can beat Harrison long term."

"I think it goes back to the fish," Evie said. "He has pounced because he thinks we are vulnerable. We have to regain the upper hand."

"How do we regain the upper hand against a man with unlimited resources?" Sam asked.

"We have to help him see the light," Evie said with a smile.

"I know that look," Sam said. "What are you thinking?"

"What if we sign a deal to sell our fish to Russia?"

"What?" everyone exclaimed at once.

"If we had a deal to sell our fish to Russia, we would not be dependent on Harrison at all."

"It's too far. It would take at least three, four, maybe five days get the fish there."

"Not if we flew them," Evie said, her smile spreading.

"My plane can't carry fish," Kat pointed out.

"We would have to have a plane that could carry the load," Evie said. "Do you know anything about international trade deals?" she asked, looking at Tamara.

"We studied it in law school, but I must confess I have never been involved in one."

"Evie, we need a reality check," Sam said. "First, we have no fish to sell. Second, we have no plane to fly them. Third, why would the Russians buy from us?"

"Sam, you're such a pessimist!," Evie responded. "We have proven that there are fish to catch north of here. I'm sure we can find a plane somewhere to borrow. And Harrison doesn't need to know that this is all a ruse."

Sam found himself speechless. Everyone was silent as they processed what Evie was saying.

"We beat Harrison at his own game, you see. Or at least we make him think we have," Evie said. "Tamara, do you think you could create official-looking documents that formed a new co-op with a contract to sell fish to Russia?"

"I'm sure I could," Tamara said with a smile. "That is so illegal!"

Sam was once again amazed at Evie's creativity. He was so grateful to have her in his life.

"Evie, you're amazing," he said as he drew a line under what he had written and put a new heading, "Russian Ruse." He added, "Contract: Tamara."

"Besides contracts and a plane, what else do we need to make this believable?" Sam asked as he wrote, "Plane?" "Fish?"

"I think we will have to lay low for a few days to make it seem legitimate that we are processing the contract," Kat said.

"Then we will need to go fishing so that we have something to sell," David added.

The crew continued to brainstorm ideas until well after lunch time. Finally with hope rising, Sam said, "This might just work! But what about Grandpa?"

CHAPTER 27

Holmes Harrison nodded at the guard. The guard turned and unlocked the cabin door. Harrison stepped in and found Skauty staring out the window, which faced south toward the harbor. Harrison slammed the door.

"Why isn't anyone responding to your request for them to sign up?"

"I didn't make a request," Skauty said.

"I did! I used your phone," Harrison said, trying to squelch his anger. "Aside from a few initial responses, there has been nothing. And no one has come by the center to sign up."

"I guess they don't like your offer," Skauty said.

"I thought you were their leader. Why don't they do what you tell them to?"

"The Tlingit are not puppets. They have minds of their own."

"What will it take to get them to sign on?"

"Perhaps you need to ask them that."

"Right now, I am asking you, and I expect a straight answer."

"Mr. Harrison, we want nothing to do with your compound. We have made you an offer. I suggest you accept it or go home and let us be."

"You don't seem to understand. I am building this compound with or without you Tlingit. You can either get on board, or the rest of your life will be very short."

"Mr. Harrison, I am old and will die soon anyway. What you say is irrelevant."

Harrison gritted his teeth. He pulled out a couple of antacids and chewed them. Then he held out Skauty's phone. "Send a message to your people in your own words that will convince them to cooperate."

"Why would I want to do that?"

"Because I have a frigate sitting about fifteen miles out that can blow this village off the map if you don't."

"That's a likely story," Skauty replied.

Harrison swallowed the rage, composed himself, and said civilly, "Mr. Hanson, I don't want to have to resort to something that drastic. It might save me some demolition costs, though. If you want to save the lives of your people, send the message."

"If you kill the people, you have no one to fish."

"Don't try me, Hanson. Send the message."

Skauty was quiet for a moment then held out his hand. Harrison breathed a sigh of relief as he handed him the phone. "I want to see what you have written before you hit send."

Skauty took the phone, typed in a message, and handed it back.

"What is this?" Harrison said pointing to the first word.

"That is 'Greetings' in the Tlingit language. It is how I start all my messages."

How do I know that is what it says?"

"If you want the message to be believable, send it. If not, I'll change that word into English."

Harrison glared at Skauty, trying to decide if he was telling the truth. He hit send and walked out the door.

* * *

Sam and David were putting up lunch fixings when Kat's phone pinged. He opened the message and read.

"What is this?" he asked and handed Sam the phone.

"Do you recognize that Tlingit word?"

"I have no idea what it means," Kat said.

The rest of the message read, "Mr. Harrison continues to offer his generous proposal to settle us in a compound so that we can continue to fish these waters. In today's world, it is the best we can do. I hope you will consider signing on. Skauty."

"Let me call Jeffery," Kat said and placed the call.

"Hey, Jeffery, did you see the message from Dad?"

"I did," Jeffery said and burst out laughing.

"What's so funny? Did you recognize that first word?"

"It says, 'This is a lie!'" Jeffery chuckled. "The old man is still crafty!"

"That he is," Kat agreed. He hung up and explained to Sam and the others.

"At least we know that Grandpa is still alive," Sam said.

"Apparently Harrison decided to force him to send a message thinking it would be more believable," Kat laughed. "Boy did that backfire!"

"Do you think we have enough details pinned down to let people know what our plan is?" Sam asked.

"No," Evie responded. "If there is someone in the community on Harrison's payroll, the plan would be ruined. We have to keep it secret."

"You're right, I'm sure," Sam said. "What can we tell people, then?"

"We tell them that in order to preserve our way of life we need to continue resisting Harrison. Never give in!" Kat said.

"That sounds perfect!" Sam said.

Kat opened the thread that didn't include Skauty's phone and sent the message. He added, "Please do not respond to the original message. We want Harrison in the dark about what we are thinking."

"I'm off to research creating a co-op and an international trade deal," Tamara said, standing up from the table.

"Thank you so much, Tamara," Kat said.

Viviana and David went up to check on the eagle, taking a fish snack.

"I think I'll go for a walk," James said and got his jacket. Tamara was still in the driveway tapping on her phone. As he walked near the car, she rolled down the window. James stopped, then realized she was waiting for him to speak.

"Oh, I was going for a walk," he finally said self-consciously. "It is great what you are doing to help them out."

"Skauty is a great leader. I would do anything to get him back and to preserve this community from Harrison's attack," she said.

"I sure hope this works," James said. The urge to ask Tamara if she would like to walk with him caught him by surprise. He was weighing his options when she turned the car off.

"Would you mind if I walked with you?" she asked.

James flashed a big smile, "That would be nice!"

CHAPTER 28

Later Wednesday afternoon, Evie walked into the den and found Sam pacing like a caged lion.

"What's wrong?" she asked.

"I don't think I can stand not doing anything to get Grandpa back," Sam said.

"But we are doing something. Remember, we have to play the long game and not do anything rash."

"I know. But it's hard just to wait."

"All right, let's do something then. Let's take a drive and see what is happening at the yacht."

Sam lit up with agreement.

Sam parked the car at Harrigan Hall, and he and Evie walked around the east side of the building.

"There is no guard," Sam whispered as soon as they could see the yacht. "Maybe we should walk on board and act like tourists."

"That's about the dumbest thing I have ever heard you say," Evie scolded.

They continued walking. When they were about even with the gangplank, a guard came out with a thermos.

"I told you," Evie said.

Sam and Evie kept walking as if they were just out admiring the scenery. They walked on down to the point where the breakwater went out and stood for a while.

"I can almost feel him," Evie said.

"We are so close. I wish we could at least talk to him," Sam said.

Evie took his hand, "We are going to get him back. I just know it."

"I wish I felt that confident."

They stood silently for a few moments gazing out at the sea. Then Sam exclaimed, "The fish!"

"What?"

"We have to get back to figuring out what happened to the fish. While Tamara is setting up our contract with the Russians, we still need to bring the fish back."

"You are right."

"What is it that we need to know?" Sam mused. Looking at the ocean, he said, "We don't know if there is anything toxic in the water."

"Maybe it's not a toxin, but something the fish just don't like, so it ran them off."

"That could be a possibility. I think we need to talk to the Sitka Sound Science Center. Maybe they can help us out. Let's go," Sam said already turning and heading to the car.

Evie hustled to catch up with him. Sam waved at the guard as they bustled past.

"Why did you do that?" Evie asked.

"I don't know. Just a wild hair, I guess."

It was 4:05pm when Sam parked at the Science Center. There was no one at the ticket booth, and the hall seemed deserted. A door opened and a lady poked her head out, "The aquarium is closed for today."

"Is there any way we could see the director? It is urgent," Sam said.

"Just a minute."

Sam and Evie waited in the hall. Another door opened and a tall woman with curly brown hair walked out with a curious look on her face. "Hello, I'm Dr. Susan Taylor. How can I help you?"

"We are Sam and Evie Hanson. It is nice to meet you. Are you aware of the disappearance of fish from the sound?"

"I have heard that the fishing industry has been struggling the last few months."

"They aren't just struggling! There are no fish whatsoever in the sound."

"That is hard to believe," Dr. Taylor said.

"I was wondering if you have tested any water samples lately."

"No, it has been a while since we have done that. We have been focusing on getting new programs up and running with the community."

"Would it be possible to test some samples to see if there is a substance in the water that could run the fish off?"

"Right now, I don't have the resources to devote to that. I am sure this is just a cyclical downturn in the fish population," she responded.

"I trust you are aware that Holmes Harrison intends to build a compound right where your facility stands," Sam said feeling irritated.

"I have been assured that Mr. Harrison will leave our facility standing."

"I see. Would you be willing to help us at all?"

"I don't see how I can help."

"If we bring in water samples from the sound, would you test them?"

"I see. Yes, we could do that."

"Do you have any direction as to how and where to take the samples?"

"I can send you the coordinates for our usual sample locations and provide you with clean containers for the samples. Just a minute," and she disappeared.

In a couple of minutes, Dr. Taylor returned with a bag of twelve plastic bottles, a pen, and a piece of paper. "If you will write down your email address, I will send you the coordinates. I will need the samples within three hours after the last one is taken, so please plan to start early in the morning. It typically takes about three hours to cover the sampling locations."

"Thank you very much," Sam said with hope they were finally getting somewhere.

* * *

A beautiful sunrise peeked over the mountains Thursday morning as Sam, Evie, David, Viviana, and James walked out the dock to Jeffery's boat, followed by four birds. Jeffery tried to shoo the birds off when they landed on his cabin.

"Those are our bird friends, Jeffery," Sam said as he handed him the list of coordinates for the sampling locations. "They will come with us."

Jeffery had a puzzled look as he entered the coordinates into the boat's navigation system.

"Thank you so much for helping us out, Jeffery," Evie said.

"Glad to do it," Jeffery said in his gruff voice. "There's no place I would rather be on a beautiful day like this, anyway."

David and James removed the mooring lines, and Jeffery glided the boat out of the harbor. The six of them chatted and enjoyed the scenery till they arrived at the first sampling spot.

Sam read the directions for taking a sample, removed the inner bottle from its container, attached it to a line and tossed it over. He let the line slide through his hands as the sample bottle sank. When it reached the depth marker on the rope, he pulled it up quickly and returned it to its container before the water could leak out the small holes on the side designed to let water in slowly in order to get samples from varying depths.

"One down, eleven to go," Sam said as he labeled the jar.

On the way to the fourth sampling location, David pointed off the port side, "Look at the dolphins! There must be forty of them!"

"I bet that's the same pod we saw from the airplane," James said. "It's odd that they are swimming in a row, side by side."

"Guys, why would a large pod of dolphins be swimming in the sound if there are no fish?" Evie asked.

"Maybe they are sightseeing," David offered.

"Does it seem odd that they are lined up in a semicircle?" Evie asked, watching as the dolphins swam west.

"That is an unusual configuration," James said.

"I think we should follow them," Evie said.

"We can't follow them," Sam snapped. "We have to finish these samples and get them to the lab."

"I guess you're right," Evie relented.

No one had noticed Rey fly off, but no one missed him when he came back, flying from the direction of the dolphins. He squawked a loud warning. Viviana looked at Rey and looked at the dolphins.

"Rey agrees with you, Evie. He says there is something fishy about those dolphins."

"Jeffery, could we come back tomorrow and see if we can follow the dolphins?" Evie asked.

"I'm afraid I can't tomorrow. I have a doctor's appointment. Have to get the old ticker checked out."

"I don't see much point in following a pod of dolphins," Sam said. When he saw the look on Evie's face, he knew he had blundered. He knew better than to question Evie's instincts, but somehow he kept forgetting.

"One of these days I may learn," Sam said. "Of course, we need to check out the dolphins. I'm sure we can find a boat."

CHAPTER 29

s soon as Tamara got back to her office Wednesday afternoon, she had her secretary reschedule her two clients and poured herself into researching how to create a company that could sell to Russia. She pulled out her old textbook on international law and scanned through the chapter on trade. Feeling rushed, Tamara slung her hair over her shoulder and scribbled notes on a legal pad.

"OK, that's a start," she thought. "All I have to do is create a company, get a business license, open a bank account, and fake a contract with Russia. Good grief! That will take forever."

Tamara opened the government trade site and made a list of documents that would be needed to do an actual trade deal with Russia. She leaned back in her chair and massaged the tense muscles in her neck. "OK, the first thing I have to do is set up the business," she thought. She did a query for obtaining a business license and discovered it would take ten to fifteen business days at best. "Good grief!"

Tamara stood and looked out her window at the mountains rising in the east. She realized she was hungry and noticed it was already 6:30pm. She peeked out her office door. As she suspected, her secretary had long since left.

"I can't do anything on an empty stomach!" She collected her purse, computer, and two law books, went by a drive-through café, and headed home. Tamara opened the door and was greeted with a sweet meow as her calico cat, Patches, rubbed around her legs. Depositing her load on the kitchen table, she turned a chair out and sat down. Patches jumped into her lap and rubbed Tamara's chin with her chin.

"I missed you, too!"

"Meow!"

"I know I'm late," Tamara said and hopped up to get the all-important treats. She deposited six morsels on the floor and sat down to her dinner. She had an epiphany when she opened the Styrofoam container with her chicken tenders, green beans, and macaroni and cheese.

"We can just use one of the fishermen's business licenses!" she said aloud.

"Meow!" Patches agreed.

She had just knocked two to three weeks off the process.

After dinner, Tamara propped up on the couch with the computer and Patches in her lap. She worked late into the night generating fake forms and contracts, leaving blanks to fill in the needed names.

Tamara felt a twinge of guilt when she hit print. "As long as I am not signing anything! I will just consider this practice in case I do ever want to help a client export something."

The sound of the printer awoke the sleeping cat. She stood and stretched and started to lie back down.

"Oh no you don't," Tamara said. "It's time for us to go to bed."

* * *

At lunch time on Thursday, Tamara left her office and took the forms she had created over to Kat and Sandra's.

"Hey, Tamara!" Kat said opening the door.

"I have made a lot of progress with our international trade deal," she said with a smile.

"Come on in. Would you like some lunch? Sandra and I were about to sit down to chicken salad sandwiches."

"Sure! That sounds great."

Kat ushered Tamara into the kitchen. Sandra was already setting another place.

"I ran into one hitch," Tamara said. "It will take at least two weeks, maybe longer to get a business license."

"Well, that won't do," Sandra said.

"You're right. So I thought we might use one of the licenses someone already has. It won't be a co-op, but at least we can keep moving forward."

"I would be happy to use my business license for the sightseeing tours. Would that work?"

"It's a stretch, but since none of this is real, anyway, I don't see why not. There is another problem. We have to have a signature from the Russian who is part of the deal."

"Does that mean it has to be in Russian?"

"I suppose our Russian could speak English and sign in English?" Tamara said uncertainly. "I don't know how official we need to be for Harrison to buy it. I am sure that he is familiar with international trade, given the business he is in."

"I wonder if the priest at St. Michael's speaks Russian?" Sandra asked.

"That's a promising idea!" Kat said.

"I'm not sure how a priest would feel about forging a signature," Tamara pointed out.

"You have a point," Kat said.

The door popped open, and Sam and the others walked in from their water sample mission. Viviana was last and had to shoo Rey back out as he tried to fly in.

"Mission accomplished," Sam announced. "Dr. Taylor said the results should be ready sometime this afternoon or tomorrow morning."

"We saw what looked like the same pod of dolphins again," James said. "Evie thinks there is something suspicious about them."

"Do you know of a boat we could use tomorrow to try to follow them?" Sam asked. "Jeffery has a doctor's appointment."

"I'm sure Jonathan wouldn't mind your using his. It's the one we took the supplies in. He has cancer and can't get out in it much. But he likes to have it run. Of course, we would have to supply the gas," Kat answered. "I'll give him a call in a bit. Right now, we are trying to figure out how to forge a signature in Russian."

"That's no problem," Sam said. "I can generate one on the computer, and we can trace it."

"But it needs to look like a signature," Kat explained.

"It will," Sam assured. "The program will even show us how to make the letters."

"That ought to be illegal," Sandra said.

"It won't be an actual person's signature, just how the word would look if you wrote it," Sam said. "All we need is a name."

"I looked up a Russian importer who deals in seafood," Tamara said. "Pyotr Poletov."

"When do we need it?"

"Now would be good," Kat said.

Sam hopped up to get his computer while David and Evie finished laying out lunch supplies.

"The next question is how do we present this to Harrison in a way that convinces him to let Skauty go?" Tamara asked.

Sam returned, opened his computer, and asked, "How do you spell that guy's name?" Sam typed it in the computer, hit translate and then print.

"That was easy," Kat said.

Sam turned the computer toward the table and hit write. The computer showed a pen writing the words in Russian.

"Wow! That's nifty!" David said.

"Back to presenting our Russian deal to Harrison," Tamara said.

"I guess we have a meeting with him and tell him that we will not be signing onto his compound because we will be selling to the Russians," Kat said. "I hope he will realize that he has no reason to keep holding Dad."

"Or he would up the stakes and threaten to kill Grandpa if we don't comply with his demands," Evie pointed out. "Maybe we should just continue ignoring Harrison and pretend he is not here."

"What?" Sam said.

"What if we send out word that we will be heading north to fish in a few days and will be selling to this Poletov guy? We could let Harrison discover it on the app. He'll be caught off guard and feel like he is losing control."

"That should make him angry, all right! But is that what we want? Isn't an angry Harrison more dangerous?" Sam asked.

"If he feels he is losing control, there is no telling what he might do," Tamara said.

"True, but then he would have to make the next move," Evie pointed out. "It may push him to compromise."

"It's risky, but I agree your idea puts more pressure on Harrison," Tamara replied.

Sam suddenly didn't want to eat. The room seemed to be closing in on him.

"What is it, Sam?" Evie asked.

"I don't like putting Grandpa's life on the line like this. I feel that we are playing with dynamite, and it could blow up in our faces any minute."

"Sometimes dynamite is what it takes to break up the rocks and free the diamond," Evie said.

Sam was silent. Everyone was silent. Finally Sam said, "I'm sure you are right, Evie. But it is still scary."

CHAPTER 30

Friday dawned with a dull pewter sky. Sam had spent another restless night and was up cooking bacon and mixing pancakes before the rest were out of bed. The smell of bacon brought David down first.

"Good morning! You do know how to wake a guy up stomach first!"

"Hey, David! Things have been so crazy that I haven't asked about your wedding plans. How are they coming?"

"We haven't talked about that lately. With all that is going on, I guess the wedding plans are on hold."

"Today is the day we roll the dice and see what happens," Sam said.

"I have said my prayers, and my fingers are crossed!" David replied, holding up two sets of crossed fingers. "We have some dolphins to chase, too."

"Does it seem silly to go chasing a pod of dolphins?"

"Not if Evie and Rey think there is something to them."

The others filed into the kitchen one by one as Sam finished the last piece of bacon. He poured the bacon grease into a jar and began cooking the pancakes. Kat came in without a word, put his phone on the table, and stared at it.

"What's wrong, Dad? You look like you're afraid the phone is going to bite you." Sam said.

"It probably will," Kat said. "I can't decide how to word the message for this morning."

"I'd say just pretend like it is really happening," Sam said.

"I'll take over pancake patrol so you two can focus your creative energies," David said and hopped up.

Sam sat down across the table from his dad. "What if we say something like, 'The international trade deal we have been working on was finalized last night. Our first expedition will set out Monday morning with the goal of delivering a nice catch of halibut to Russia on Wednesday. All who are interested are welcome to participate?'"

"You made that seem easy," Kat said.

"Well, I have been stewing on it most of the night."

"Do you think you need to spell out the price they will get for their catch?" David asked.

"You do realize that there will be a million questions since people have never heard of this idea," Evie remarked as she took a seat at the table.

"Yeah, I don't know what to do about that," Sam said.

"I think we have to take a chance and explain to people what is going on before we release the invite. We are less likely to be sunk by a spy in the community than the obvious lack of understanding that will come from the random message," Evie said.

"Evie, what would we do without you?" Kat said. "You are absolutely right. We have to take the chance and let our people know what is going on before we send out the message."

Kat picked up his phone and began pecking away. After what seemed like forever, he said, "How does this sound? 'My fellow Tlingit, we are about to send a message over the app that Holmes Harrison can see in an attempt to get Skauty released. The message will say that we have finalized an international trade deal with Russia and will be selling our fish to them. That is not true, but please play along like it is. The message will say that our first expedition will set out Monday morning and that we plan to deliver the catch to Russia by Wednesday. In order to carry out the ruse, we may have to head north on a fishing trip Monday morning, so please be preparing. My hope is that once Harrison thinks we have gone around him and don't need him, he will let Skauty go. Please go along with the message and act like you are interested in the deal.

'Thank you so much, Kat.'"

"It sounds good to me," Sam said while watching for Evie's reaction. He then realized everyone was looking at her.

"Should we add a picture of the contract?" Evie asked. When she realized everyone was staring blankly she added, "I mean in the message that Harrison receives."

"That is a clever idea," Kat said. "Is everyone good with the original message?"

Heads nodded around the table. Kat hesitated a moment, then hit send. He slid his phone over to Sam, "It's your turn."

Sam picked up Kat's phone and began typing in the message he had come up with earlier. Kat's phone rang, and Sam jumped and dropped it. Recovering, he picked it up off the floor and answered, "Hello."

"Hi, it's Susan from the Science Center. We finished testing the samples and found nothing unusual. Just traces of boat fuel and plastic residue. I don't see anything that would explain the disappearance of the fish."

"Thank you so much, Susan. I really appreciate your help," Sam said. He hung up and announced, "There is nothing in the water driving the fish away."

"I'd say you're wound a little tight this morning," David offered.

"It's not every day you send a message on which your grandfather's life depends," Sam answered.

When Sam had finished typing, he read the message out loud. Evie pulled out the last page of the contract with the signatures. Sam took a picture of it and added it to the message.

"I can't believe how fast my heart is beating," he said. His palms were sweating, too. Sam looked up, and everyone read the question on his face.

"Send it," Kat said.

Sam sent the message, and David placed a huge pile of pancakes on the table.

Before the butter made its rounds, celebratory responses began coming in on Kat's phone. He read some of the responses.

"Yay! We're back in business!"

"I am so glad this worked out!"

"It looks like we don't need Harrison after all!"

"Yay! I'm all in and will be ready Monday morning!"

"It looks like they took the bait and ran with it!"

"I wonder how long it will be before Harrison sees it!" Sam said.

* * *

Holmes Harrison was in the dining room drinking coffee and reading the news on his computer. Dirk Donegan walked in. "There was a notification on Hanson's phone," he said handing over the phone.

Harrison opened the phone and read. He felt the familiar burning in his stomach but kept his face placid.

"So that's why they have been so quiet," he said as he fished three Tums out of his suit coat pocket. "Dirk, they have established a contract with a Russian to sell fish. Can you believe that?"

"No, sir, I can't imagine they would try such a thing."

Harrison scanned through some of the responses, "They certainly seem happy about it. That was a bold and unexpected move. What do you think we can do about it?"

"I'm sure you will come up with a devastating response," Dirk said.

"Yes. Yes. Devastating," Harrison said absent mindedly. "Dirk, leave me, please. This will take some pondering."

"Of course, sir," he said and left the dining room.

Harrison walked over and looked out the window facing Harrigan Hall. "It's been a while since I have had this good of a fight," he said out loud. "Do you people really not care about your leader? I will have to find something you do care about then."

Harrison called Dirk, "Meet me at Hanson's room, please."

"Yes, sir."

Harrison and Dirk strolled into Skauty's room, "Good morning, Mr. Hanson."

"Good morning."

"I trust you enjoyed your breakfast."

"It was quite nice, thank you."

"It appears that your people really don't care about you," Harrison said as he handed Skauty his phone. "Look at how they have treated my generous offer."

Skauty read over the message and smiled, "That was creative wasn't it? So there is no need for your compound after all."

"Mr. Hanson, you are free to go."

Skauty's mouth dropped open. "You mean just like that?"

"Yes. Your presence here is no longer helpful. You may leave."

Harrison noticed the look of concern on Dirk's face. "It's OK, Dirk. See to it that Mr. Hanson has all his belongings and escort him off the ship."

Harrison stepped out of the room, then poked his head back in, "Don't assume that this is over, Mr. Hanson."

Skauty walked away from the gangplank, half expecting to be shot in the back. When he reached the other side of Harrigan Hall, he called Kat.

"Hello," Kat said.

Skauty could hear the wariness in Kat's voice. "It's me, Kat. Harrison let me go."

"Wow! That was quick!"

Skauty could hear Kat telling the others that he had been set free. "Do you mind coming to pick me up? I'm at Harrigan Hall."

"I'm on my way!" Kat said. "He is waiting to be picked up at Harrigan Hall," Kat explained after hanging up.

Everyone got up as if to go with Kat.

"I don't think we all need to go," Kat said. "I'll be right back."

"I'm going with you," Sam added and would not be deterred.

When Kat and Sam reached Harrigan Hall, they jumped out and hugged Skauty.

"Man, am I glad to see you!" Sam said.

"Same here," Skauty replied. "I've had enough of the yacht life!"

"I can't believe that worked," Kat said.

"Let's not get our hopes too high," Skauty replied. "Before I left, he did say this isn't over."

"At least you are free," Sam said.

"Now, tell me more about this deal with Russia," Skauty said.

"I'm afraid that was a ruse to get you released," Sam said.

"Well, it sounds like a good idea. Maybe we should try it for real," Skauty said.

"Maybe you are right," Kat agreed. "But, for now, let's get you home and celebrate!"

* * *

"Come in," Harrison responded to the knock on his office door.

"The clone of Hanson's phone is ready," Raymond Sands said, placing the phone on Harrison's desk.

"Thank you very much, Sands," Harrison said.

The phone pinged, and Harrison said, "Perfect timing." He picked up the phone that already had the Tlingit app open and read, "We are happy to celebrate that Skauty is now free!"

"That will be all, Sands." Sands left the room. Harrison stood and walked to his window. "Yes. Yes. Enjoy your little celebration. It will be short lived."

CHAPTER 31

Skauty could barely get through the door when they arrived at Kat's house. Everyone crowded in for a hug and to congratulate him on his freedom. Even Viviana gave him a hug, which surprised David.

When things calmed down, Viviana said, "There is someone you need to meet."

"Oh? And who is that?" Skauty asked.

"Come upstairs."

"Oh my! Isn't she a beauty!" Skauty said as he took in the eagle. "Is that the one that attacked the goons when they dragged me out of the boat?"

"Yes."

"She put up quite a fight till one of the idiots shot her. But she's OK?"

"I think she is healed enough that we can take the wrap off," Viviana answered. "Are you familiar with her? Do you know her?"

Skauty looked deep into the eagle's eyes, "I do believe I have seen her hanging around my house some. She looks familiar."

"This is your eagle friend. She has picked you to protect and assist. You just haven't realized it until now."

"You mean like you and Rey?"

"Yes."

"Well, who would have ever thought I would have a bird friend," Skauty said as he drew closer to the cage. He thought he saw a look of compassion in the bird's eyes and knew the answer before he asked, "Will she bite?"

"Not you," Viviana said and opened the cage. The eagle waddled out, and Viviana removed the wrap to free her wings.

"Are you sure it's a good idea to take that off in the house?" Sandra asked from the doorway.

The eagle spread her wings so that Skauty and Viviana had to step back. She flew about three feet off the ground and landed back down.

"She looks like she can fly again!" Viviana said.

Skauty got down on his knees and looked closely at the eagle. "What is her name?"

"That is for you to say," Viviana replied.

Skauty studied the eagle, and she seemed to be studying him as well. "What shall we call you? … Nadashée?"

The eagle bowed her head.

"I think she likes that name," Viviana said. "What does it mean?"

"Helper. She is my helper," Skauty said. He reached out and tentatively rubbed the feathers down the back of her head and neck. "Thank you for trying to save me."

The eagle eyed Skauty with a tender expression. Then she spread her wings and lifted up to the ceiling.

"I think this girl is ready to go," David said.

Viviana came and sat on her knees in front of Nadashée. She looked her in the eye for a moment, then crawled to her side and lifted the wing. "It looks good. No infection or bleeding. I think she is well enough to release."

Viviana looped her arm around Nadashée and picked her up. The others stepped aside and followed them out. Viviana released Nadashée, and she flew over the house, high above the trees, and landed in a hemlock tree on the side of the yard.

"I'll have to keep an eye out for that bird and see if she sticks around," Skauty said. "I wouldn't blame her if she abandoned me after being shot and then stuck in a pen."

"I don't think she will leave you. She seems very loyal," Viviana said.

They heard a car coming down the road and looked up to see Tamara driving toward the house. She got out and ran to Skauty, giving him a bear hug.

"I'm so glad they let you go!"

"I am, too!" Skauty said. "But Harrison did say that it's not over. I don't know what he is planning next."

"Well, at least you are safe! We can do battle with Harrison when he makes his next move."

"I know the Russian deal was fake, but it actually sounds like a good idea. Do you think we could really work out something like that?" Skauty asked.

"I suppose it would be possible," Tamara said. "I think we would need a lawyer who specializes in international trade to set it up for real."

"Let's see if we can get a Russian company interested in our fish. That is the only way I see to bypass Harrison."

"OK, I'll send out some messages to see if we get any bites," Tamara said.

The group started filing back into the house. Skauty paused and looked up at Nadashée one more time before going in. "I wonder how long you have been watching out for me," he mused.

"What's next?" David asked as everyone settled in the kitchen and Sam put on coffee.

"We were going to track those dolphins today," Sam said.

"Track dolphins?" Skauty asked.

"We've seen a huge pod of dolphins in the sound twice," James explained.

"And you think it is worth the energy to track them?" Skauty puzzled.

"They were swimming in a semicircle last time like they were herding fish," James explained.

"But there are no fish to herd," Skauty said.

"That's precisely why we think we need to follow them," Sam said.

An idea popped into James' head, and he could feel his mouth getting dry. He summoned his courage and looked at Tamara, "Tamara, would you like to go with us?"

James registered the surprised look on Tamara's face. She paused for a minute, then said, "I am supposed to be working today."

James' shoulders drooped slightly.

"But, I only have one client coming in. It's been a tough week, and I feel like celebrating. Why not!"

* * *

James piloted the boat out of the marina and into the sound. The heavy gray sky had begun to break up into puffy white clouds. The sun broke through in places, sending rays that danced on the water.

"It's turning out to be a beautiful day," James said loud enough to be heard over the engine.

Tamara was sitting near him in the wheelhouse, "The sun on the water is gorgeous! I need a picture!" She went out to the bow and took several pictures with her phone.

"Those turned out nice," she said when she was back inside. "Would you like me to send them to you?"

"I would love that," James said. "But my phone is on the side of a road in Virginia."

"Well, that won't work at all," Tamara said. "I can't think of any other way to get your number."

James' cheeks flushed. "Oh. I guess you will just have to give me yours then. I think I need to get a new phone!"

"That would be helpful," Tamara said. "What's with the birds perched on the top of the boat?"

"It's a long story."

"I have plenty of time today."

"Apparently these birds befriended Sam, Evie, David, and Viviana and helped them escape from a compound in Virginia. They flew into Kat's plane and came with us to Alaska."

"That's odd! How did you come to be a part of this group?"

"They hijacked my truck during their escape and took me prisoner."

"Prisoner? You don't look like you are being kept prisoner."

"I didn't have any reason to stay where I was, so I convinced them to let me come with them. And here we are!"

"You're not prone to making up whoppers, are you?"

"It's the truth! You can ask one of the others," James said gesturing toward the bow where Sam, Evie, David, and Viviana were taking turns scouting for the dolphins with binoculars.

"Um hum," Tamara said with a smile. She walked over to James, looped her arm around his and took his hand off the wheel. "Well, however you got here, I'm glad you did."

James felt his heart flutter and squeezed her hand. "Me, too."

James had set a track east across the sound in the northern third. Lunch time came and everyone ate sandwiches from the cooler. After he finished, Sam took over piloting the boat so James could eat. James turned the boat south before handing it over to Sam. James and Tamara took their lunches to the stern and ate and talked and laughed for a while.

"I haven't had this much fun in a long time," James said as he stood up. Tamara stood up, too, and she was so close. He looked into Tamara's dark eyes, reached out and pulled her to him. They enjoyed a long embrace and a delicious kiss.

"Wow! That was better than lunch!" James said.

"Yes, it was," Tamara replied with a smile.

"There they are! I see them!" Evie's excited call broke James' reverie. He and Tamara hurried to the bow. Evie was pointing to the southwest.

"It looks like they are swimming in a semicircle again," Evie said.

David had hurried over and was searching with the second pair of binoculars. "I see them, too!"

Evie passed her binoculars to Viviana and David handed his to James. James studied the direction the dolphins were swimming. "I think if we keep our current course, we will intersect their path," he said as he handed the binoculars to Tamara. She stepped in front of him. James put one hand on her shoulder, leaned in, and pointed toward the dolphins with the other.

"I believe you two had a nice lunch," David said with a grin.

James felt his cheeks flush again, but he didn't pull back until Tamara had spotted the dolphins. James went into the wheelhouse. "If we keep the same course, we should intersect the dolphins' path."

"Sounds good," Sam replied.

James was right. In about twenty minutes the dolphins crossed about a quarter of a mile ahead of the boat.

"OK, let's follow those rascals and see where they are headed," Sam said and turned in a southwestern direction.

"I would stay about this far back," James recommended. He could just see the silver backs flashing in the sun as they surfaced.

They left the sound about two miles from Biorka Island.

"Whoa!" David suddenly exclaimed. "There is a mountain of a ship up ahead!" Handing the binoculars to Viviana he called, "James! Get out here!"

"What is it?" James said coming out on deck.

"Look at this monster!"

Evie handed James the binoculars, and he looked ahead. "That's the frigate Kat and I saw the other day."

"Well, the dolphins are headed straight for it. And so are we!" David said.

"We need to follow the dolphins to see what is going on," Evie said.

"I was afraid someone would say that," David responded.

Sam continued following the dolphins, staying about a quarter of a mile behind them. Soon no one needed the binoculars to see the frigate.

When they were about a mile from the frigate, a call came over the radio, "We are a research vessel mapping the ocean floor. Please do not come any closer. You may disturb our readings."

Sam replied, "We were just following these dolphins to see if they would lead us to some fish."

"If you continue your current course, we will consider it an act of aggression and will defend ourselves."

Sam looked at James, "What do you think?"

"I'd place my bet on their being serious. If this thing actually belongs to Harrison, I'm sure they would attack."

Sam picked up the mic, "Your objection is duly noted. We are turning around." He turned the boat around to head back toward Sitka.

Evie came flying in the door, "What are you doing! We need to get close enough to see what is going on!"

"They threatened to blow us out of the water," Sam replied.

"They wouldn't do that! Turn back around!"

"I'm afraid they would," James said. He could see the anger spread over Evie's face.

"There is something not right about this, and it has to do with that ship!" Evie stood and patted her foot. "What if we tell them we are having engine problems and ask for help?"

"I don't think they would go for it since they have watched us running just fine for the last half an hour at least," James said.

Without another word, Evie went to the stern and trained her binoculars on the dolphins. She watched as long as she could see them, which took the dolphins close to the frigate.

CHAPTER 32

At two o'clock on Friday afternoon, Harrison called Anne Solomon, Hal Anderson, and Dirk Donegan to the conference room. He popped a couple of Tums into his mouth before they arrived. He was in a sour mood.

When everyone sat down, Harrison said, "Well?"

There was silence. Finally, Donegan ventured, "Well what, sir?"

"Does anyone have any ideas as to how we proceed?" Harrison said in an icy tone. He was greeted with blank looks. "We are not leaving this room till we have a plan."

Anderson opened his note pad and began sketching boxes, making a diagram of where they were and where they needed to get. It helped him to see things on paper. Solomon closed her eyes to think. Donegan found himself thinking, "He doesn't pay me enough for this kind of crap!"

Finally Solomon opened her eyes and said, "I say we give up on the Tlingit and start a recruiting campaign for fishers from other areas. We should be able to entice enough people to come. That will give us a workforce of people who want to be here, which will make the whole operation better."

"That's a great idea, Solomon," Anderson said. "Even if we could coerce these people into signing on, they would be nothing but trouble."

Donegan had enough sense not to venture a comment.

Harrison was quiet for a full three minutes. Then he said, "What you say has merit. But if we let this bunch of ingrates defeat us, it will set a precedent for other ventures. I have no intention of letting that happen. We need a better plan."

Anderson resumed his sketching. Solomon closed her eyes again. Harrison leaned back, put one foot on the table, and drummed his fingertips together.

After five minutes of tense silence, the slightest smile came over Harrison's face. He put his foot down, sat up straight in his chair, and said, "Have you ever heard of the Trail of Tears?"

They all nodded in agreement. "What do you mean, sir?" Anderson ventured.

Harrison just smiled, "Donegan, I want half of the militia transferred from the frigate to the cargo ship. We are going to need them."

"Yes, sir," Donegan replied.

"Anderson and Solomon, I want you to create a communication strategy that tells people I have reconsidered my offer and want to present a new proposal. And I want it to sound good enough that the whole village will show up."

"Yes, sir," they said together.

"Donegan, how long will it take to have the militia here?"

"We should be able to have them transferred and back at the dock by sometime tomorrow morning."

"Good. Good. Go ahead and set that in motion."

"Yes, sir," Donegan said and left the room.

"I will be at the A-30 summit Sunday through Tuesday. Let's call the people to a meeting on Wednesday evening. Say, seven o'clock? Meanwhile, have the building crew create a huge outdoor pavilion and enclose it with fencing."

"Yes, sir," Anderson said and gave Solomon a questioning look.

"Don't just sit there, people. Get to it!"

* * *

James took over piloting the boat saying, "Do you want to see if you can calm her down?"

Sam hesitated, feeling uncertain. "I know better than to try to calm her down, but I will go be with her," Sam said. He went out toward the bow, where David and Viviana were snuggled together. David pointed toward the stern.

Sam found Evie with the binoculars plastered to her eyes. He walked up and put his arm around her, "I'm sorry we couldn't follow the dolphins all the way there."

"That's where the fish are," Evie said calmly.

"What do you mean? On the frigate?"

I don't know, but don't you see?"

"See what?"

"The dolphins are herding the fish to that frigate. Harrison has used dolphins to herd all of the fish out of the sound."

"That's...." Sam started to say, "Ridiculous," but was able to catch himself and recover with, "Possible?"

"Of course, it's possible! Dolphins can be trained to do all sorts of things. They use swimming in a semicircle to herd fish to a place where they can catch them more easily."

Sam was amazed at his wonderful wife once again. "But where would they put the fish? That's a big ship, but I don't think it would hold that many fish."

"He has been running fish out of the sound for a long time. I bet he started when the people first noticed a downturn in their catches."

"But where would they put them?" Sam asked again realizing Evie was in her own world and had not heard him.

"I don't know, Sam. I guess they could have a fleet of fishing boats that have been catching them. But I feel like the fish are out there."

A series of loud warning caws startled Sam and Evie. They had not realized Rey had flown off the boat. He came flying in from the direction of the frigate. He flew past Evie and Sam and up to the bow. They followed him.

Rey continued to caw loudly from the top of the wheelhouse, flicking his wings and bobbing his head.

"What's he saying?" Sam asked.

"I'm not sure," Viviana said. "But he doesn't like what is going on at that ship."

"We have to find out what it is!" Evie said. "I say we turn around and go back."

"We can't risk that," Sam said. "They were very convincing about firing on us."

"We have to do something!" Evie demanded.

Everyone fell into silence trying to produce a plan. Sam felt pressure to come up with some way to find out what was going on because he sensed that Evie was right.

"If we had a drone, we could try to sneak it over there and have a look," David said.

"We would need one that had a long range, at least a mile," Viviana pointed out.

"Maybe Dad could get close enough in his plane to have a look," Sam said. "That may be our best bet."

As they got close to the marina, Sam noticed the cargo ship slowly heading out into the sound.

CHAPTER 33

Sam pulled Sandra's Suburban up to the house and noticed that the Tesla was gone. He found a note on the door. "Hey, folks! Skauty is resting at his house. We are at the high school putting together a cookout for the village to celebrate his release. Extra hands would be appreciated!"

After a quick round of showers, they headed to the high school. Quite a crowd was already there, and a motley assortment of grills were fired up. People hustled to set up tables for serving stations and place their chairs in the student parking lot.

"It looks like a huge tailgate party!" David said.

Sam found Kat tending his grill in the middle of the crowd. "Hey, Sam! I'm glad you made it! It looks like we have everything but ice. Would you mind going to get about twenty-five bags?" he said as he fished out his credit card.

"I'll be glad to," Sam said.

"How did the dolphin expedition go?"

"We were able to track them to the frigate. The frigate warned us off when we got close."

"They warned you off?"

"Yeah. They said if we came any closer they would consider it an act of aggression. I didn't ask them to explain."

"I see."

"Evie thinks that Harrison has used that pod of dolphins to herd the fish out of the sound. We need to get a closer look to see if they are somehow trapping them there."

"That doesn't sound very likely," Kat said. "We have a celebration to get ready for. Hustle after that ice. You may have to buy out two or three stores!"

Sam realized he needed to put his request that Kat try flying over the frigate on hold. So he said, "I'm on my way."

"Oh, see if James will go pick up Dad."

"Got it. He'll need your key."

Kat pulled his key out of his pocket and handed it over. "Ask James not to tell Dad what is going on. He doesn't know about the celebration yet."

"Will do," Sam said and headed off to find James.

* * *

James and Tamara picked up Skauty and drove back to the high school.

"You took a wrong turn. Kat's house is the other way," Skauty said as soon as James veered from the direction to Kat's house.

"Kat wanted us to meet him at the high school for some reason," James improvised.

Skauty sat quietly the rest of the way and wondered what was up. When James pulled into the parking lot, he could see all the cars and activity.

"What is going on here?" Skauty asked.

"I guess you might as well know," James said. "We're having a cookout to celebrate your release."

"That's silly, but it looks like fun," Skauty said with a smile.

They got out and began walking toward the crowd. Skauty had made it only fifty feet from the car when he was swarmed with people congratulating him. That was as far as he got for twenty minutes as people just kept coming.

Skauty greeted each person and thanked them for their concern. More times than he could count, he had to assure people that he was all right. "No, I wasn't tortured. Other than keeping me in a nice room, they treated me fine. Yes, I had plenty to eat."

Finally, Skauty made it to the area where the grills were smoking happily. He found Kat and scolded him, "You know you should be ashamed for doing this."

"We haven't had much to celebrate lately. I thought it would be good for everyone to get together," Kat answered.

"You are probably right," Skauty said. He noticed the PA system had been set up. "What is that for?"

"You know they are going to want to hear from you."

"I guess I'll have to try to think of something to say while I eat. You sure know how to ruin a good hamburger!"

"Sorry about that," Kat said.

When almost everyone had finished eating, Kat went to the microphone. "Thank you so much for coming out tonight. I know we are all delighted and relieved to have our leader released from the hands of this crazy man who has come to disrupt our lives."

People applauded long and hard.

"I think it only fitting that he come and share a few words with us this evening." The applause resumed while Skauty walked to the microphone.

"Thank you so much for your warm welcome tonight. It is a sharp contrast to the breeze that is chilling this old man's bones. I think we have to realize that Holmes Harrison is out to build his compound no matter what. I am not sure why he released me, but I am sure that this is not over. He will try another tactic to get us on board. We all have to be vigilant in standing our ground if we want to preserve our way of life.

"I love the ruse you used to help secure my freedom. Harrison did not mention that when he released me, so I don't know what he thinks of it. I mean, I don't know if he believed it. While it was a fake story, a Russian trade deal sounds like a good idea. If we could sell to Russia, we would have no need for Harrison to buy our fish. I have asked our own Tamarack Woods to see if she could find some potential buyers in Russia."

The applause fired up again.

"We are Tlingit. We have lived in these lands since Raven created the world. We are meant to be free. I trust you will join me in doing everything we can to keep it that way!"

People stood applauding and shouting. It was quite a celebration. As the applause quieted down, Skauty walked away from the microphone. The crowd started breaking up and heading home. When Skauty found James, he said, "I'm looking forward to sleeping in my own bed tonight. Will you be staying with me or at Kat's?"

"I'll come back to your place if that's OK," James said.

Skauty noticed that Tamara was still close by. "I am grateful to you for looking into the possibility of finding a Russian buyer."

"I am glad to do it," Tamara said.

"I'll have to drop Tamara off at Kat's and pick up my toothbrush," James said.

When they got to Kat's house, James and Tamara hopped out while Skauty stayed in the car. James walked Tamara to her car, "Can I see you tomorrow?"

"That would be lovely," she said.

"I have a feeling we are going to be doing a fly over of that frigate sometime tomorrow. Do you want to say supper time?"

"Sure, that sounds good."

"I hate to say this, but I guess you will have to pick me up," James added.

"No problem. I'll be here at five."

"I look forward to it," James said and reached to take her hand.

CHAPTER 34

Saturday dawned with a threatening gray sky that fulfilled its promise with a downpour at seven thirty. Sam, Evie, David, Viviana, Kat, and Sandra sat down to breakfast with lightning and thunder in the background. Yesterday evening had been so busy, and they had finished so late that Sam had not had the chance to fill Kat and Sandra in on their dolphin chase.

"Yesterday, we found the pod of dolphins and followed them to the frigate," Sam began. "Evie thinks that Harrison is using the dolphins to herd fish out of the sound. The question is, what are they doing with them when they get to the ship?"

"I find it hard to believe that dolphins could herd all the fish out of the sound," Kat said.

"They could if they worked at it for months," Sam countered. "I bet they have been at it since before people started noticing a downturn in their catches."

"How else can you explain the fish disappearing?" Evie asked. "There was nothing in the water to run them away."

"She does have a point, Kat," Sandra said.

"OK, let's suppose that is a possibility. Then what?" Kat asked.

"We assume they have either caught them and hauled them away or are trapping them somewhere near the frigate."

"Maybe they have one of those things people are using to breed and grow fish in the ocean. It's like a giant net that keeps the fish contained until they are ready to harvest." David said.

Everyone looked at David with amazed expressions.

"That's brilliant, David!" Evie said.

"I can't imagine how large of a net it would take to hold all the fish in the sound," Sam said.

"Or, it could be a bunch of smaller ones," Evie added.

"Let me get this straight," Kat said. "You are thinking that Harrison has set up a bunch of nets, and the dolphins are herding the fish into them. Then Harrison will release the fish once we sign onto his compound, and fishing will magically be restored."

"That sounds just like something Harrison would do," Sandra said.

"It is beginning to sound more plausible," Kat said. "If that is the case, what do we do?"

"What we were thinking is maybe we could fly close enough to the frigate to see if there is anything like nets or buoys that might be marking where the fish are being kept," Sam answered. "What do you think?"

"I think it's risky if they warned you off by radio," Sandra said.

"Maybe we could fly south and then come like we were flying up from Port Alexander," Kat offered. "We wouldn't fly directly over the frigate but should be able to get close enough to see with binoculars."

"That should work!" Sam.

"Well, you're not going right now. The weather is terrible" Sandra pointed out.

Kat pulled out his phone and checked the weather app. "It looks like this should pass over in a couple of hours. Then the weather should be fine for flying."

"I don't like this at all," Sandra said. "It is too dangerous. Why don't you just go over and ask Harrison if that is where the fish are?"

"I'm sure he would get a kick out of that!" Sam said. "There is no way he would tell us the truth."

"How about satellite images?" David asked. "Do you think we could see anything with them?"

"Another brilliant idea!" Sam said and went for his computer. He searched for images near Biorka Island since that was the closest land to the frigate. His search pulled up nothing. Three other searches yielded no results. Frustration started to set in. He did a search for Sitka, and it was blank, too. The others had begun chatting small talk and weren't paying Sam any attention until he started muttering.

"What are you muttering about?" Evie asked.

"I can't find any satellite images of this area. It's like they have been wiped from the internet."

"That sorry dog!" Evie said. "I bet he had that done so no one could see what he is up to."

"But these are government images. Surely he doesn't have that much influence."

"Why not?" Evie asked.

Sam was stunned and felt as if he was going numb. The realization that Harrison could have had the satellite images hidden was terrifying.

"Maybe this guy is more dangerous than I realized," Sam finally said.

"I'm glad you are starting to understand," Evie said. "Sam, the people who made it as part of the A-30 didn't get there on their charms. They are ruthless, and the quest for power is what drives them. You saw what a horrible person Mitch Carter was and what he was up to. I don't think we can expect anything better from Harrison."

"You're right. I guess I need to learn to think like Harrison," Sam said and drifted off into thought, his blue eyes staring blankly into space. "Why would I have satellite images removed? Because I am up to something that I want no one to see. Why would I have a frigate parked out of sight of my project? Because I will make this happen by force if necessary. Why would I lie and say that the frigate is a research vessel from France?" He muttered, "I have no idea."

"Now what are you muttering about?" Evie asked.

"I have no idea why Harrison would lie and say that his frigate is a research vessel from France."

"Maybe because you don't want your cronies to know what you are up to?" David asked.

"Of course!" Evie said. "He wouldn't want his fellow A-30 members to know that he is such a low life and has to resort to such drastic measures to get what he wants."

"Aww, he does have a soft side," David said.

"Soft and moldy," Evie added.

Kat's phone chimed a notification. He opened it to the Tlingit app. "What? This is from Harrison. How could he have sent something on our app? It says that he has a new offer and has set a meeting at Harrigan Hall for Wednesday evening at seven o'clock. But how could he be using the app?"

"The conniving scoundrel!" Sam said. "I bet he cloned Grandpa's phone so he could track what we are saying on the app."

"I'm glad he let us know before we tried to communicate something we didn't want him to hear," Evie said.

"Do you think he has reconsidered and will accept our original offer?" Kat asked.

Evie burst out laughing. "I'm sorry, but that was a funny thought. I can't imagine that he will ever do that. It would be more likely he will come back with an offer that is worse for us."

"I don't know. Maybe if he thinks we are going to sell to the Russians, he will take what he can get to keep our fish," Sam said.

"He has probably already contacted our Russian importer to see if the deal is for real," Evie pointed out.

"This guy sure is irritating," David said. "What is it going to take to get him to go away and leave Sitka alone?"

"He may consider it a fight to the death," Viviana said, surprising everyone since she had been so quiet.

"That's not a pleasant thought," Sam said, fearing she might be right. "Well, all I know to do is take it one step at a time. And the next step is to figure out if the fish are really penned up near the frigate. And if they are, can we release them?"

There was a knock on the door, and Skauty and James walked in.

"Good morning!" Skauty said. "It is nice to be a free man again."

Evie jumped up and gave him a hug, "I'm so happy you are safe!"

"I'm also happy to report that James has a date this evening," Skauty said.

"Oh?" Sandra asked.

"Yes, with Tamara," Skauty added.

"I'm not surprised," David said. "You two seemed to be getting quite close on the boat."

"That's nice. I think you're a good match," Sandra said. "Have you had breakfast?"

"Yes. James cooks a wonderful omelet," Skauty said. "But another cup of coffee is always in order."

"Coming right up," Evie said and headed to the coffee pot.

"I saw Nadashée outside the house this morning," James said. "I guess she is still watching over Skauty."

"I'm not surprised," Evie said. "Our birds have stuck with us through all sorts of craziness."

"OK, folks, we need a plan to get the fish freed," Sam said, trying to pull the discussion back.

"Operation Fish Freedom," David offered.

"That's great, but how are we going to do it? What else do we need to know?" Sam asked and pulled the paper out of his pocket.

"First, we need to know if the fish are actually there," David said. "Then, how in the world could we set them free? We can't just drive up to the frigate and say, 'Let my fish go!' Though that did work for Moses."

"That brings us back to the fly-by. That's the only way I can think of to see if they are there," Sam said.

"And if they are, then what?" David asked.

"I have been thinking about that," James said. "If we could get hold of scuba gear and a DPV, I could swim over and cut through the netting if that is what is holding them."

"A DPV?" Sam asked.

"It's a diver propulsion vehicle, a device that scoots you along underwater. Is there a dive shop in town? We might be able to rent the equipment."

"I imagine Sandi and Stan would let us use the equipment for free if they knew what we were doing," Kat said.

"Do you really think you could do that?" Evie asked.

"It should be no problem," James answered. "I will be underwater, and they won't be able to see me. I'm thinking we could take the boat to within a mile of the frigate, and I could hop off the opposite side. Then the boat could come back by in an hour and a half or so and pick me up."

"But I thought scuba divers could stay down only about forty-five minutes," Kat said.

"That's true, but with the DPV I won't be exerting much energy, and I'm trained to breathe as little as possible to conserve the air. Trust me, it will work. If I do run out of air before the boat gets back, I can minimally surface to breathe."

Everyone was silent, processing what James had said. Sam's heart quickened with hope at this plan's potential.

"That's cool as cat feet!" David said. "I think it might work."

"OK," Sam said. "Dad, how do you feel about flying when the weather breaks?"

"It sounds good to me!"

"I still think it's dangerous," Sandra said. "Why don't you just let James swim over and see if anything is there?"

"We'll stay well away from the frigate. If they don't like us, I'm sure they will give us a warning like they did with the boat," Kat said.

CHAPTER 35

The rain slowed and the clouds blew over. By eleven o'clock the sun was shining, and everything seemed cleansed.

Sam said, "It looks like it's time. Are you ready to go, Dad?"

"I need to go so I can see how this thing is laid out. That way, I'll know how to approach it in the water," James said.

"That does make sense," Kat said. "Why don't you stay here and do your computer magic? See if you can come up with any way to humble the mighty Mr. Harrison."

"OK," Sam said. "But don't fly too close."

"You don't need to tell me twice," Kat said.

With James armed with a camera, telescopic lens, and binoculars, Kat took off and flew south over the interior of Baranof Island so that he could approach the frigate as though he were flying up from Port Alexander.

James watched the beautiful mountain scenery go by, but mostly he thought about his training days as a Navy SEAL. He had been fortunate not to have to serve in active combat, but that meant he spent a lot of time training for all sorts of possibilities. James felt excited and realized he was looking forward to this adventure.

"This feels like the good old days when I was in the Navy," James said.

"I can see that," Kat answered. "We're doing reconnaissance before the big mission."

James lapsed back into thought, trying to run through all the things he needed to know about this underwater cage, if it existed. "I'll have to be sure to try to see if there is more than one cage and try to determine what it is made of," he thought. "I'll really need good close-up pictures."

James checked the camera to make sure image stabilization was on for the close-up shots. Then his mind drifted from his mission to his date with Tamara that evening.

As though reading James' thoughts, Kat said, "We have to get you back in time for your date tonight."

"I am looking forward to it," James confided. "I like Tamara."

"She is a wonderful person. I've known her since she was a little girl. I'm not sure why she never married. I guess she just didn't find the right person. Maybe you will change her luck."

"I don't think it's time to start talking marriage," James said.

"I guess that's true. But I hope you two have a good time tonight."

"Thanks."

Kat flew till he saw Benzeman Lake and turned the plane southwest, following Necker Bay out to the ocean.

"Here we go," Kat said as he aimed the plane northwest.

Soon James saw the frigate with his binoculars. "There it is. I think it would give us the best view if you flew to the west of the frigate. That seemed to be where the dolphins were headed."

"Got it," Kat replied.

About the time Kat could see the frigate, the radio sounded. "Please alter your course and don't come within a mile of this vessel. A direct approach will be considered an act of aggression."

"That's the same thing they said to us on the boat," James said.

Kat picked up the mic, "Sorry. I'm on a sightseeing tour from Port Alexander to Glacier Bay National Park. No harm intended. We are just passing by."

They were close enough for James to see blue buoys in the water. "That's odd," he thought. He got the camera and started snapping photos.

"I repeat, do not come any closer," the radio squawked.

"Roger that. I don't mean to upset you. Would you prefer we veer east or west?" Kat said trying to buy time for James to get a better look as he continued his course.

"It doesn't matter which way!" the man from the frigate barked.

"What do you think?" Kat asked James.

"Veer to the west. That way I can continue taking pictures."

Kat made a gentle turn to the west and spoke into the microphone, "Roger that. We are veering west. Again, no harm intended. I didn't even know you were there till you came on the radio."

There was no response. Kat made a semicircular loop around the frigate. Just as he was about to turn back north, they heard the boom, boom, boom of the twenty-five-millimeter chain gun. Glass exploded, the plane rocked, and the engine sputtered and billowed smoke. James heard Kat groan and saw blood oozing from his neck where a piece of glass had lodged.

Kat pulled out the glass and yelled, "The engine is hit! I don't know if we will make it back!"

Another round of fire exploded the plane around the engine. "I'm sure we're going down, now!" Kat yelled.

The engine continued to sputter for another minute, then died altogether.

"Try to glide as far as you can," James said.

"That's what I'm doing!" Kat said as he wiped blood from his neck. "It would help if we were higher."

James lurched to the floor and pulled out two life jackets. He put his on and said, "Lean forward so I can put this on you."

Kat threaded his right arm through, then leaned forward. James pulled the vest around, and Kat stuffed his left arm through. James zipped it while Kat battled the plane.

"Fly as close to shore as you can. Then we will have to jump just before the plane hits the water."

"Jump?" Kat asked.

"Yes. We don't want to be in here when it crashes!"

A third round of fire hit the tail section and obliterated the rudder. The plane pitched and began to loop toward the northwest side of Biorka Island.

"I'm not feeling so good," Kat said, his speech slurred.

James looked and saw that he was pale. "He's losing a lot of blood," he thought.

"Get up and let's jump!" James said.

Kat was trying but moving slowly. James pulled him to his feet and dragged him to the side door of the plane. James steadied Kat on his feet. "Jump and turn so you land with your back facing the direction the plane is going."

Kat gave a feeble jump, but it was more of a fall. James knew he would not land well. Giving Kat a couple of seconds to clear, James jumped. He heard the plane crash into the water just before he hit. The force of the water knocked his breath out. When he slowed enough to regain control, James fought his way to the surface, the life vest helping to lift him.

James broke the surface and gasped for air. All of his limbs seemed to be working. He spun around looking for Kat and found him floating about fifty yards away. James swam as fast as he could to get to Kat. Kat was definitely unconscious but still breathing.

"His neck may be broken," James thought when he saw the odd angle of Kat's head. James saw the shore in the distance. He grabbed the back of Kat's life jacket and started swimming madly toward shore. After about thirty yards, James realized there was no way he could keep up that pace. Slowing down, he switched hands so he could pull with the other.

James paused and looked at Kat. He was still breathing, but very lightly. The panic was strong, and James wanted to hurry. But he knew that he couldn't, so he continued to swim at a pace he could sustain.

James was tiring severely. He paused to switch arms again. Kat was no longer breathing. James' heart sank. He knew he would have a better chance of making it to shore if he left Kat, but he could not do that. He continued the slow, agonizing swim.

After another thirty minutes, James began to shake. It finally dawned on him how cold the water was. He changed grips again and continued to pull Kat and himself toward the shore. It didn't seem to be getting any closer.

James got colder and colder. The shivering got so strong that he could hardly swim. Finally, the shivering stopped, and he began to feel numb. He looked at the shore, and it seemed farther away. It got blurry and darker as he looked. James realized he was about to pass out.

"I have to keep moving," he said out loud and took a few more strokes. The light faded. James' ears began to roar. The last thing James thought before everything went black was, "Is that an engine?"

CHAPTER 36

Sam thought about what Kat had said about finding something to humble the mighty Harrison and opened his computer. "What could that be?" he thought. David and Viviana had gone for another of their walks to the river. Sandra and Evie were tackling chores. Skauty was in the den watching the news.

"Power and money," Sam thought. "Those are the things Harrison values. Is there any way I can disrupt one of those?" Sam sat back and thought. "I could put a virus in his payroll system. That would at least give someone in his organization a headache. But I don't think it would affect Harrison much. If someone did that at MC2, I would simply have fixed the problem."

Thinking about money and payroll led Sam to think about his and Evie's account. He had just assumed that Mitch Carter had frozen his account or confiscated the money. He had not risked checking since they fled the compound. "I think it's time to check. It would be nice to have money again."

Sam logged into the account. To his surprise it was neither frozen nor emptied. "I guess Carter was too distracted by all the fallout from his nuclear disposal disaster." He started to reactivate their pay direct features that allowed them to pay with their phones. They had let them lapse after moving to MC2 since all they needed was the ID chip to pay for anything. Then he thought, "What if Carter is just waiting for me to access the account so he can trace where I am?"

Sam leaned back and pondered the situation. "I think the best thing to do is to transfer the money into a different account out of MC2's control. Maybe I'll set up one in Mom's maiden name with a fake Social Security number. That shouldn't be traceable."

Sam thought about it more, trying to make sure he wasn't missing something that could lead Carter to him. Once he decided the bases were covered, he opened the Solutions Financial website, the banking platform used by anyone that was not part of the A-30 system. He set up an account in his mother's maiden name, Sandra Pullman, making up a Social Security number. Sam wrote the name and number down and put it in his computer bag.

Once the account was open, Sam transferred the money from his MC2 account into it. It worked perfectly. Sam was happy to have their sizable savings at his disposal again.

Evie declared it was lunch time, and Sam joined her and Sandra in the kitchen.

"David and Viviana took a picnic, but I don't think Kat and James took anything to eat," Sandra said.

"I'm sure they'll be OK," Sam said. "They should be home before too long. Guess what! I transferred our money into a Solutions Financial account. It's in your maiden name, Mom, in case anyone comes asking questions."

"Yay! We're not broke anymore," Evie said.

"That doesn't sound legal," Sandra scolded.

"It's not, but I was afraid Mitch Carter might try to track us "down if I put it in our names."

Sam got out the fixings for turkey sandwiches while Evie produced the drinks.

"Grandpa, it's time for lunch," Sam called, but Skauty didn't answer. Sam went in and found him asleep on the couch.

"I think that ordeal on Harrison's boat drained Grandpa more than he thought," Sam said coming back into the kitchen. "He's sound asleep."

"I'll make him a sandwich, and he can eat when he wakes up," Evie said.

Sam took the last bite of his sandwich and froze, eyes wide.

"What's wrong, Sam?" Evie asked.

He spit out his bite of sandwich. "Did the TV say what I think it said?" He ran to the den. Evie and Sandra followed.

"The report about the plane crash just off Biorka Island was called in by workers at the National Weather Service radar site. So far there is no word on survivors. The Coast Guard is dispatching a ship to the crash site even as we speak. We will bring you updates as we have them."

"Oh no!" Sandra said.

Skauty woke up to find everyone staring at the TV. "What is it?"

"They are reporting a plane crash off Biorka Island," Sam said.

"That's where Kat would have been," Skauty said.

"What are we going to do? We have to go out there. We need a boat," Sam said frantically.

Evie grabbed Sam by the shoulders, "Look at me. The Coast Guard is on their way. They would beat us there anyway. Besides, we don't know that it was Kat and James. Just calm down. All we can do is wait."

"Wait and call Dad!" Sam said. He pulled out of Evie's hold and ran to Sandra's phone to make the call. The phone rang six times then went to voicemail. "No answer," Sam said as hope started to drain from his soul.

Evie wrapped him in a bear hug, "We have to keep hoping and trusting."

Tears were flowing down Sandra's cheeks. Next, Evie went to her with a hug. Then she went to Skauty, who was standing in a daze.

"We have to do something!" Sam said weakly. "Maybe they are far enough out to sea that he didn't have a signal. I'll call again in a few minutes."

"Yes, do that," Evie said.

Sam could read on her face that she didn't really think Kat would answer. Sam's heart was racing. He felt his world was falling apart.

He realized Evie's hands were on his shoulders, and she was pulling him to sit down on the couch.

"....breaking development in the plane crash off Biorka Island," pulled Sam back. The announcer continued, "The workers at the radar center located two people in the water at the crash site. They report one is alive but unconscious and one appears to be dead. Ambulances are set to meet them at the marina in Sealing Cove, and the victims will be transported to Mt. Edgecumbe Medical Center. We will be back as we have new developments in this story."

"Now we know what to do," Evie said. "Let's go to the marina." No one said a word as they filed toward Sandra's Suburban. Evie thought to leave David and Viviana a note on the way out.

Sandra was still crying, so Evie took the keys. As they were coming off O'Connell Bridge, they saw two ambulances pulling onto the road. Evie followed them to the hospital and parked near the ambulance bay.

Sam jumped out and ran toward the ambulances. A security guard held him back.

"My dad might be in one of those!" he said trying to push around the security guard.

"OK, if you can identify these people, that would be helpful. Come with me," the security guard said. He eyed Sandra, Evie, and Skauty suspiciously as they caught up.

"They're family, too," Sam said.

The back doors of the first ambulance opened, and the paramedics hustled the stretcher out and rushed into the emergency room.

"That is James," Sam said, feeling stunned.

The paramedics in the second ambulance weren't in a hurry. They unloaded the stretcher. There was a sheet over the patient's head.

The security guard stepped up and said, "I think this man can identify your victim."

The paramedics summoned Sam over and pulled the sheet back to reveal Kat's lifeless face.

In a voice they could barely hear, Sam said, "That's my dad, Kat Hanson."

Sam felt Evie's arm around his waist. He just wanted to collapse on the asphalt, but she held him up. Tears began to flow. Evie turned him from the stretcher and pulled him away. He embraced his mom, and both began sobbing.

Evie went to Skauty, who stood straight as an arrow. She put an arm around his waist, and he put his arm around her shoulders. Skauty's embrace released Evie's tears. He asked the security guard, "What happens now?"

In a comforting voice, the security guard said, "A physician will pronounce him dead and then an autopsy will be done to determine the cause of death."

"Thank you," Skauty answered. "What about James?"

"He will be treated. You can see him as soon as he is stable. Please go to the waiting room and let them know that you are there for James."

Skauty started to steer them toward the emergency waiting room.

"Oh," the security guard called. "Could I have James' last name?"

Sam looked at everyone and realized he couldn't remember. The others looked blank, too.

"He's a friend that we haven't known too long. We will have to get back to you on that," Skauty said.

The security guard gave them a suspicious look and said, "OK, but if you remember, please let someone know."

"We will," Skauty replied, and they found seats in the waiting room while Sam told the intake clerk that they were with James and Kat.

About the time Sam sat down, a woman came rushing through the waiting room and up to the clerk, "I need to know who was brought in from the plane crash!"

"I'm sorry, but I can't tell you that," the clerk responded.

"Tamara?" Skauty said.

Tamara turned around to see Skauty and the others. "Oh, no," was all she could say.

Sam watched as Tamara walked over and sat next to him. The world seemed dull and fuzzy, unreal. He felt that he should say something, but no words came. Finally he was able to get out, "Dad didn't make it."

Sam looked over to Tamara and saw tears spilling over and running down her cheeks.

"I'm so sorry, Sam," she said. "Do you know what happened?"

"Not really. The news just said the plane crashed. I wouldn't be surprised if they were shot down."

"Who else was with him? The news said there were two," Tamara asked.

"James."

Sam noticed Tamara stiffen.

"How is James?" she asked quietly.

"We haven't heard anything but that he is alive. He looked unconscious when they took him out of the ambulance," Sam said.

Silence followed. Sam watched people coming and going. He had no idea how long it had been when he heard someone call, "Katlian Hanson?"

The clerk pointed in their direction and a physician walked over.

"Hi, I'm Dr. Martin, and I'm sorry for your loss. Do you know who was piloting the plane?"

"It was Dad, I mean Katlian Hanson," Sam said.

"Because of the circumstances of his death, we will have to perform an autopsy. His body should be released within forty-eight hours. Do you have a funeral home preference?"

The world went blank again for Sam. Finally, Sandra spoke up and said, "We'll use Prewitt. They handled his mother's service."

"Thank you. We'll contact them when it is time," Dr. Martin said.

"Do you know how James is doing?" Tamara asked.

"No, Dr. Woods, I mean your brother, is treating him. I'm sure he'll let you know as soon as he can."

Dr. Martin walked back to the ER, and Sam and the rest sat back down to wait. A wave of guilt flooded Sam's soul. "I shouldn't have suggested that they fly over the frigate," he said. "This is all my fault," and tears began to pour.

Evie wrapped her arm around Sam and squeezed, "Sam, this is not your fault. It's not your dad's fault, either. No one could have known this would happen. If you need to blame someone, blame Harrison. He is the aggressor here."

Sam leaned into Evie. The tears continued to flow. He knew she was right, but he still felt awful. "I can't believe this is happening. It feels like a dream. I hope I wake up soon."

Evie squeezed Sam again and rubbed his back. Sam felt soothed by Evie's gentle touch.

"James?" a voice called.

"We're with James," Tamara called.

"Tamara? What are you doing here?" Dr. Woods said as he walked over to his sister.

"James is with the Hansons. He has been helping do battle with Harrison," Tamara said. "How is he?"

"He should be fine. Mostly hypothermia, though he does have some contusions. I assume they are from the crash. He is conscious now."

"Can we see him?"

"Sure, but just two at a time. It's ER policy."

Tamara looked around, and Sam could see the intensity in her eyes. "You go first," he said.

Tamara hesitated, and Evie said, "I'll go with you."

They walked with Dr. Woods into the ER. Tamara rushed up to the bed and grabbed James' hand. "How are you feeling?"

Dr. Woods gave Evie a curious look. Evie nodded.

"I've been better," James said. "Did Kat make it?"

Tamara shook her head and leaned down to hug James. He hugged her back.

"I tried to save him. He was hit in the neck with glass and losing blood. I think he was nearly unconscious when he jumped, and he didn't hit the water right." James slung out the words in a hurry.

"Jumped? What do you mean jumped?" Tamara asked.

"The plane was going to crash. I knew it would be better not to be inside when it hit the water, so we jumped just before it crashed."

"James, do you know why the plane crashed? We need to know," Dr. Woods asked.

James hesitated, and Tamara thought she saw a guilty look on his face.

"It's OK, James. You can tell him. He needs to know the truth," Tamara assured him.

"The frigate shot us down," James said.

"The frigate shot you down?" Dr. Woods repeated, not comprehending.

"Don't you know? Harrison has a frigate anchored a few miles out from Biorka Island. We were flying over to see if we could determine for sure if he is holding the fish there."

"Can you tell me what day it is?" Dr. Woods asked as he pulled out his pen light.

"I think it's still Saturday, October thirteenth. Why?"

Dr. Woods shined the light in James' eyes, checking his pupils' response.

"Everything he said is right on target, Yani," Tamara said. "We think Harrison has been using a pod of dolphins to run fish out of the area and into huge nets out by the frigate. That is why the fishing has been so poor the last several months. Kat and James flew out to determine if the net cages are really there."

"Yani? You just called the doctor Yani?" James said with a puzzled expression.

"Yes, Yani, Dr. Woods, is my brother."

"Well, it's nice to meet you," James said with a weak smile and extended his hand.

"It's nice to meet you, too. I take it you and Tamara know each other."

"We do," Tamara said. "James was supposed to take me on a date tonight. Some men will do anything to avoid taking me out."

"Who said we're not going out tonight?" James said. "I'll be out of here soon, won't I?"

"I don't see why not," Dr. Woods replied. "Everything is looking normal now that we have you warmed back up. I wouldn't advise too wild of an evening, though. You do probably need to rest."

"You noodle head, we can't go out tonight. I was just teasing about your trying to get out of it. We have to take care of you and Kat's family," Tamara scolded.

A nurse popped into the bay and handed Dr. Woods James' lab report. He looked it over and then looked at James, "How do you feel?"

"I'm feeling OK. Just kind of tired and beat up."

"Your lab results are good. I don't see any signs of broken bones. Let's see if you can stand up."

Tamara pulled the large pile of blankets back to find James in a hospital gown. "I like your new outfit."

James looked down at the gown and said, "Thanks! I'll have to wear it more often." He swung his legs off the narrow bed and sat up.

"I'm afraid we had to cut your clothes off," Dr. Woods said. "We couldn't leave you in those wet things."

Dr. Woods took one arm and Tamara took the other. "OK, let's see how you do."

James stood, and his head swam for a few seconds. Dr. Woods nodded his head toward the IV pole, "Would you pull the pole along?" he said to Evie, and she hopped to the task.

James walked out of the room and down the ER hall. After a few steps, Dr. Woods let go of his arm. After several more steps, Dr. Woods said, "Tamara, you have to let go, too. I need to see how he's walking."

Tamara blushed as she let go of James arm. James seemed stable as he walked on his own.

"I think you are good to go, James," Dr. Woods said, looking over the lab report one more time. "But, we still don't know your last name," he said and looked at Tamara. Tamara blushed again and looked at James.

"It's Carson. James Carson," he said. He looked at Tamara. "I guess we hadn't gotten to last names yet."

"I'm sure you could figure out that mine is Woods."

"Hey, Tamara Woods," James said.

"Oh brother! We have to get you two out of here," Dr. Woods said. "I want you to rest and drink plenty of fluids for the next couple of days. Then you should be ready to tackle the world."

CHAPTER 37

David and Viviana laid out a blanket in a grassy area next to Indian River. They ate lunch and then lay back on the blanket. The grasses blocked some of the breeze, and the sun felt warm. Viviana snuggled up and laid her head on David's shoulder.

"This is nice," she said.

"It is. I can't wait till we can do this all night, every night."

"Me either."

"Have you thought any more about the wedding?" David asked.

"Obviously, we can do nothing until this mess with Harrison is over," Viviana replied. "I would still love to have the wedding down by the water."

"That's what I was thinking."

"What will we do after the wedding?"

"That will be the fun part!" David said grinning.

Viviana whacked him on the chest, "No, I mean where will we live? How will we survive? All I know is how to live in the woods."

"I kind of like this place. I could see if I can find a church here," David said.

"That sounds nice. I wonder what Sam and Evie will do? And James?"

"I don't see any options for them but to stay here, either. They certainly can't work for an A-30 company again."

"Umm," Viviana said.

A few minutes later, David guessed from Viviana's steady breathing that she was asleep. He relaxed and fell asleep, too.

A shrill chirp from Canto and loud splashing pulled David out of his sleep. He lifted his head to locate the cause of the splashing and saw two large bears pouncing in the river. An even larger bear was on the bank opposite him. David was afraid to move.

Viviana awoke and sat up, "Oh look, a mother and her cubs!"

"Those are cubs?" David squeaked. "What should we do?"

"Do you want to feed them?"

"Feed them! Don't you think we should get out of here?"

"They're not after us, silly. She is teaching them to fish. Come on, let's find a stick!"

"Find a stick? I don't think a stick is going to help us."

"A stick for fishing," Viviana explained as she got up and walked toward the trees.

David sat frozen for a moment, then decided he needed to stick with Viviana. He followed closely as she searched the forest floor. Finally, she picked up a long, straight stick and tested it to see if it would break. She pulled out her knife and whittled the end into a sharp point.

"Are you going to try to catch a fish with that?" David asked.

"How else would I catch one?"

Viviana sat down on the blanket and slipped off her socks and shoes. She stood up and pulled off her jeans.

"I guess you are allowed to look all you want," she said as David stood transfixed.

Unfortunately, her jacket hung down to mid-thigh. David followed Viviana to the river, keeping a wary watch on the bears. Viviana stepped into the river just down from some rapids.

"Whoa, that's cold!"

She walked upstream a few steps, then stood statue still. From his vantage point on the bank, David could see trout in the water. One swam near Viviana's leg. Like lightning, Viviana thrust the stick into the water and popped out the fish. She tossed it on the bank.

"Don't let it flip back in!"

David grabbed it and held on. A couple of minutes later she tossed another one on the bank.

"We need one more," she said.

David eyed the bears, who were now eyeing him as he held the fish.

"They're looking at me," he said.

"Of course," Viviana answered. "You're holding their snack."

She tossed the third one on the bank and climbed out of the river.

"My toes are about to freeze!"

"Now what?" David said with his foot on the third fish.

"Let's give the bears a treat." She picked up the third fish. "Come on."

David followed Viviana as she walked toward the bears, who were still in the river. They stood on their hind legs and watched the humans closely. When she was even with the bears, Vivian held up her fish and laid it on the ground. David did the same with his two fish.

"Now we walk away," Viviana said.

She walked slowly back to the blanket. David watched as the two cubs and the mother crossed the river and gobbled up the fish. When he looked back, Viviana had dressed and gathered up the blanket and lunchbox.

"We need to leave now. They might come looking for more."

"OK," David agreed.

Walking back toward the house, David saw the Suburban and Tamara's car pull up. As they got out, David could read in their body language that something was wrong.

"Something bad has happened."

They quickened their pace and went into the house just after the others.

"What's wrong?" David asked.

"They shot down the plane. Kat didn't make it," Tamara said.

"Oh no. I'm so sorry," David said.

"That's terrible," Viviana added.

Sandra sat down in a kitchen chair. The weight that pushed her down seemed to fill the air, and the silence was thick. David looked over the hurting faces and tried to think of something to say. He knew the usual platitudes were useless. "It happened for a reason. This is part of God's plan. He's in a better place," had been spoken to him when his friends were killed on the battlefield, and all it did was make him angry.

David walked over and sat beside Sandra, "This is a dark and difficult time, but we will walk with you through it."

Sandra put her elbows on the table and sobbed into her hands. David sat still, letting her cry. An awkward silence surrounded Sandra's sobs.

Tamara broke the silence. "James, you need to sit down," she said, pulling out a chair.

"I'm afraid the backside is a bit sore," he replied.

Tamara hustled to the den and returned with a pillow. She plopped it into the chair and patted it. James obliged and sat down.

David walked over to Skauty, who was standing stoically in the corner. "I'm so sorry, Skauty."

"The man who is trying to take our village took my son's life. I can't believe there is such greed and evil in the world," Skauty said. "Now we have to live the rest of our lives without Kat."

Evie came over and hugged Skauty, "We will be with you, Grandpa."

"I think it must be a hard thing to lose a son," David said.

"Yes, it hurts a lot. The whole circle of life has been dented."

"We have lost a good man," David said and looked around. He noticed Sam had disappeared. "Should I look for him or let him be?" he thought.

David found Sam in the den, elbows on his knees and face in his hands. "How are you doing, Sam?"

No response. David looked closer and realized Sam was trembling. He sat beside him on the couch.

Finally Sam lifted his head and said, "That was an act of war. If war is what he wants, war is what he will get."

David could feel the rage in Sam's voice. "So you are angry about your father's death," he said hoping to encourage Sam to talk about it.

"Yes, I'm angry! I'm beyond angry!" Sam exploded and stood up. "That scum of the earth killed my father. And he will continue trying to take our village. And what can we do about it? So far, nothing. But that is going to change! That has to change! He is going to pay for what he has done. I will see to that!" Sam was pacing like a lion in a cage. "The question is, how?"

Sam's outburst seemed to have shifted Sandra's gears. David heard, "We need to think about supper. I don't think I am up for going to church tomorrow, but any of you can. Let's see what we can fix for tonight."

David heard the refrigerator open and realized that Sandra was now in mom mode. The phone rang, and Sandra answered it, "Hello… I understand... Yes, we could come tomorrow at two… Thank you. That was the funeral home. We have an appointment to plan the funeral tomorrow at two." David heard a chair pull out, and Sandra's sobbing resumed.

Sam continued pacing, seeming oblivious to the world around him. "You know that we will help you any way we can," David said.

Sam's shoulders sagged, and he sat back down. "I don't want any help. Look what happened to Dad. I have to do this alone."

"Like that's going to happen," Evie said as she marched into the room, sat down beside Sam, and hugged him. "Alone is something we Hansons don't do. We are a team, remember? We will tackle this together or not at all."

Sam melted into Evie's arms, "What am I thinking? There is no way to defeat Harrison. It would be best to just let him have his way so no one else gets hurt. It would have been better if I had died in that drone attack. Then Dad would still be alive."

"Sam Hanson, I will have none of that kind of talk. Kat's death was not your fault. I want you to believe that and quit telling yourself that it was. It is a terrible tragedy, and it will take us a long time to get over it. But we will get over it if you will quit talking nonsense," Evie said.

Sam sat silently in Evie's arms, tears rolling freely down his face. Her words made sense in his head, but his heart was reluctant to accept them. "If only I hadn't suggested they go out in the plane," he said weakly.

CHAPTER 38

I t was a long hard night. Sam had fitful bits of sleep between bouts of beating himself up with guilt, rage at Harrison, and feelings of emptiness over the loss.

A bout of rage pulled him out of bed at five o'clock. Fuming at Harrison, Sam walked quietly down to the kitchen, put on coffee, and booted up his computer. "Let's see what kind of damage I can do to you," Sam thought as he prepared to hack into Global Food Source's system. "Money and power are close to your heart, so I think I will start with money."

Evie walked in and Sam said, "Sorry, I tried to sneak out without waking you."

"What are you doing?"

"I am going to find a way to hack into GFS's system and see what kind of damage I can do to Harrison as payback.

"Are you sure that is a wise thing to do, given he has that frigate ready to attack the whole town?"

"Well, I have to do something. I can't just let him get away with killing Dad. He has to pay!"

Evie held a finger to her lips as Sam's voice got louder. "I'm not saying to do nothing. But we do need to consider the consequences. We also need to plan a coordinated attack that will have Harrison running with his tail between his legs."

"So you think I should stop?"

"Hmmm," Evie thought. "Why don't you go ahead and look around. See what kind of options you have, but don't do anything yet. Let's work out the timing for how we are going to send this guy packing."

"Why couldn't he have gone for the original idea of letting us live in our own homes and fish for his company? It seems so logical. And Dad would still be here." Sam put his head in his hands.

"Obviously, logic is not one of Harrison's strong points," Evie said as she walked over to give Sam a sideways hug. "Do you think your synapses are firing well enough to figure out this hacking business after not sleeping much?"

"How did you know I didn't sleep much?"

Evie gave Sam her "I can't believe you just said that" look. "I was there, remember? Right next to you?"

Sam looked into her bright green eyes, her red hair still messy from the bed, and felt loved. He stood up and pulled her into his arms as a tear worked its way out. "I love you. I don't know what I would do without you."

Evie hugged him back, "That's good, because you are stuck with me." Feeling Sam tremble, Evie squeezed tighter.

"I wish we could do yesterday over and not send Dad out in the plane."

"I know. I wish that, too."

Sam reeled in his tears. When he pulled away from the embrace, he saw that Evie was crying, too. He took her back into his arms and held on until she had finished her cry.

"We still make a good team," Sam said.

"We always will. Now see if you can get into that computer system." Evie poured glasses of orange juice for herself and Sam and began looking over breakfast possibilities. "I'm tempted to make chocolate gravy and biscuits," she said.

"I don't think we need to be that adventurous this morning. You'd better stick with something more traditional."

"I thought you liked my chocolate gravy."

"I do. I just think the rest of the crew doesn't need the challenge of something new on top of what we are already going through."

"You're right. How about bacon and egg biscuits?"

"That sounds good," Sam said absent mindedly as he pored over GFS's computer system.

"It's way too early to start cooking, though," Evie said as she pulled a granola bar from the pantry. "Do you want a snack to go with your coffee?" Sam didn't answer, so Evie took it as a yes. She poured the coffee and set a granola bar by Sam's cup.

Sam noticed the bar and said, "Thanks." He stopped long enough to peel open the wrapper. Evie sat and watched Sam work, eating her granola bar and sipping on coffee. Finished with the bar, she took a bag of sunflower seeds and put some out for their four bird friends, thankful that Viviana had started letting them sleep outside.

Azul was the first to show, then the others quickly followed. Evie watched them eat for a couple minutes, then said, "Guys, it's cold out here. I'm going back in." Azul chirped, and Evie took it as a thank you. "You're quite welcome," she answered.

Sam had a near smile on his face when Evie came back.

"I can't believe that after all of the cyber-attacks in recent years a company like this would still be so easy to penetrate. I found a way in," Sam said.

"That was quick! Maybe they just didn't expect they would have to defend themselves against a computer ninja like you!"

Sam looked up and grinned. He sipped his coffee and continued exploring. After about ten minutes, Sam muttered, "Now that's interesting."

"What's interesting?" Evie asked.

"Harrison has his personal bank account linked to the payroll program. I might be able to access that!"

"Access Harrison's own money?"

"Yeah. If I can, we could drain it all out. That ought to hit him where it hurts."

"That would be helpful. But it would be so illegal. I don't think you should risk tampering with his money. You could end up in jail for a long time."

"OK, I won't do anything right now. But I bet it will take something like that for him to back off."

"You are probably right. Keep looking and see what other sort of mischief you could cause."

Sandra walked in and sat down without a word.

"I'm sorry Mom. We didn't mean to wake you," Sam said.

"You didn't. I didn't sleep much and was awake when I noticed the light come on. After a while, I decided there wasn't much point in just lying there, so here I am."

"Would you like some juice or coffee?" Evie asked.

"Thanks. Both would be nice. You and that computer, Sam. How can you possibly be messing with it this time of day?"

"I'm hunting for ways to attack Harrison through his computer system. I have found a trail to his personal bank account that I think will be useful."

"You have always been good at beating bullies," Sandra said. "But I'm afraid this one has beaten us. I don't see any way around it."

"We have to keep trying. For Dad's sake," Sam responded.

"I guess you're right, but I'm about ready to throw in the towel. This just doesn't seem real. I don't know if I can take going to the funeral home today," Sandra said as she rested her head in her hand with her elbow on the table.

Sam could feel the heaviness weighing on his mother. "We will have to hold each other up this afternoon."

"Why did he have to fly over that ship?" Sandra fumed. "I told him not to. But did he listen? No! I don't believe he did such a stupid thing!" She got up and stormed toward the coffee pot. "That's just like him, though! He won't listen! And now look what has happened!"

Sandra's rage drew Sam to his feet. He hugged his mom. "This is so hard but try to calm down."

"Calm down! How can I calm down? I will never again see the man I love more than life itself, and you want me to calm down! All because he wouldn't listen! If only he hadn't gone!"

Sam could feel his mother shaking and didn't let go.

"If only he hadn't gone," she said again and began sobbing on Sam's shoulder. Sam gave Evie a pleading look and saw she was crying, too.

Evie came and joined the hug. "This is going to be a hard day."

* * *

"It's one thirty. I guess we should go soon," Sam said. His words seemed to echo in the silence. He looked around and saw eyes cast to the ground. He realized everyone was dreading this as much as he. James had announced that he was staying at the house, and Tamara had come to make sure he behaved and rested like the doctor said. David said he planned to go, but Viviana was staying put.

Ten minutes passed without a word. David got up and said, "It's time," and opened the door to the garage. Sam, Evie, Sandra, and Skauty filed out, and David closed the door as he left.

Tamara sat on the couch and patted her legs. James laid his head in her lap, "I could get used to this."

"How are the bruises?"

"Still sore, but nothing terrible."

"Are you sure you're OK?"

"Actually, right now, I don't think I have ever been better," James said with a grin. Tamara bent down and kissed him.

"OK, now I'm even better! We still need to plan a date, since I messed up the first one."

"I could cook dinner for you tomorrow evening," Tamara offered.

"That sounds wonderful!"

"Say six o'clock?"

"Um, you still might have to pick me up," James said.

"I'll be happy to. I'll come by around five after I leave the office."

"It's a deal."

"Or maybe I'll leave the office early and take you to get a phone. It would be nice to be able to call you."

"I'll be at your disposal whenever you show up!"

The door opened, then James heard someone in the kitchen. "Viviana?"

"Yes?"

"Just checking to see if that was you," James said.

Viviana walked into the den, "We need to talk. This situation is getting dangerous, and they are liable to get us all killed."

"That is true," James replied. "The biggest threat is that frigate. We need to disable it somehow."

How would you disable a frigate?" Tamara asked.

"Mainly with explosives," James answered and sat up.

"We don't have any explosives," Viviana pointed out.

"That does present a problem," James said. "So you have never done any scuba diving?"

"No," Viviana answered.

"I have been thinking of a possibility for the frigate, but I would need some help, someone to carry extra oxygen."

"I'm sure I could learn. How hard can it be?"

"It's not hard. You just have to learn to breathe and relax. Kat said there is a dive shop where we can get the scuba gear. I probably shouldn't ask a lawyer this, but do you know of a place we could get some C-4?"

* * *

It was a gray afternoon, and clouds crawled down the ridge behind Prewitt Funeral Home. Sam steeled himself as they walked toward the front door of the modest building. Nadashée landed at the peak of the roof and watched silently.

Skauty looked up at her and smiled. "Thanks for being here, my friend."

Mike Mitchell, the funeral director, opened the door and welcomed them in, his gray hair blending nicely with his charcoal suit. "I am so sorry for your loss. Kat was such a wonderful man. Please come into the conference room, and we will talk about the service."

"Thank you," Sam said and followed him.

A man whom Mike introduced as Jim was busy running water into tumblers and placing them on the table as people sat down.

"I understand that Kat's body is to be cremated," Mike said and waited for confirmation. Sandra nodded her head.

"Have you thought of when and where you would like to have the service? They are releasing Kat's body this afternoon, so we could have everything ready tomorrow."

Sam felt like he was in a tunnel. Mike's voice seemed disconnected from reality. When he said, "What do you think about having the service on Tuesday, Mom?" he wasn't sure anyone could hear him. He felt too far away, numb.

Sandra responded, "I think Tuesday is good."

Sam heard her voice, but it seemed filtered through cotton.

"I think Kat would have liked the service to be at the church," Sandra said. "Could we do that?"

Sam saw Skauty nod and say, "I agree. Let's have the service at the church."

Sam felt that his spirit was disconnecting from his body, as if it just couldn't bear talking about his dad's funeral. He finally noticed that everyone was looking at him, but he didn't know what to say.

"Is having the service at the church OK with you, Sam?" Mike asked.

"Yes," he managed. He sat and observed as they set the time for 11:00am and noticed that Jim was taking notes. Sam suddenly wanted to run, just get up and run.

"Sam, are you OK?" Evie asked, taking his hand.

Her touch calmed him down. Sam drifted back to the present. Mike was asking, "Whom would you like to do the service? Pastor Kylie is out of town on vacation, but I'm sure she would be willing to come back."

"No, don't call her back. That wouldn't be fair," Sandra said.

"David, would you be willing to handle the service?" Evie asked.

"I would be honored to, if that is what the rest of you want," David replied.

"I think that's a great idea," Sam said. Everyone nodded in agreement.

"Would any of you like to speak at the funeral?"

"I would like to say a few words," Skauty answered.

Sam felt he ought to say that he would speak, but he didn't think he could do it. A wave of guilt rushed over as he sat silently.

"All right, all we have left is to decide on music, select an urn, and go over our fees," Mike said.

Those words sounded so final. Sam felt himself slipping back into the tunnel.

CHAPTER 39

Back from the funeral home, Sam pulled into the driveway and noticed that Tamara's car was gone. Once in the house, Sandra announced that she was going to try to take a nap.

"I think I need coffee to make it through the rest of the day," Evie said.

"Me, too," Sam agreed. "I'll put on a pot."

David headed up the stairs and came right back down. "Viviana is gone, too."

Skauty's phone pinged, and he checked the message. "Listen to this. 'Global Food Source has reconsidered the plan for Tlingit Bay. Holmes Harrison invites you to a meeting Wednesday, October 17, 7:00pm, at Harrigan Hall. Come and see the wonderful new ideas!'"

Sam could see the irritation in Skauty's face when he looked up.

"Here we go again," Skauty said.

"Do you think he reconsidered the proposal for us to live in our own homes and fish for him?" Sam asked.

"I doubt it," Skauty said. "He probably changed the color of some of the paint. But I guess we will have to go."

Evie set out mugs, and Sam followed behind pouring coffee. David set out a variety of creamers.

"We need a plan that totally derails Harrison by Wednesday," Sam said.

"We know how to release the fish," Evie said. "But I don't think Sandra will be able to tolerate us going near the frigate again."

"I think it will take more than releasing the fish to stop this man," Sam said. "He will have to run up against people who are stronger than he is."

"If the Tlingit aren't stronger, then I don't know who is," Skauty said.

Sam felt proud when his grandfather said that. It was an odd feeling. Sam had always felt shame when he thought of his Tlingit heritage, but now he had a realization. "I am beginning to think of myself as Tlingit."

The sound of a car pulling into the driveway pulled Sam from his thoughts. Sam heard a few clinks in the garage. Then, James, Tamara, and Viviana walked into the house carrying wet suits.

"I don't think we have to guess what you guys have been up to," Sam said.

"We picked up scuba gear from the dive shop," James said. "They were generous and happy to help."

"Maybe we had better hide those. We don't want to upset Sandra," Evie whispered.

"Can we put them in your car, Skauty?" James asked.

"Of course."

When James and Viviana came back in, Evie was saying, "I think Harrison has just given us our timeline. Let's release the fish and do the cyber-attack on Wednesday morning so he will have tons of problems on his mind by the time of the meeting. I hope it will be enough to get him to back off."

"Evie, did I ever tell you that you are brilliant?" Sam said. "If we can show Harrison that his computer system is crippled and the fish are back, what else can he do but give up? We have homework to do. James, we need a plan for how to get close enough to the frigate without getting shot. I have to figure out all of the nasty things I can do to Harrison's computer system. And David, you have a service to plan."

"I noticed you had two wet suits, James," David said.

"I did. I think I am going to need extra oxygen, so Viviana is going to carry that for me."

Sam watched as David's eyes grew wide.

"It's OK," Viviana said. "James is going to teach me how to scuba dive tomorrow."

"I don't think I like that idea. Why don't you let me do it?" David protested.

"Just think, David," James said. "It will be a lot safer underwater than on the boat."

"I hadn't thought of it that way," David mused.

"You need to make sure none of Harrison's people can see you training," Evie said. "They might put two and two together."

"I hadn't thought of that," James said. "Any ideas where we can go?"

"Stephen Walker has a private dock at his rental house just south of here. I'm sure he would be willing to let you use it," Skauty said.

"How deep is the water?" James asked.

"I'd say fifty to one hundred feet," Skauty answered.

"That sounds perfect," James said.

"I'll give him a call. Do you have a time?" Skauty asked.

James looked at Viviana. "We might as well start in the morning. Nine o'clock?"

Skauty started to dial the number.

"Wait, Grandpa," Sam said. "If they have a clone of your phone, they could listen in on your calls." He fished Sandra's phone out of her purse and handed it to him.

"Sam, you have to fix our phones so we can use them again," Evie scolded.

"You're right. I'll disable the GPS tonight, and we can get a new carrier tomorrow."

* * *

James arrived at nine o'clock sharp, driving Skauty's car. Viviana was ready to go, and David showed up with his backpack.

"I thought I'd bring stuff to work on my message for the service while you two do your thing," David said.

"That sounds good," Viviana responded. "You do like to write near water."

The day was crystal clear and fairly warm for that time of year. James entered the address for Eagles Landing into the car's GPS system and took off. They arrived fifteen minutes later. The house seemed empty, and the dock was deserted. There was a set of green chairs and a heavy table on the dock. David took a seat at the table while James launched in to explaining the basics of scuba diving.

David started listening intently at first, but found the talk about the mask, how to empty it if it fills with water, and how to breathe rather dull. He pulled out his Bible and notepad and turned his thoughts to his message for the funeral. He didn't turn his attention back until Viviana stripped down to a one-piece swimsuit in order to wiggle into the wet suit.

James was explaining buoyancy and how to use the buoyancy compensator device as he went through her instruction. He went through breathing, equalizing ear pressure, and descending and ascending while he donned his suit.

When they were ready, David asked, "You do know how to swim, don't you?"

Viviana came over and gave David a quick kiss. "Thanks for being concerned, but I've got this." She climbed down the ladder and went into the water. James was right behind. David couldn't quite make out what James was saying. After a couple of minutes, Viviana fiddled with something and slowly sank under the water.

David walked to the edge of the dock and could see their shadowy forms for a few seconds. After that, he could tell where they were only by the bubbles coming to the surface.

Knowing he would be scolded if Viviana surfaced and found him staring at the water, David went back to trying to concentrate on his message. His heart drew him to II Timothy 4:6-8, "As for me, I am already being poured out as a libation, and the time of my departure has come. I have fought the good fight, I have finished the race, I have kept the faith. From now on, there is reserved for me the crown of righteousness, which the Lord, the righteous judge, will give me on that day, and not only to me but also to all who have longed for his appearing."

"That sounds like Kat," David thought. "He was certainly fighting the good fight when he was murdered." David felt anger rising in his veins at the surfacing of the word murder in his mind. "Harrison needs to be prosecuted for this," he thought.

David heard a change in the water and looked up to see Viviana and James bobbing in the gentle waves. They climbed up the ladder.

"How did it go?" David asked.

"It was wonderful!" Viviana replied. "I haven't had that much fun in a long time!"

"Next we will have to work on going deeper," James said. He launched into a discussion about nitrogen, how to surface slowly, and what to do if she started feeling the bends.

David listened intently. When James was finished, he asked, "Any questions?"

Viviana shook her head no.

"Be careful," David said as she pulled her mask back on and started down the ladder.

*　*　*

"I'm starved," David said as they pulled up to the house. Sam and Evie pulled in right behind them.

"We have phones again!" Evie announced.

"I need to get a phone. Someone tossed mine out the window!" James said, eyeing Viviana.

"It was necessary," Viviana replied.

Walking into the house, they found Sandra sitting at the kitchen table with wadded tissues all over the place. Evie ran and wrapped her in a hug, "Oh Sandra, I'm so sorry. We shouldn't have left you alone."

"Alone is exactly where I needed to be," Sandra said. "It was easier to bawl my eyes out that way."

"Still, we should have been here. Maybe you wouldn't have been so sad," Sam said.

"If losing Kat is not worth a good cry, then I don't know what is," Sandra said. "What have you guys been up to?"

"We got our phones activated," Sam said.

"I got started on my message for tomorrow," David said.

Sam realized when Sandra fixed her eyes on James and Viviana that she knew before they said anything.

"Um, we were with David," James said.

"You don't have to tiptoe around me," Sandra said. "I know you were out teaching Viviana to scuba dive."

"How did you know that?" Sam asked.

"It was quite obvious the way you all have been sneaking around. It is important to me that we finish what Kat gave his life for. So when do we release the fish?"

"We're planning to launch a cyber-attack and release the fish on Wednesday morning before Harrison's meeting," Sam answered.

"The only stipulation I have is that I will be on the boat with you," Sandra said.

"You don't have to do that, Mom."

"If all of you are going to get blown up, do you think I want to be left behind? Besides, maybe I can stop you from doing something stupid," Sandra replied.

"I just realized we need clothes for the funeral! It looks like a shopping trip is in order after lunch," Sam said.

CHAPTER 40

Tuesday morning dawned with a heavy gray sky, mirroring Sam's heart. "Dad is really gone. He's not coming back," Sam said aloud as the realization crashed in.

"It is hard to believe," Evie replied as they all sat around the table waiting for the time to go to the funeral.

"I remember when my dad died. For months I kept expecting him to come tell me good night after I went to bed," Viviana said. "Then I would remember, and the sadness would start all over."

"I had the same feeling when my brother died," James said. "But by the time my parents died that didn't happen. I guess the reality that death was our way of life had taken hold in my heart."

"How did your family die?" Tamara asked.

"We weren't part of one of the A-30 compounds. Basically, they starved to death, even though it was pneumonia that killed all three of them. I would have been next if I hadn't gotten into the Navy."

"That must have been awful," Tamara replied.

Sandra came into the kitchen in her black dress, "Let's go so we're not late. I want all of you to sit with us in the family section. I think we'll need two cars." And in that business-like manner, she walked to the door.

James drove the Suburban and Sam "drove" the Tesla. As the Tesla turned off Indian River Road onto Sawmill Creek Boulevard, Sam noticed a freshly graded area with what looked like a giant pavilion going up. "What is going on there?"

"It looks like Harrison is already starting on the prison he calls a compound," Evie said.

"But what is it?"

"I have no idea."

As the Tesla neared St. Peter's by the Sea Episcopal Church, Sam noticed cars lining the narrow streets. He took over driving because people were walking everywhere. People nearly covered the grounds of the church. He pulled up to the small parking lot to find that the parking spaces were still open. "They saved the parking places for us," Sam said, touched.

James pulled in beside the Tesla, and everyone got out. It took fifteen minutes to get inside the church, which was packed, because so many people stopped them to express their condolences. The ushers led them to seats up front, and David arranged his Bible and notes on the pulpit.

The ushers signaled for everyone to be seated, and Tlingit musicians began a medley of Tlingit and Christian music. Sam reached and squeezed his mother's hand, feeling at home with the familiar music. Evie took Sam's other hand, and he felt that somehow he would make it through losing his father. David gave opening remarks and led a prayer. He invited Skauty to come and speak.

"When Raven created the world, he had to, by cunning and deceit, steal from the greedy in order to give us the things we need for life. Once again, our life is being threatened by the greedy. My son lost his life in a fight to snatch our freedom out of the grasp of this man. Kat was a good and honorable man. I am proud of my son and am grateful that he was willing to give his all in the effort to keep our freedom intact.

"I will miss Kat greatly, as I know all of you will. But in the midst of our grief, the fight continues. We must be unflinching in resisting the establishment of this compound that Holmes Harrison plans to force upon us. We must let Kat's spirit lead us on in the battle and do him the honor of following in Raven's trail."

Sandra pulled out a tissue from her purse and glanced at Sam. She passed him two, and he passed one onto Evie. David led them in a prayer and then read the scripture passage from II Timothy.

"It is amazing how well Skauty's words fit with this passage. The Holy Spirit does work in mysterious ways. I had only known Kat for a few days. The reason I met him is that I was the beneficiary of one of his rescue missions. He flew down to Virginia and lifted us out of the grasp of another greedy soul. I am now convinced that rescuing, helping, and saving other people was an innate part of Kat's life. His wonderful life will continue to bear fruit in all of us as we, in turn, share the love and compassion that he showed us."

When the service was over, the family was herded to the fellowship hall, where long tables were covered with food. Sam, Sandra, Evie, and Skauty greeted people as they filed by on their way to fill a plate. Since there was no room for chairs, everyone took their plates out on the grounds.

"I'm thankful that it isn't raining," David said as he came up and put his arm around Sandra. "I'm sending these folks to get a plate and have a seat," he announced while pulling Sandra toward the serving line.

"I can't believe how many people are here," Evie said as David nudged them on.

"I'm not surprised," Sandra said. "Kat was loved by the whole town."

* * *

Back home and inspired by the service, Sam launched into exploring the havoc he might could wreak through the entry he had found into GFS's computer system. He followed the trail to Harrison's bank account and was amazed at the huge amount of money in his checking account: $16,204,383.21.

"Wow! I wish I had that!" Sam said to himself.

"What are you muttering about?" Evie asked as she continued putting up the food they had brought from the service.

"Harrison has over sixteen million dollars in his checking account!"

"Oh," Evie said.

Sam was miffed by how unimpressed she was. "Don't you think that's a lot of money?"

"Yes, it's a lot of money. But all he has is money. I sure wouldn't want to trade places with him."

"Your moral compass always points true," Sam replied. "That gives me an idea! I think it would benefit Harrison to make a sizable contribution to the Sealaska Foundation to help preserve Tlingit heritage."

"Can you do that?" Evie asked with a grin.

"I think so. As long as he doesn't have a limit on how much can be transferred at one time, it should work. Does five million sound about right?"

"Five million what?" David asked as he walked into the kitchen.

"Five million dollars. Harrison is about to develop a humanitarian streak and donate to the Sealaska Foundation," Sam answered.

David laughed, "I love it! Let operation Heaving Holmes begin!"

"Heaving Holmes?" Evie asked.

"Yeah. We're going to heave him right out of here!" David said.

"Should I go ahead and do it?" Sam asked.

"I think you should wait until tomorrow and let everything crash in on him in one day," Evie said.

"OK. Tomorrow will be an exciting day!"

CHAPTER 41

A gentle pink hue rested on the mountains as Sam looked out the window Wednesday morning and stretched. He had already been up for an hour putting the finishing touches on the program he planned to use to lock down GFS's computer system. Sam had decided that anything less than totally disabling GFS's operations would not be effective. He began creating a ransomware program to hold GFS hostage until Harrison relented on the compound plans.

Sam looked over the code he had written. "This ought to do the trick," he thought. The night before, they had discussed the timing and decided to wait until after the mission to release the fish so as not to stir up Harrison's suspicions.

Anger warmed Sam's veins as he thought about Harrison. "Revenge will be sweet," he thought. "I should put in a virus that will wipe out everything in their system. I still want to do that. But Evie was right. Then Harrison would have no incentive to back down on the compound."

Sam heard footsteps upstairs as Evie, David, and Viviana arose and began getting ready. "Today is going to be a stellar day," Sam thought. "I just wish Dad were here to go with us."

Sam was wiping away a tear when Sandra walked into the kitchen. She had been crying, too, and put her arm around Sam.

"I know," was all she said. She busied herself with breakfast, and Sam continued looking over his program. There was a knock on the door, and James and Skauty walked in.

"Good morning," Skauty said. "Getting up this early is rough on an old man."

"Grandpa, you didn't have to get up," Sam said.

"If Sandra is going, then I am, too," Skauty answered.

"Some people will do anything for a free breakfast," Sandra teased as she put the first pancakes on the griddle.

"That is another perk," Skauty replied.

The others came down and devoured the pancakes as quickly as Sandra could cook them. Then they made an assembly line to fix sandwiches for lunch, packed the cooler, and were ready for the day. James checked items off a list as he loaded the diving gear into the Suburban. They all piled in and headed for the dock.

With the boat underway and chugging slowly out of the harbor, Sam pulled out a map of the sound. Pointing to Biorka Island, which was a few miles east of the frigate, Sam said, "I think we should come around the island and head northwest on a path that takes us about a mile from the frigate. We could even put the nets down. Maybe that would help avoid suspicion."

"That's exactly what I was thinking," James said. "And Viviana and I could slip off the boat when we are at the closest point."

"How long do you think you'll need before we pick you up?" David asked looking over from where he was piloting the boat.

"I'm thinking about an hour and a half," James said.

"I thought you could only go about forty-five minutes on a tank of oxygen," David stated with a worried tone.

"They had two-tank systems at the dive shop, so we should be good," James said.

"You will be wearing all the oxygen you need?" David asked.

"Yes," James answered.

"Then why does Vivian need to go?"

"We've added a bit to the mission," James answered.

"And what is that bit?" David said turning and letting go of the wheel.

"You'd probably rather not know," James said.

"I think I would very much like to know!"

Seeing that David had lost track of what he was supposed to be doing, Sam took the wheel. Viviana walked over and put her arm around David's waist, "It will be OK. We are going to blow the rudder and one of the propellers on the frigate."

"You're going to what?"

"We have C4. While Viviana is cutting the fish cage, I'm going to plant the C4. It has timers, and I'll set it to go off after we are back in dock," James explained.

David was beside himself. "Why didn't you tell me about this?" he pleaded with Viviana. "I don't think it's a good idea. Wait, you have explosives on this boat?"

"I think it's a great idea," Evie said. "Harrison won't be able to bring the ship in to fire on the village."

"I'm hoping that he didn't get his hands on any missiles," James said.

"It's OK," Viviana said again, hugging David tightly. "James is handling the explosives. All I have to do is cut a fish net."

It dawned on David that he was no longer at the wheel, and he jerked his head around to see Sam there. "Thanks, Sam. I sort of lost it."

"No problem," Sam replied.

"Why didn't you tell us about the explosives before now?" David asked.

"We didn't want anyone to be upset or worried, especially Sandra," Viviana answered.

"Do you think we should tell her?" Sam asked.

"Tell her what?" Sandra said as she walked into the wheelhouse. "I know about the explosives, if that's what you mean."

"What is the plan with the C4?" Skauty asked, coming in behind Sandra.

"It looks like we don't have any secrets to keep now," James said. "I am going to disable the frigate so it can't navigate."

"You'll have to blow the rudder and propellers for that," Skauty said.

"That's the plan," James said.

*   *   *

Holmes Harrison arrived back at his yacht late Tuesday evening. He was pumped with lofty ideas after the A-30 summit. All thirty sectors represented by the A-30 were prospering. They had begun discussing the possibility of expanding their operations into Mexico or Canada. The possibility of expanding his power enlivened Harrison. He had felt goose bumps when Steve Sterling, the owner of ConnectX, the communications conglomerate, had voiced the possibility.

The one irksome notion Harrison brought back was the realization that he was behind the others in developing compounds. This was a dark cloud hanging over the otherwise exciting meeting. Harrison paced in his small office on the yacht feeling a tiring mixture of exhilaration and angst. He stopped his pacing long enough to pop a couple of Tums into his mouth.

"I should call a meeting and make sure everything is ready for tomorrow," Harrison thought. He looked at his watch and realized it was 11:15pm. "Oh bother, I guess it can wait." He knew his crew would be ready and waiting at 8:00 in the morning.

At precisely eight o'clock, Harrison strode into the conference room and sat down at the head of the table, where his cappuccino was waiting on the coffee warmer.

"First things first," Harrison said. "Is the pavilion ready?"

"The structure is complete, and the last section of fencing is going up this morning," Hal Anderson said.

"It will be ready by this evening?" Harrison more stated than asked with a raise of his eyebrows.

"Absolutely. By lunch time," Anderson responded.

"Have you advertised tonight's meeting sufficiently?" Harrison asked, looking at Anne Solomon.

"I have sent out reminders three times a day, had announcements on the local radio and television shows, and sent two direct mailings," Solomon answered.

"Good. Good," Harrison said, sinking deep in thought. He was silent for a couple of minutes while his three top staff members were watching and wondering. Finally Harrison looked up. "Oh, are the militia on the cargo ship?"

"Yes, sir," Dirk Donegan said.

"Good. Good. Anderson, I'm sure you will see to it that we have an ample supply of contracts to sign."

"Yes, sir. They are printed and already at Harrigan Hall."

Harrison took a sip of his cappuccino, "Is there anything else we need for this evening?"

Solomon, Anderson, and Donegan looked at each other. "Not that I can think of, sir," Solomon said.

"Lady and gentlemen, this is going to be a stellar day!" Harrison said, taking another sip of his cappuccino. "That will be all."

CHAPTER 42

It was 10:35am when Sam stopped the boat on the northwest side of Biorka Island to lower the nets.

"This is just about where we crashed," James said.

Sam winced as a shock of grief flowed over. "It feels strange thinking the plane could be right under us." Sam stuffed the sadness so he could get back to the task at hand.

While Sam, David, Evie, and Viviana lowered the nets, James and Skauty positioned the dive gear and C4 on the starboard side of the wheelhouse where it would be out of view of any prying eyes on the frigate.

With everything in place, Sam took the wheel and started the boat on its path to cross within a mile of the frigate. Evie and David helped James and Viviana to get the oxygen tanks on. Skauty and Sandra positioned themselves in the back to appear ready to haul in a catch.

Sam's nerves tensed as he moved past the island and closed in on the frigate. "If they fired on Dad, they might fire on us, too," he thought. "I wish Evie had stayed home. I can't bear it if anything happens to her."

It seemed like an eternity, and Sam was sweating before the frigate finally came into view.

"Frigate ho!" Sam heard David say. Sam realized how tightly he was gripping the wheel and tried to relax. He tried to focus on steering the boat so that its path came as close to the frigate as he dared. "Our closest point will be when the frigate is perpendicular to the side of the boat," he thought, digging back into his geometry. He watched for that closest moment while the others finished their preparations.

Viviana stood up from strapping her knife onto her leg, and David grabbed her in a bear hug. "Please be careful. I don't know what I would do without you."

"I'll be careful. You be careful, too. Remember, it is probably more dangerous on this boat than under the water," she tried to reassure him.

James started to say that he wished they had rebreathers so the bubbles wouldn't show but realized that would increase David's worry.

Viviana could see the frigate through the wheelhouse windows. The time was getting close. She worked to hide her nervousness for David's sake.

"When we jump, turn facing the back of the boat, land on your heels, and fall backwards into the water. And try not to let go of the DPV. But if you do, remember it is strapped to your wrist," James said to Viviana. "Push your mask tightly onto your face while you land."

"Got it," Viviana said.

They all watched the frigate get closer. "Let's get up on the box," James said.

David steadied Viviana as she climbed onto the storage box they would use to jump over the rail and handed her the flippers.

"Why do you need flippers when you have the DPVs?" David asked.

"They are a precaution in case something goes wrong with the DPVs," James said. He checked his watch and stored the GPS coordinates. "It's 11:07am, so we should meet back here at 12:37pm," he said.

"12:37," David repeated to help himself remember.

"Good luck!" Viviana said, and James jumped.

"I love you!" David said as Viviana followed James. David stood watching as the boat sailed away from his heart.

Viviana watched as James got his bearings and dived. She followed, trying to relax and let the DPV pull her along. All she could hear was the hum of the DPV. Down about thirty feet, the light was muted, but she could see James well enough to follow him.

After about twenty minutes, Viviana saw a dark wall up ahead. It was massive, and Viviana couldn't see the end. As she got closer, she could see that the darkness was moving. She realized that she had let up on the PDV and slowed to nearly a stop, looking in awe at the massive structure. Seeing that James was leaving her behind, Viviana snapped back into gear and zoomed the DPV to catch up.

When Viviana looked at the wall again, it was like a cliff with rocks that were in constant motion. She finally realized that she was seeing fish swimming inside the net wall. "That's a lot of fish!" she thought.

They reached the wall, and James signaled for Viviana to start cutting. He pointed to the box with the C4 and in the direction of the frigate, and she understood that he was going on to the ship while she cut the net.

James zoomed off to the left, and Viviana rose to about ten feet below the surface. She pulled her knife from its sheath. "I hope I don't get stampeded by fish," she thought as she started to cut. The material seemed to be nylon and was tougher than she expected. It took some force to cut through it.

Viviana was totally focused on cutting through the netting. She had cut down about twelve feet when she was hit hard on the hip and knocked sideways. She looked and saw a shark swimming away. It looked like it was making a circle to come back. Feeling her hip, she discovered that the shark had made a rip in her wet suit, and she was bleeding.

The shark turned to make another attack. Viviana's adrenaline surged, but she didn't panic. Two thoughts flashed into her mind: "Try to stab the shark. Get behind the net." Viviana grabbed the net and pulled herself through the cut she had made as quickly as she could. The DPV caught in the opening as the shark charged. Viviana jerked it through and gave a hard kick with her flippers, propelling herself away from the opening.

The shark turned toward her and crashed into the netting, knocking Viviana backwards. Viviana's vision was suddenly cut off, and she was spun around, engulfed in a huge school of fish. She had lost her sense of direction and didn't know which way was up or which way the net was. "I have to get back to the net," she thought as an unending wall of fish continued to zoom by. "Facing the shark is better than this."

Viviana kicked with her fins, trying to aim herself perpendicular to the direction in which the fish were swimming. She was surprised that only a few fish bumped into her as she continued to swim. Finally she burst through the jungle of fish and was back at the net. She regained her orientation and now knew the direction of the surface. She was surprised to find the knife still in her hand.

Viviana felt for the cut she had started but couldn't find it. "I must have been swept away by the fish." She looked at the fish, turned on her DPV, and swam in the opposite direction. When she found the cut, she was surprised at how far the fish had carried her. She was not so surprised that the shark was still there.

Viviana kept a wary eye on the shark as she resumed cutting. She got about three feet farther with her cut when the shark snapped itself in her direction and charged. Viviana pushed backwards along the net and braced herself for when the shark hit.

She saw a flash of silver to her right. A dolphin exploded onto the scene and rammed the shark in the side, knocking it off course. Before the shark could recover, another dolphin rammed it. The shark turned and fled with the dolphins in pursuit. A third dolphin stopped and eyed Viviana, seeming puzzled that she was in the net.

Viviana heard the dolphin making clicking sounds, and in no time three more dolphins were there eyeing her. She looked closely into the eyes of the first dolphin and thought she saw amusement.

"He thinks I'm a funny looking critter. I wish I had a way of thanking the dolphins for running off the shark," Viviana thought as she hung suspended in the water looking at these amazing creatures. After what seemed like a long time but was probably less than a minute, the dolphins took off toward the surface.

Viviana quickly resumed cutting the net. She went down about thirty feet, then started cutting horizontally. She cut what she estimated was about another thirty feet, went back to the top, and began cutting horizontally again. She would soon have a door.

She was nearly though cutting when James appeared. The door was wide open, but none of the fish were leaving. They just kept swimming in the same direction they had been since she got there. Viviana looked at James, and he shrugged his shoulders.

It dawned on Viviana that the fish had grown so accustomed to their boundary that they may not realize there was a way out. She sheathed her knife and swam into the swirl. Swimming against the flow of fish, Viviana was able to divert some on the outer edge to the door. Once she had succeeded with getting about a hundred to go out, others began to follow on their own.

Viviana swam out the door just in time as a flood of fish followed. Soon there were so many fish trying to exit the cage that they almost clogged the opening. Viviana looked at James, and he signaled a thumb up then waved his hand to say, "Let's go." Viviana got hold of her PDV, turned it back on, and followed James away from the cage.

Viviana realized how tired her right hand was from all of the cutting. She tried to just hold to the DPV with her left hand but couldn't keep it steady. By the time they had gone twenty minutes and James stopped, her hand was cramping and hurting.

James motioned to his watch and gave another thumbs up, which Viviana barely noticed as she tried to stretch the cramp out of her hand. As the cramp released, Viviana noticed a hum. "That must be the boat," she thought. She noticed James pointing at her and followed his finger in the direction of her thigh. She signaled OK.

Viviana was startled by a silver flash that suddenly came into view. Before she knew what was happening, she was surrounded by dolphins. She was certain that one of them was the one into whose eyes she had looked earlier. The dolphins came close and nudged her. "I think they want to play."

She looked over and saw three dolphins checking out James. She reached out and touched the closest dolphin, and it seemed to like it. The dolphin nudged her again, and she reached out and hugged it. James seemed to be having fun, too.

The sound of the boat got closer, and Viviana looked toward James and saw only fins. He was headed to the surface. Viviana took time to touch the dolphin one more time and then followed James.

Pulling her mask up when she had reached the surface, Viviana looked around and found James. Then she tried to locate the boat. Seeing a bright yellow inflatable dinghy headed their way caused her breath to freeze.

"Uh oh," James said. "It looks like someone from the frigate has been following our bubble trail."

"Should we dive?" Viviana asked, ready to make a run for it.

"No, they could still tell where we are."

As the boat got closer, Viviana saw one man with an assault rifle across his lap and another driving the boat.

"I think we are caught," James said.

Viviana tensed and a rush of adrenaline went through her body. "Maybe we can find a way to escape once we are on the boat," she said.

The dinghy circled around them, and the man with the assault rifle said, "You will come with us."

James obeyed and swam to the side of the boat. Viviana held back and felt a dolphin brush her legs. "What a terrible way to end such a pleasant visit," she thought.

"I'm not waiting all day," the man barked at her.

Viviana grabbed the side of the dinghy and started to pull herself on as James lay across the side at his waist. The dinghy tipped a little toward the side they were on, and the man with the rifle stepped back. Viviana pulled hard to heave herself up. There was a jolt to the boat. The man with the rifle flew over Viviana's head. The boat flipped over and landed with Viviana and James underneath.

"We found our chance!" Viviana said. They put on their masks and dived. Under water, they were greeted by seven dolphins who were shaking their heads up and down. The one Viviana had hugged came over and nestled to her. Viviana stroked the dolphin again and thought, "You guys rammed the boat!"

She hugged the dolphin then noticed James. He was frantically pointing at the two men who were clinging to the upside-down dinghy, then pointing away. She understood that he thought they needed to leave in a hurry. She grabbed the dolphin's dorsal fin, and the dolphin whisked her away. She looked back at James and grinned.

After the dolphin had come up for air three times, Viviana let go and looked around for James. She was about ten feet under the water and didn't see him. Waiting for a couple of long minutes, Viviana wondered if she had made a mistake letting the dolphin be her motor. Finally James came into view holding to another dolphin. The rest of the dolphin crew was swimming with him.

The dolphins seemed in a playful mood. "Maybe they like being heroes," Viviana thought as she swam up to the surface. The dolphins put on a show, leaping, flipping, and making all sorts of sounds.

"They are celebrating rescuing us," Viviana said to James.

She saw an incredulous look cross James' face, then he smiled, "You may be right!"

The low hum of a boat engine registered in Viviana's ears, and she tensed. Looking around, she breathed a sigh of relief when she saw the tiny outline of the fishing boat in the distance.

James checked the GPS coordinates on his watch. "We're about half a mile from the meeting spot. I guess we should swim back."

"Wait," Viviana said, watching the boat. It veered in their direction. "Do you think they saw us?"

"I don't think they could from that distance. Maybe they are staying away from that raft."

The boat came closer, and Viviana and James waved their arms. It turned and aimed directly at them. The dolphins continued their antics until the boat arrived. Viviana hugged her friend one more time, threw her fins onto the boat, and climbed the ladder.

David was there to help her over the rail and immediately noticed the tear in her wetsuit and a trickle of blood. Rey was cawing like crazy and landed on Viviana's shoulder.

"I missed you, too," she said.

"You're injured! What happened? Are you OK? You need to sit down!" David spewed.

Viviana twisted to look at her hip. "It will be OK," she said.

Sam popped out of the wheelhouse, "They are telling us to get out of here," he said.

Viviana pointed to the dolphins and started to tell how they had helped when she heard a whiz overhead then a heavy splash.

"I think the stories will have to wait," James said. "That was the proverbial shot across the bow. We have to get out of here!"

Sam hurried back to the wheelhouse and gave the throttle all it had. As the boat headed for home, James said, "I hope they don't find the explosives."

CHAPTER 43

Sam charged through the door with determination. "Harrison thinks he has the power to enslave the whole Tlingit population and have us do his bidding. We're sure not going down without a fight!" he said heading for his computer.

David ushered Viviana upstairs to tend to the wound on her hip. Sandra tossed him a tube of antibiotic ointment on his way up the stairs.

Viviana pulled off her jeans and was still in her swimsuit. She twisted around to the mirror, "You don't think they need stitches, do you?"

David looked carefully at the three shark-tooth shaped wounds. "I don't think so."

"I can't imagine how bad it would be if I hadn't had on the wet suit," Viviana mused.

David went to apply the antibiotic ointment and was so distracted by the shape and softness of her hip that he missed. Viviana looked down and rubbed his head. He wiped off that round and succeeded with getting the ointment in the right place. He applied band aids, pulling them tight so that they applied pressure to keep the wounds closed.

He stood up and grabbed Viviana in a tight embrace. "I hope the wedding can be soon."

Sam booted up the computer and rubbed his hands together. "It's time for you to make a generous donation to the Sealasaka Foundation," he said out loud.

Sam got into Harrison's bank account and set up a five-million-dollar transfer. Then he changed the five to a six. "That's for the shot across our bow," he said. "Now to put you in jail for being such a bad boy." He backed out of the bank account and installed the ransomware program.

Sam hit the button to activate the program and grinned. "Let's see what you think about that!"

* * *

At precisely three pm, Holmes Harrison sat down to check his emails as was his custom. While opening his computer the phone rang.

"Homes Harrison here," he answered.

"Sir, this is Captain Kilpatrick. I have some bad news."

"Well, what is it?" Harrison urged.

"It appears some divers have cut open the fish cage. They are all escaping."

"They are sneaky rascals, aren't they?" Harrison replied.

"I am sending divers out to try to repair the breach."

Harrison laughed, "Don't bother, Captain. I was going to release the fish tomorrow anyway."

"I thought we were keeping them penned up until you had the Tlingit people signed up for the compound."

"That's right, Captain. They will all be signing up tonight."

"Yes, sir. I'll call off the divers."

"Thank you, Captain," Harrison said and hung up. He rubbed his hands together and woke up the computer. When he logged into his email, the computer screen went black with a white-lettered message: "ACCESS DENIED UNTIL FURTHER NOTICE."

"What?" Harrison said. His phone rang again.

"What's up, Solomon?"

"Sir, it appears our computer system has been shut down with a ransomware program."

"Well, if it's not too exorbitant, let's pay it so we can get back to business."

"So far there are no demands."

"You mean they aren't after money?" he said, scrunching his eyebrows.

"I don't know what they are after. I put in a call to Henry Warren so he could get to work on it."

"Thank you, Anne. You are always on top of things, and I appreciate that."

"You're welcome, sir."

Harrison hung up and started to pace. "This is not what I need right now," he said out loud. "Who would want to shut down our system?" He stopped pacing long enough to eat a couple of Tums. Then a light came on in his head. "That Hanson guy was the head of IT for Mitch Carter! Well, Hanson, you will be singing a different tune this evening!"

* * *

Sam stood up from his computer feeling like there was something else he needed to do. "That seemed too easy," he thought. Then a light came on in his head. "I need to let the rest of the Tlingit people know what is going on!" Sam pulled out his new phone and downloaded the Tlingit app. He was entering a message when it occurred to him that Harrison would be able to see it. He almost called out, "Dad," but caught himself, and his heart did a somersault. Then he went to find Sandra.

"Mom, I just almost called for Dad to let me borrow his phone."

"I know, Sam. I keep expecting him to walk through the door any minute. It is hard to believe that he is really gone."

Sam saw the tears welling up in her eyes and gave her a hug. After a minute he said, "I need to borrow your phone so I can send a message to the people using the thread that left Grandpa's phone out." Sandra fished the phone out of her purse and handed it to Sam.

"Thanks," he said and opened the Tlingit app. He read a few of the entries to make sure he was on the right thread then began entering his message.

"Here is an update on today's events. We were able to release the fish that have been caged near the frigate. They should be swimming back into the sound at this very moment."

Sam paused wondering whether to say anything about the bombs on the frigate. He decided he'd better not mention it and continued the message.

"I have locked down GFS' computer system with ransomware. With the fish released and Tamara exploring a real option of selling to Russia, we have no need to capitulate to Harrison's demands. I have no idea what he is going to propose this evening, but I doubt it will be anything to our advantage. Let's all hold tight and stay united. We can defeat this guy and save our way of life." Sam paused before hitting send. He went to the den and found Skauty in the recliner with his eyes closed.

"I'm not asleep," Skauty said.

"Grandpa, would you look over this message and see if you think it's OK? Is there anything we need to add?"

Skauty took the phone and read it over. "That sounds perfect! Do you want me to add my name to it?"

"Sure."

Skauty went to the end of the message and added, "Sam and Skauty." "There you go," he said."

Sam took the phone and felt a sense of pride seeing his name with his grandfather's. He just looked at it a few seconds before hitting send. He took the phone back to his mom.

"Sam, I'm proud of you," she said. "You and your friends have done everything possible to defeat Harrison and preserve our way of life. Just remember, no matter what Harrison says or does tonight, I'm one proud mom."

"Thanks, Mom," Sam said. "That means a lot."

Sam went back to the kitchen and found Evie looking through the fridge.

"Should we celebrate our success with grilled salmon for supper?" she asked.

"That sounds yummy!" Sam said.

"We'll have to eat early if we want to get to the meeting on time. Say around five thirty?"

"I'm sure everyone will be hungry after spending the day at sea," Sam said. "I'll have the grill ready by five."

At 4:15, Sam dragged the barrel shaped grill out of the garage to fire it up. The grill was his dad's baby. Sam had always wondered why he wouldn't keep it on the deck until he had asked one day. "I want to keep it out of the weather," his dad had explained.

Sam opened the top and picked up the brush. He could almost feel his dad with him. In fact, Sam looked around to see if Kat was there. The feeling brought goose bumps to Sam's arms. A powerful sense of love washed over him, and tears welled up in his eyes. "I'm going to miss you so much," Sam said as he reached out and touched the grill.

The crunch of gravel startled Sam. He wiped the tears from his eyes before looking around to see Tamara pulling into the driveway.

"Hey, Sam! How did the mission go today?" Tamara asked before even getting the door shut.

"Other than a shark bite, James and Viviana nearly getting captured, and a shot across our bow, it went great. The fish are released."

"Who got bitten by a shark?"

"Viviana, but she's OK," Sam said.

"So James is OK?" Tamara asked without stopping as she headed into the house.

Sam smiled as he went back to pouring in charcoal and lighting it. "Somehow all of the chaos we have been through in the last few weeks has brought two couples together," he thought not needing to ask why Tamara was in such a rush. "I guess God works in mysterious ways, mixing life and death, joy and grief, success and failure. Life is such a messy mixture."

Sam came back into a quiet house. He found Skauty asleep in the recliner, James with his head in Tamara's lap on the couch, and Evie and Sandra in the kitchen talking quietly.

"It looks like everyone is tired," Sam said. "I could go for a nap, too."

"It has been quite a day," Evie said.

Sam went up and stretched out on the bed. He tried to nap, but so many thoughts were running through his head that he never went to sleep. At five o'clock, he got up and grilled the salmon.

Everyone gathered around the table to celebrate the day's victories.

"This smells exquisite!" David said. He said a blessing, and everyone dug in. "You know, Jesus celebrated his resurrection with fish. I think having salmon is perfect for a day like this."

"I agree," Tamara said. "And I'm glad you all made it home safely, even if Viviana is a bit ragged."

"I can't wait to see what Harrison has to say about all of this," Sam said.

CHAPTER 44

Sam, Evie, Sandra, Skauty, and Tamara gathered coats and the other things they needed to go to Harrigan Hall. James and Viviana begged off the meeting, pleading that they were tired after the dive. David said he was staying with Viviana.

Sam stepped out of the car into the crisp October evening and was surprised at how many people were filing into Harrigan Hall.

"It looks like everyone is coming to hear what Harrison has to say," Sam commented.

"I just hope he has had a change of heart," Tamara said. "There might be a riot if he proposes the same thing."

As they headed toward the hall, they were swarmed with people expressing their condolences over the loss of Kat. Sam was warmed by all of the wonderful comments and compassion. They made their way into the hall, which was already filling up.

"It looks like there will be standing room only tonight," Skauty said.

"The only seats left are near the front left," Sandra noticed.

"I want to sit up front anyway," Skauty said. "I may need to speak."

Sam sat between Skauty and Evie. He looked over and noticed that Evie was fidgety and had a tense expression. "What is it?"

"Something is not right. We need to leave," Evie said.

"We can't leave," Sam said. "We have to hear Harrison's proposal so that we'll know how to respond. Besides Grandpa has to be here, and I don't want to leave him."

"You're right, Sam. But I have a bad feeling about tonight."

Sam's nerves tightened at Evie's words. "She's just tense after all we've been through today," he tried to convince himself. But his gut was telling him that Evie was right.

Sam looked around and noticed that the same six men in black suits were stationed around the room. One of the men reached into his coat pocket, and Sam held his breath. He breathed again when he saw him pull out a phone. Sam realized that Evie's comment had him on edge. "I have to relax," he thought.

Sam leaned over to Skauty. "It looks like the whole town is going to be here."

"That's good. I hope everyone will hold out against Harrison. I see he has the sign-up table loaded with contracts."

Sam looked where Skauty was pointing and saw four long tables piled high with papers. "He's optimistic," Sam said.

As Sam spoke, a huge artist's rendering of the compound appeared on the screens around the room, and Harrison came wheeling in on his Segway. He hopped onto the stage with his usual flair and addressed the crowd.

"I have come to this town to create an exceptional place where we can all live, work, and enjoy life. Tlingit Bay will be a top-of-the-line compound with modern housing, great recreational opportunities, and the chance to do the work you love to do. You can see the wonderful proposal on the screens.

"So far, most of you have resisted my proposal. I realize that change can be hard. But change in life is inevitable. This is the way of the future. If you look around the United States, you will see that compound life is thriving. Now you have the opportunity to have this in Sitka.

"I have gathered you here to make a proposal that you can't refuse! I mean literally, you can't refuse this. It is time for the creation of Tlingit Bay to move forward. You have one more chance to sign up for the compound tonight. If you refuse, I have purchased land inland and will allow you to be resettled there.

"Your decision must be made tonight. If you sign on, you will be allowed to live in your homes until the compound living quarters are ready for you. If you refuse to sign on, you will be removed to the resettlement area tomorrow."

About twenty militia men filed through the door in full combat gear, including assault rifles.

Harrison continued, "I realize that many of you are carrying guns. I think you would agree that it would be better to go about this peacefully. There are many more militia outside. Please understand that you are out-gunned.

"Now, my staff will gladly sign you up for the Tlingit Bay compound at the tables to your left. Any of you who decline this generous offer will be escorted to a holding pen. Good evening, my friends and future coworkers!"

Harrison hopped onto his Segway and rolled out of the building. Sam went numb. His heart was pounding, but he couldn't seem to feel his body. He looked over at Evie, and she seemed in shock, too. Before he could recover, he felt Skauty getting up. Skauty marched straight toward the line of militia men. Sam, fearing for his grandfather's safety, caught up with him. The men had their guns aimed at Skauty and Sam's chests as they approached.

"I am the clan leader and need to speak," Skauty said and pushed through them. Sam followed as Skauty got to the stage and took the microphone.

"Holmes Harrison has come to test the will of the Tlingit. Throughout our history as a people, we have had to do battle with the greedy. Sometimes we have won. Sometimes we have lost. But we have never capitulated to anyone's demands that we change our ways."

Sam stood amazed at the authority with which his grandfather spoke. "I think I really understand why he is clan leader," Sam thought.

Skauty continued, "I cannot tell you what to do. We face a hard decision. It appears we must either give ourselves over to this man's control or rebuild our lives elsewhere. I can tell you what I will do. I will never submit to this man's control. I will refuse to sign his contract until I am dead. He can do what he will with my body, but he will never own my spirit!"

The crowd exploded with applause. Sam noticed some of the militia jump at the loud sound. Somewhere in the room, a chant began, "Freedom! Freedom! Freedom!" The chant grew as it spread through the crowd. Caught up in the moment, Sam held up his fist and joined in the chant. He was surprised when he saw Evie and his mother chanting, too.

After five minutes of the chant growing ever louder, Dirk Donegan angrily grabbed the microphone from Skauty. "I see you have made your decision," he shouted five times before the crowd quieted enough to hear him. "I'm sorry you didn't choose wisely. We will begin with the front row and exit single file. You will deposit any firearms and phones in the bags near the door, write your name on the bag, and it will be returned to you at the resettlement area.

Skauty and Sam were the first to be ushered out. The guards frisked them and found no weapons. Walking out of the building, Sam saw a line of guards on both sides of the sidewalk. The path led to a bus, onto which they were directed. Sam stepped on the first step and looked back. He saw Evie, Sandra, and Tamara coming close behind. The guard gave Sam a push, "Go on! File to the back." The last thing Sam heard as he stepped onto the bus was Wingston's scratchy fuss.

"Now I guess we know what that pavilion is for," Skauty said as they waited for the bus to fill. Two militia guards got on after the final Tlingit was onboard, and the bus drove off. Evie sat next to Sam, and he reached out and took her hand, "I'm sorry."

"At least we're in this together," Evie replied.

There was another line of guards that formed a path to the gate. The guards directed people into the pen. Sam noticed a line of port-a-potties along one part of the fence.

"They treat us like cattle," Skauty said as he walked into the pen and looked around at the worried faces.

Sam heard one man say, "He can't do this to us! It's illegal. Someone should let the police know."

Sam walked over to him. "I'm afraid all but one officer was with us. I don't think our police can do anything about this situation."

Buses continued to arrive and pour people into the pen. Sam found himself moving farther away from the gate as the crowd grew. Jeffery Troutman walked up to Skauty, "You don't think he will really go through with this, do you? Surely he is just trying to scare us into signing."

"I'm afraid he is serious. Harrison is a selfish man and resents not getting his way."

"If he offers to let us sign again, are you going to?" Jeffery asked.

"There is no way I will ever sign anything Harrison offers," Skauty said.

Sam put his arm around Evie. "It's ironic. I've always wanted to leave Sitka and get away. But tonight, when it's not a possibility, I want to stay."

"That's because your roots are here, Sam. You are a part of this soil, this sea. It's in your blood," Evie said.

Sam felt a tear well up in his eye as the truth of what Evie said lit his heart. "Well, I'm glad I left the first time, or I would never have found you."

Evie pulled him into a hug, "I'm glad, too."

"You wanted to get out of MC2's compound, but I don't think this is what you had in mind."

"You're right. But we'll make it, Sam. We have to."

Suddenly Evie pulled back and had a worried look.

"What is it?"

"We need to warn the others! What are we going to do?"

Sam rubbed his hands together thinking. "I have no idea. I imagine they will come looking for us when we don't come home."

"Oh no! They'll be caught and tossed in here with the rest of us," Evie said.

Worried, Sam stood silently and watched the pen fill up. It was an hour and a half before the last bus dumped its load. The pen was crowded, but there was some space left over. Sam looked around for Skauty and saw him moving from group to group.

He pulled Evie by the hand to catch up with Skauty and heard him say, "It's going to be cold tonight. We will need to huddle together for warmth."

"We'll have to be like the emperor penguins in Antarctica," Sam added. He saw one man looking at him like he had lost his mind. Sam explained, "They huddle in one huge mass in the Antarctic cold while they are incubating their eggs. They even take turns with who has to be on the outer edge."

"I don't think I want to stand up all night," the man grumbled.

CHAPTER 45

Viviana directed David to the end of the couch so she could lie down on her non-shark-bit side. She grabbed a pillow and placed her head in his lap. James was stretched out in the recliner, and the television was going. It wasn't long before Viviana drifted off to sleep. David watched Viviana sleep for a while, feeling full of love. Then he laid his head back and fell asleep, too.

Viviana bolted upright to the sound of urgent tapping on the den window. The sound was accompanied by loud chirping. Viviana rushed to the window and pulled it open to find Wingston and Azul on the ledge. They flew in and back out several times.

The noise awoke David and James.

"What is going on?" David asked.

"I don't know. Something is wrong," Viviana said. She heard Rey and Canto tune up in a tree nearby. When Nadashée's loud cry pierced the night, Viviana knew. "Something has happened at the meeting. We have to see what it is."

Viviana ran upstairs and came back down with her bow and arrows. James and David were still sitting. "Come on! Let's go!" she called.

They sprang into action. "I have the keys to Skauty's car," James said to Viviana's back as she rushed out the door.

James drove west on Indian River Road. As they approached Sawmill Creed Boulevard, Viviana pointed out lights shining in the new pavilion. "What is going on there?"

The car got closer, and they could see hordes of people in the pavilion. "Are they having a picnic?" David asked.

"I don't think this is a picnic," James said. "It looks more like a holding cell." He hit the brakes when he saw the militia guards in full combat gear, stopping right in the middle of the road.

"They have taken everyone prisoner!" Viviana said.

Three of the guards started walking toward the car. "We have to get out of here!" James said and whipped the car around, spinning in the dirt on the side of the road as he accelerated. James saw a road to the left and skidded into a turn.

"Where are you going?" David asked.

"I want those guards to think we went this way rather than straight back to the house." James came to a road to the right and turned. Then came another road to the right, and he took it. "This should take us back to Indian River Road, I hope." James turned off the headlights and slowed to a crawl.

Coming to an intersection, James rolled through it without hitting the brakes. The only sound in the car was the soft hum of the engine. After what seemed like an eternity, the Hansons' driveway appeared in the darkness. James released the accelerator and coasted into the driveway, finally having to hit the brakes to keep from rolling into the house.

Viviana was shocked. "I should have known something like this would happen."

"What if they come after us?" David asked.

*　*　*

Harrison summoned Donegan, Solomon, and Anderson to the conference room. He was pacing and rubbing his hands together. The three walked in, and Harrison said, "Well, what do you think of our little surprise?"

Solomon gave Donegan an accusatory glance, "I'm afraid this is going to cause a PR nightmare, sir. Once word gets out, the rest of the A-30 could turn on you."

"I think they will understand. Business is business after all. Dirk, how did the transfer to the pavilion go?"

"Without a hitch, sir. Everyone cooperated. There were no sign-ups for the compound, I'm afraid."

"I'm not really surprised," Harrison said. "These are stubborn people. We will have to arrange transportation to the Telegraph Creek site as soon as possible. I'm afraid Dirk will have his hands full with security, so I'm going to ask you to handle that, Hal. This is a new community, after all," Harrison laughed.

"Could I ask where Telegraph Creek is?" Hal Anderson asked.

"It's east of here. I understand that it is accessible by plane or helicopter, or something. We will need several. I'm sure you can figure it out," Harrison responded. "I suppose everyone is aware that someone sabotaged our fish cage earlier today. It is not a big loss since we don't need to keep the fish confined anymore. What we haven't circulated yet is that the saboteurs also planted explosives on the frigate. Divers reported that the rudder and one of the propellers were blown off. The frigate will have to be towed to a shipyard for repair.

"I say this to point out the kind of people with whom we are dealing. I think getting rid of this bunch is a wise move. Our next big problem is the computer system. We are severely hobbled until we can get that up and running again. Anne, have you had any word from Henry Warren?"

"Not yet," Anne replied. "He assured me that he has his whole team working on it."

"We may be able to speed things up," Harrison resumed. "I suspect Sam Hanson was the author of this malicious attack. He was the IT chief for Mitch Carter and caused all sorts of trouble there. Dirk, go collect Sam and bring him to the yacht. Let's put some pressure on him and convince him to release the ransomware."

"Yes, sir," Dirk replied, and Harrison noticed the enthusiasm in his voice.

"Yes, you might enjoy this, Dirk."

* * *

Kyle Cagle, one of the militia guards, hustled over to Chris Smith, the head of the guard detail at the pavilion. "A car just spun around and took off down that road," he said excitedly while pointing down Indian River Road.

"Thanks, Kyle. I'll check with Dirk Donegan to see if he wants us to pursue it." Chris dialed Dirk's number.

"Dirk Donegan here."

"Sir, this is Chris. One of my men spotted a car that turned around and sped away. Would you like us to pursue it?"

"I was just about to call you, Chris. I need you to transport Sam Hanson back to the yacht. He's one of the prisoners. Send two or three guards to make sure he doesn't get away."

"Yes, sir," Chris responded. "And what about the car?"

"If you have enough extra guards and everything is under control, then have them see if they can locate it."

"Yes, sir," Chris said and hung up. He called over three guards. "Dirk Donegan wants you to take Sam Hanson to the yacht. Use one of the buses and make sure he doesn't get away."

The three guards moved to the gate. Joey began to call out, "Sam Hanson. Sam Hanson. Come to the gate, please."

Sam heard his name being called and looked at Evie, "Now what?"

"It's probably about the ransomware lockdown," Evie said.

Sam looked around for Skauty, but he was lost in the crowd. "I wish Grandpa was here to give me some advice," he said. "I guess I'd better see what they want."

Evie took his arm and walked with him. By the time he reached the gate, Sam's throat was dry and tight. He wasn't sure the words would come out when he said, "I'm Sam Hanson."

Joey unlocked the gate and said, "Mr. Harrison has asked that we bring you to his yacht."

"I'm going with him," Evie said.

Sam noticed Joey's surprised look. He recovered quickly and said, "I'm afraid not. Mr. Harrison only requested Sam."

Sam noticed the other two guards hugging their weapons as though Evie might charge and attack. "It's OK, Evie. I'll go." Sam stepped through the gate.

"Turn around," Joey ordered and placed Sam in handcuffs.

"Really?" Sam said. "Do I look dangerous?."

"Mr. Harrison said to take no chances," Joey responded.

Sam looked at Evie and saw worry in her eyes.

CHAPTER 46

Turn out all the lights," Viviana urged. James and David scrambled to turn out the downstairs lights, while Viviana rushed upstairs.

"We need a plan to get the people out of that pen," David said.

"Did you see how heavily armed the guards are?" James replied. "I don't see much hope in that."

"We have to do something," David said.

"You're right. We do need to do something."

Viviana came trotting down the stairs. The evening twilight had just given over to dark. David sniffed and touched Viviana's shoulder, "You put on your deerskin dress."

"It is better for what we have to do tonight," she said.

"What do we have to do?"

"Get everyone out of that pen safe and alive," Viviana said.

"That's what James and I were just saying. But how?"

"I'm thinking the guards are staying on the cargo ship. Maybe most of them will go back and sleep there tonight."

"The ones that don't still have assault rifles," James pointed out.

"Shhh," Viviana said as the sound of a vehicle registered on her ears. They watched out the front window as a bus drove slowly by.

"Look around for guns," James ordered.

"There's a gun locker in the study where I sleep," David answered. They ran upstairs and found Kat's hunting rifles and ammunition.

"It's locked," David said.

"Look in the desk," Viviana said.

David found the key and unlocked the cabinet. He pulled out a rifle and handed it to James. The second one he held out to Viviana, but she patted her bow.

"I'm better with this."

David got two boxes of ammunition and locked the cabinet back. Downstairs, they were loading the rifles when the bus came back and stopped.

"We got these just in time," James said.

"Out the back door," Viviana ordered and took off. David and James followed. Viviana held a finger to her lips and quietly slipped out. James locked the door and closed it as quietly as he could.

Viviana walked quickly across the back yard and into the woods, not making a sound. Under the cover of the trees, she stopped and looked back. Lights were coming on in the house.

"I can't believe they just walked in," David said. "That was rude."

"These folks aren't playing," James said.

"Let's move deeper into the woods," Viviana said. "They may come looking for us when they realize we aren't in the house." She moved east until she found the path that she and David used to go to the river. She led them to the last point from which they could still see the house and stopped.

Looking back, she saw the back door open. Two guards came out, stood on the deck, and looked out into the woods.

"I hope they give up now," David whispered.

The guards walked off the deck and spread out in the yard. "It looks like that was wishful thinking," James whispered.

"Now what do we do?" David asked.

James jumped when Rey landed on Viviana's shoulder. "We wait," Viviana whispered.

The guards, with assault guns at the ready, walked to the woods line. They peered into the trees for a couple of minutes.

"I don't see anything," one guard said.

"I guess it was a different Cherokee," the other one answered. Maybe these folks are already in the pen. Let's go." The guards turned and walked back around the house. Their taillights moved down the road back toward the pavilion.

Rey squawked, and David said, "Where is Canto when I need him?" He jumped when the little bird landed on his shoulder. Canto flew back to a tree limb. "I should have known you were here, buddy," David said.

"Let's go back to the house and see if we can come up with a plan.

* * *

"Welcome aboard, Mr. Hanson." Holmes Harrison oozed a fake charm. "I believe we have some business to tend to."

"That is for sure," Sam said angrily. "You have a whole village of people penned up that need to be let go."

"Yes, that was right clever of me. I will be rid of you people and can finally move forward with this project. I knew this was going to be a stellar day. But the business to which I referred is that I suspect you are the one who shut down my company's computer system. Before the evening is over, I expect you will agree to undo your mischief."

Sam tried to decide whether to admit it or deny it. He decided that there was no use in denying what Harrison had already decided was true. So he said, "You are right. I locked down your computer system and will release it only after you release my people, give up on this compound, and leave."

"Those are mighty big demands from such a puny person," Harrison smirked. "I expect my engineers will be able to remove your little program in a day or two. You could save us all some time and trouble if you will go ahead and do it," Harrison replied. "You might even save your life," Harrison added with a wicked grin and walked out, leaving Sam with Dirk Donegan and two security guards.

* * *

Evie found Skauty in the crowd, "They took Sam!"

"What do you mean, 'They took Sam?'"

"Security guards called him to the gate and said that Harrison wanted to see him."

"Why would they take Sam?" Skauty asked.

"I wonder if they figured out that he is the one who locked down their computer system," Evie said feeling the worry build. "What are they going to do to him?"

"I had forgotten about the computer system," Skauty said. "You could be right. I'm afraid they won't let him sit in the room and enjoy niceties like they did with me."

Tamara walked up, "Do you think he really intends to ship us inland? I can't believe he would actually go through with that. It is illegal in so many ways."

"He seems pretty ruthless," Skauty said. "I imagine that is exactly what he plans to do."

A sense of dread settled into Evie's soul. "In that case, we have to find a way to get out of this jail."

* * *

"Uncuff him and leave us," Dirk said as he laced his fingers and stretched as if getting ready for a boxing match. "All right, Hanson. What is it going to take to get you to remove that ransomware program?"

"Weren't you listening the first time?" Sam said with a surge of anger.

Dirk stepped forward and punched Sam in the gut. "Maybe that will help you see the light."

Sam's rage overpowered his sense of caution, and he charged Dirk, knocking him into the wall. Sam drew back his hand for a punch but stopped short. Dirk had drawn his revolver and had it aimed at Sam's chest.

"You like to play rough, do you?" Dirk said. "I think we can accommodate that. Guards!"

The two security guards popped into the room.

"Kindly handcuff Mr. Hanson's arms to these chair legs," Dirk said pulling out a chair. The guards slammed Sam into the chair and roughly handcuffed his hands to the back legs.

"Now, Sam," Dirk glared, "I want you to think clearly about your situation. Your life depends on your cooperation."

"You're right," Sam said. "I was very rude. I forgot to thank Mr. Harrison for his generous donation to the Sealaska Foundation."

Sam watched confusion creep into Dirk's countenance and realized that the system was so locked down that they didn't even know about the transfer of funds. Sam thought he had regained control until Dirk backhanded him.

Sam felt blood trickling in his mouth from the smack, and the pain lingered. Sam wasn't eager for another blow, so he just sat silently and watched Dirk pace the room. Sam thought Dirk seemed to be trying to process what he had said and to decide on his next move. He tried to anticipate what Dirk would say next but realized he had no idea. So he waited.

Dirk finally stopped, delivered a menacing look, then walked out of the room. Sam wondered what Dirk was up to. His anxiety grew the longer Dirk was gone. "I have to get control of myself," Sam thought and began to do deep breathing exercises that he had learned from Evie. He was beginning to feel calmer when the door opened.

Dirk walked in with a small black bag that he unrolled and placed on the table. Sam saw various implements of torture, and his nerves tensed again.

Dirk looked over the implements and pulled out a slender metal device that he could run under Sam's fingernails. "This should do nicely," he said. Without another word, he sat down behind Sam, grabbed his little finger, and jabbed the device deep under the nail.

Sam tried not to scream, but he couldn't help himself.

"Oooh. That was fun!" Dirk said as he pulled the device out. He grabbed Sam's ring finger and did it again. Sam cried out again and decided he needed to do something to buy some time. His mind grasped for ideas and finally landed on one.

"I can't do anything without my computer."

CHAPTER 47

Viviana, David, and James gathered around the kitchen table with brains hard at work. It was almost 10:30.

"OK, they should send most of the guards back to the ship soon to sleep and leave only a few to guard the pen overnight," Viviana said. "I think sometime in the middle of the night would be the best time to attack."

"You're right," David said. "The guards that are there should be sleepy and struggling to stay awake.

"I'm thinking they will still have at least four guards around the pen, and there are only three of us. We don't have night scopes and shooting that accurately at night would take sheer luck. One call would bring the rest of the militia running," James said.

"Are you always such a pessimist?" Viviana asked.

"I'm not a pessimist. Just being realistic."

"Remember that Tamara is in that crowd, too," Viviana pointed out.

"I am well aware of that, which is why I'm thinking cautiously. I don't want the guards to turn their guns on the crowd."

"OK," Viviana said, realizing that they were getting testy with the stress of the situation. "If they couldn't call in the rest of the militia and we had help, do you think we could do it?"

"That would be better," James said.

Viviana suddenly held up her hand, then the others heard the sound of a vehicle pulling in the driveway.

"It sounds like we have company again," David said. "Why would they come back?"

"I don't know, but I'm tired of people showing up uninvited," James said. "Let's capture this bunch and see what they can tell us. Grab your rifle, and let's get behind the door." James hurried and pressed his back against the wall on the side where the door would open and hide him. David quickly joined him, and Viviana hid behind the wall leading into the kitchen. She heard car doors close.

The front door opened, and the first guard stepped in, revolver drawn. He proceeded into the room, and the second guard entered. As he shut the door, James whacked him in the head with the butt of his rifle and hollered, "Don't move!"

The first guard spun around to see two rifles aimed at his chest. He held up his hands.

"Drop the revolver," James ordered, and the guard dropped it.

"Get down on the floor on your back," Viviana ordered stepping out from the kitchen. The guard turned his head to see Viviana with an arrow aimed at him. She saw fear on his face, and the guard did as she had ordered.

Viviana stood at the guard's side with her arrow aimed at his heart. "What are you doing here?" The guard hesitated. "We shoot intruders in Alaska," Viviana added, pulling back on the arrow a little more.

"Wait," the guard said. "We were sent to pick up a computer. That's all."

"Why are you trying to steal a computer?" James asked.

"We aren't stealing it. We are taking it to Sam Hanson so he can remove the ransomware program."

"Why would Sam do that?" David asked.

The first guard, whom James had whacked on the head, moved and tried to get up. David picked up the guard's revolver and aimed it at him, "I think you had better just stay on the floor."

"You didn't answer David's question," Viviana said and jabbed the arrow point into his shoulder. The guard yelped and grabbed his shoulder, feeling a trickle of blood.

"Mr. Harrison has him on the yacht. Dirk Donegan was torturing him, and he requested his computer. We are supposed to pick it up and bring it back. That's all I know, lady."

Viviana looked at James, "I say we kill them, so we don't have to worry about their giving us away."

"You are probably right. I think this night is going to get ugly," James replied.

"We can't just kill them," David said.

"Do you have a better idea?" Viviana asked.

"Not yet, but I'm working on it," David said.

The first guard grabbed Viviana's arrow and pulled her down. Before he could wrap his arm around her neck, the point of a knife dug into his throat.

"Let go," Viviana said and pushed the knife in a bit. The guard's eyes were wide open with fear, and he did as she said. Viviana kept a little pressure on her hunting knife while she stood back up. "I told you we need to kill them," Viviana said.

"Let's tie them up and leave them here," David suggested.

"When they don't come back, Harrison will send others looking for them," James pointed out.

Viviana noticed David's consternation. She didn't want to kill, either. "OK, but we have to hide them where they won't be found."

"David, go to the garage and see if you can find some rope," James said.

Viviana pulled her knife back and scooped up that guard's revolver, aiming it at him. He rolled over to get up, and Viviana kicked him in the head, knocking him back down. "This is a stubborn one, James. I don't think he is going to make it."

"I see what you mean. If you want to live, you will have to cooperate. That was your last chance," James said.

"I thought they said there was no one here," the second guard said, his head clearing.

David returned with a large coil of rope, "This ought to do the trick."

Viviana pulled her hunting knife out and cut two lengths of rope. "Does that look OK?" she asked looking at James.

"Perfect. Now, roll onto your stomachs," James ordered. Viviana crunched her knee down onto the guard's neck. "Hands behind your back and don't try anything."

David bent down to tie his hands, then paused. "Wait, we need to strip them first."

"What are you talking about?" James asked.

"He's right," Viviana said.

"We will need their uniforms to get on the yacht and deliver Sam's computer."

"Why would we do that?" James asked.

"So Sam can send an order from Harrison to have the militia transferred back to the frigate," David said.

"How is he going to do that?" James asked.

"I have no idea, but he can do things like that."

Viviana released the pressure on the guard's neck. "Take your clothes off."

Both guards regarded Viviana suspiciously but did as she said. David trained a gun on them while Viviana and James tied their hands.

"Now what?" James asked.

"I know!" David said. "We can drive them down the road and into the woods. They can spend the night enjoying nature."

"That's a great idea," Viviana said.

"Do we need gags?" James asked.

"They won't make a sound but once," Viviana said sternly.

Viviana and James marched the two guards in their underwear and socks to the car. David came out with two throws.

"What's with the blankets," Viviana asked.

"They might get cold," David said.

"Good grief," Viviana said. "Sit down and leave your feet out."

James and Viviana tied their feet and closed the back doors. David drove the car the guards used while Viviana kept watch with one of the revolvers. James followed in Skauty's Cherokee.

David found what looked like an old logging road going off to the right and turned. The car bumped and scraped until it was out of sight of the road. He stopped.

David tucked the throws around the guards and said, "Sleep tight."

"How is anyone going to find us?" the second guard asked.

"I'm sure someone will come along to go fishing one of these days," David said as he closed the door.

It was almost midnight by the time Viviana, David, and James got back to the house. David and James changed into the guards' uniforms, which were royal blue long sleeve polos with the GFS emblem and black nylon cargo pants. James' fit fairly well, but David's was a bit short.

"I hope no one realizes we aren't the same two that left," David said.

"Oops, we made a mistake," James said. "We should have kept the guards' car."

"We can park behind Harrigan Hall and hope no one notices," David offered.

"I think you need to get the computer to Sam, let him send that email David was talking about, and then get Sam out of there." Viviana strategized.

"Maybe we can convince anyone we run into that Sam has removed the ransomware program, and Harrison is sending him back to the pavilion," David said.

"Somehow we will have to become the ones guarding Sam to do that," James pointed out.

"So as long as we can get on board without being recognized as imposters, find Sam, convince the other guards that we are taking over, and sneak him out in the middle of the night, we should have no problems. Why do I feel nervous?" David said.

"Where is Sam's computer? Maybe we can find a layout of the yacht before we go," James said.

David found the computer in Sam and Evie's room, connected to the charger. "Got it!" he announced and unplugged the cord. David started to exit the room, then turned back and pulled the charger out of the wall.

Downstairs, he opened the computer but could get nowhere. "It requires biometrics to get in," he said.

"We'd better get going. They'll wonder what is taking so long," James said.

They walked out to the car, and Viviana said, "Good luck!"

"Aren't you coming?" David asked.

"Don't you think my presence would raise suspicion?" Viviana said.

David looked at her deerskin dress. "You are right."

CHAPTER 48

James parked the car on the opposite side of Harrigan Hall from the yacht, and David's muscles tightened with stress.

"Suddenly this doesn't seem like such a promising idea," David said.

"If you have a better one, I'm all ears."

"I don't guess I do," David said. "Now is as good a time as any to die. Let's go."

David held the computer and charger. As they walked around the corner of Harrigan Hall, David spotted the guard at the end of the gangplank and nearly froze.

"Here is our first challenge," James said followed by a laugh.

"What are you laughing about?"

"Just act like we are two guards having fun," James said quietly, then laughed again. David joined in the laugh this time. But as they got closer to the guard, his nerves began to take over.

"We finally found that computer," James said as he approached the guard.

"What computer?" the guard asked.

David's throat went dry.

"Oh yeah, you weren't on when we left," James covered. "Harrison sent us to get Hanson's computer so he could remove the ransomware program."

"I see. Word is Dirk has been having a field day torturing the poor guy," the guard said.

"I guess he gave in and agreed to remove the program then," James responded.

They walked onto the gangplank. David realized he had no idea which way to go at the end of the plank. He looked at James and saw that he was puzzling, too. Just as they got to the end, where it was decision time, they heard a scratchy fuss.

Looking up and seeing Wingston and Canto sitting above a door just to the right of the gangplank, David breathed a sigh of relief. "Thanks, you two," he whispered and ushered James to that door.

James went in first, and David followed holding the computer and charger. He wanted to be holding the guard's revolver but resisted thinking, "That wouldn't look right."

The yacht was dead quiet except for the sounds of their footsteps. They followed a hall that led to the center of the yacht. James stopped and looked both ways along a hall that led forward and aft.

David started to suggest they go right when a voice to the left called, "It's about time you got back. Donegan is fit to be tied. He gave up and went to his quarters and said to let him know when you got back."

"The guy had it hid under his mattress," David lied, holding up the computer. "We almost gave up searching."

The guard stood up from the folding chair he had placed by the door and pulled out his phone. "I'll let Dirk know you're back, but you have to stay here and face his fury. I'm going for coffee." Without another word, the guard tapped on his phone and headed toward the galley.

When he was sufficiently down the hall, David looked at James and said, "That was easier than expected."

"We need to get the computer to Sam and see if he can send the email before that guy gets here," James said and opened the door.

Sam was still tied to the chair. He looked up with surprise, opened his mouth, but no words came out.

"Are you OK?" David asked.

"I'll live," Sam replied.

"Can you send an email from Harrison ordering the cargo ship to take the militia back to the frigate?" James asked.

"I can if I have the time," Sam said. "But I would have to remove the ransomware program first."

The door burst open and Donegan flew in. "What are you two doing in here?" he demanded.

"Delivering the computer, sir," James said.

"You're not the two I sent to collect it. Where are they?"

"They went for coffee, sir," James replied.

David could see suspicion in Donegan's eyes.

"I haven't seen you on the yacht before," Donegan said.

James launched himself into Donegan, knocking him to the ground and had his revolver aimed at Donegan's face before he knew what hit him.

"You ask too many questions," James said.

David's eyes popped, and he stood there gawking for a moment before thinking to pull his revolver, too.

James pulled Donegan's revolver out of the holster and slid it toward David. He fished Donegan's phone out and slid it toward David, too.

"Now what?" David asked feeling perplexed by the turn of events.

"I think it's time for us to leave this boat," James said.

"What about him?" David asked pointing at Donegan.

"Guys, this is Dirk Donegan, the cruel head of security for Harrison," Sam added.

"I guess we either have to kill him or take him with us," James said.

"Could we knock him out and tie him up?" David asked.

"I don't see any rope," Sam said.

Dirk tried to get up, and James smacked him on the temple with the butt of his gun. "Try that again, and you're a dead man."

"We could put him with the other guards," David said.

"I think that's our best option," James said. He stood up and said, "Get up. If you value your life, you will lead us off this boat without making a sound, understand?"

Dirk nodded his head and stood up while David was untying Sam.

David, keep your gun on Sam to make sure he doesn't get away," James said.

"I don't think he'll try that," David said before he realized this was a show for the guard at the gangplank.

James put his gun to Dirk's back, "OK, let's go. I will do the talking."

David tensed a little tighter as Dirk pulled the door open. Out in the hall, the guard who had been at the door was walking back with his coffee. David gulped. He noticed that James had lowered his gun. David remembered what he was supposed to be doing and aimed his gun at Sam's back. "I hope the safety is still on," he thought.

Dirk cooperated all the way off the boat and to the gangplank. He led the way down the gangplank toward the guard, who stepped aside for the procession. He touched the GFS insignia on his shirt as he approached the guard and kept walking.

"We're taking the prisoner back to the pen. Mission accomplished," James explained.

David relaxed a bit as he walked past the guard. But his breath froze when he heard, "Don't move and drop your weapons."

David looked back, stunned to see the guard aiming his revolver. David lifted his hands and then dropped the gun to the side. Then he heard, "Fire at will, son."

James had spun Dirk around so that he was between him and the guard.

"I suggest you drop your weapon. Now!" James barked.

The young guard looked confused but did as James had ordered. David gathered up the two revolvers and said, "This party is getting out of control."

"You will need to come with us," James said. "I have Donegan. You take this guy, David. And give Sam the third gun."

David handed Sam the gun and computer and moved around behind the guard, and they marched to the car. When they reached the car, James said, "Hmmm."

"What is it?" David asked.

"Just trying to figure out who is going to sit where," James answered. "Oh, check him for a phone," he added pointing to the guard.

"Hands on the car," David said and frisked the guard. "Got it," he said pulling the phone out of the guard's pocket. He noticed that Sam had been quiet and that his left hand was tucked under his arm.

"Are you OK?" David asked.

"My fingers hurt where this scumbag rammed metal under the nails," Sam said. "It hasn't sunk in that I don't have to worry about his next attack."

"You are a scumbag," James said. "We can let Sam return the favor before we deposit you. OK, Sam can you drive?"

"I think so."

"You, in the front seat," James said pointing to the young guard. "Dirk, you are right behind him. I'm in the middle, and you're next to me, David. Keep your gun trained on, wait, what's your name?"

"John," the young guard answered.

"David, keep your gun aimed at John's head. If he makes the slightest move toward Sam, shoot."

"Roger that," David said. Then, trying to sound more in control than he felt, "Everyone in the car."

David closed the door when John was in and heard a crash and a yelp.

"Oops, sorry about that," James said. Dirk pushed himself off the car where James had jammed his head into the frame. He glared at James without a word, then got in.

Sam drove one handed, using the left hand gently only when necessary.

"We have to stop by the house for rope," James announced.

At the house, David said, "Sam, we need that email sent to the cargo ship as soon as possible," then headed into the house for the rope. "Viviana," David called as he pulled out his trusty Swiss Army pocketknife and cut four lengths. "Viviana?" Hearing no answer, David ran upstairs as he continued calling.

"I can't find Viviana! What if they captured her!" David said, worried as he handed the rope to James.

"If they did, I'm sure they would have just taken her to the pavilion."

"I don't think she would have gone willingly. I hope she is OK."

"Dirk, we'll let you have the honors first," James said. While Dirk was leaning against the car and James was tying his hands, Wingston landed on the hood fussing for all he was worth. When Dirk's hands were secured, Wingston flew at his face and pecked at his eye, leaving an injury.

Dirk yelped, "What's with that bird?"

"I believe he doesn't appreciate how you treated his friend," David answered.

"Sam, you are welcome use David's pocketknife to return the favor," James said. David noticed Dirk stiffen.

"No, I won't lower myself to his level. We Tlingit value life, even if it is in a sorry soul like his," Sam answered. "I have a better idea than the email. Since the system is down, no one on the ship is likely to be checking email. Why don't you two deliver a message from our dear friend Dirk?"

David's nerves went taut again, but he said, "I have been wanting to practice my acting skills."

With Dirk's and John's hands tied, Sam drove out to the hidden car. Pulling in, David could see the two guards sitting back-to-back. "They're untying their hands," he said.

Sam skidded to a stop. David and James jumped out and ran to the car. "I don't think so," James said as he opened the door and aimed his gun. "David, keep an eye on the other two while Sam and I get these tied back up."

"It's a good thing we had another deposit to make," David said.

"These must be good knots," James observed. "You haven't made much progress, I see." He tied the guard's hands a little tighter. "Are you sure we can't just shoot them and be done with these pests?"

"I don't think we need to go that far," David answered. "Remember what Sam said."

"OK," James answered. "I think we'll buckle you in this time. That ought to prevent any further mischief."

When James reached in to buckle the seatbelt, the guard on the other side leaned over, bit his collar, and pulled him down. The guard under James bit down on the arm that held the gun.

Sam smacked the one biting James' arm with the butt of his gun three times before the guard slumped over. He ran around the car to the other guard, but he had already released James.

James pulled himself out of the car, walked around to the other side, and punched the guard in the mouth. "If you try that again, I'll put a bullet there instead of my fist."

He leaned in to buckle the seatbelt, and the door of the Cherokee flew open. Dirk jumped out and ran into the woods, heading in the direction of the yacht. David aimed his gun but couldn't see Dirk at all with the glare of the car's lights.

David was cursing himself for getting distracted when he noticed John wiggling to get hold of his door handle. David quickly rounded the car and was there just as John opened the door. "I don't think so," David said.

"Let's get his feet tied and tuck him into the car," James said.

"Shouldn't I go after Dirk?" David asked.

"He's too far ahead," James answered. "Besides, we know where he's going. We can catch him there."

CHAPTER 49

James fastened the seatbelt around John. "Someone will probably find you guys in a week or so," he said as he shut the door.

"I'm going to need lots of coffee if we are going to pull an all-nighter," Sam said. "And lots of Tylenol would help, too. Let's stop by the house for a minute."

"If Dirk gets to the yacht, all is lost," James said.

"Wait, he doesn't have to get to the yacht," David said. "He only has to get to the pavilion!"

"That's just a couple of miles away. So much for my coffee break," Sam said.

"David, you drive. Drop Sam and me near the pavilion and then hurry to the cargo ship," James said. "You have to get that ship underway before they realize what is happening."

"Keep an eye out for Dirk while we are driving. He will probably be hiding just off the road," Sam added as his adrenaline started to creep in and replace the sleepiness.

Having seen no sign of Dirk, David stopped about a quarter of a mile from the pavilion. Sam and James hopped out.

"Make sure you catch this guy," David said. "I don't want to be tucked away in the hold of that ship to rot."

"Now what do we do?" Sam asked, looking to James for guidance.

"I'm sure he won't just walk up the road. You go north, and I'll go south. Go about a hundred yards and find cover so you can still see."

"What do I do if I find him? A gunshot will alert all of the guards at the pavilion."

"It would be best to tackle him and knock him out. And try to keep him from calling out," James guided. "If all else fails, shoot him and run."

Sam looked west toward the pavilion. He could see that some of the people had sat down in groups. Others were lying down, trying to sleep. Some were still walking around. What he really wanted to see was Evie's red hair. His heart yearned to storm the pavilion and get Evie out. "I can't do that. We have to neutralize this bigger threat first," he said to himself.

Sam forced his heart to turn and follow his feet in the direction James had sent him. He found a thick tree to hide behind and took his position. His fingers ached miserably, and he held them up to slow the throbbing. "I hope he goes on James' side."

* * *

David drove up Sawmill Creek Boulevard and turned north on Halibut Point Road. "Where is Viviana," he thought. "I wish she were here. She would know what to do. I have to figure out what I'm going to say when I get there."

David stressed more with every turn of the tires. He was going twenty-five miles an hour over the speed limit but figured all of the police officers were in the pavilion. It was nearly two am when he saw the lights of the cargo ship looming ahead.

He started to pull into the parking lot but decided that since he was supposed to be on official business he would just park at the gangplank. There was a guard on duty. David took three deep breaths to steel himself and got out of the car.

The guard had unshouldered his assault rifle but lowered it when he saw David's uniform. "Halt! Who goes there?" the guard said with a big grin.

"I have an urgent message for the captain," David said.

"The captain is sleeping."

"Harrison wants him to return the militia to the frigate," David said feeling his throat getting dry. "He's afraid the optics won't look good if news organizations get word that there was a whole militia after these people."

"I don't think herding them up and hauling them off is going to look good any way you spin it. I'll let the captain know first thing in the morning."

"Actually, Harrison wants them gone tonight."

"Great!" the guard said with frustration. "You get to wake up Captain Swanson then. Come with me."

David froze, having expected that the guard would deliver the message. The guard was halfway up the gangplank when he looked back, "Well, come on. Let's get this over with."

David followed quickly, hoping the guard had not surmised why he hesitated.

"I'm going to enjoy this," the guard said and led David up a series of stairs and hallways. Stopping at a door labeled, "Captain Swanson," the guard knocked.

Nothing.

After what seemed like forever, the guard knocked again.

"Come in," David heard muffled by the door. The guard opened the door and ushered David in.

David's throat was tight and dry, but he managed to croak out, "Sir, I have a message from Mr. Harrison."

Sitting up on the edge of the bed, Captain Swanson said in a loud, raspy voice, "This had better be important!"

"Yes, sir," David said, reverting to his military days. "Mr. Harrison wants you to take the militia forces back to the frigate tonight. He said he doesn't want any sign of them present in the morning in case there are journalists around."

"Great Scott, man! Are you crazy! The whole ship is asleep."

"Sorry, sir. I'm just delivering the message," David responded.

"Why didn't he call me himself?"

"He said he thought you'd be asleep and wouldn't hear the phone."

"Well, I'll need to speak with him myself. Not that I don't trust you, but this is awfully sudden."

"Yes, sir. He did go to bed, though."

"If he woke me up, then I'll return the favor," Swanson said reaching for his phone. He hesitated then lowered the phone. "This is going to be bad enough without having to listen to Harrison gripe. Puckett, quit lurking in the doorway and rally the crew. Let's get this hulk of iron underway."

"Yes, sir," Puckett answered and disappeared.

"That will be all… What did you say your name is?"

"John," David lied quickly, thinking of the guard they had just tied up.

Swanson got up and started getting dressed without another word. David turned to leave. He wasn't sure he could find his way off the ship. "I should have paid more attention."

* * *

Sam was looking toward the pavilion, which was about one hundred yards away, and feeling guilty that Evie and the rest of the village were stuck there. His eyes searched the crowd hoping for a glimpse of Evie's bright hair.

"I have to get her out of there," he was thinking when a stick snapped close by. Sam stiffened as a shot of adrenaline hit his system. Without moving, he turned his head to the left, scanning the darkness for Dirk.

He saw movement in his peripheral vision. Then the last thing Sam wanted to see moved into focus: Dirk Donegan.

Sam froze, and his mind started reeling, "What do I do?" He waited as Dirk moved forward on his left. Sam realized he had to do something. He waited till Dirk was just past his position.

Remembering that James had said to tackle him, Sam launched himself at Dirk as fast as he could. Dirk turned at the sound so that he was facing Sam. Sam hit him as hard as he could with his shoulder, knocking Dirk to the ground. Dirk curled his knees into his chest as he fell, then used his feet to launch Sam over his head. Sam landed on his back with a thud and scrambled to his feet.

Dirk, with his hands still tied, was already on his feet and running at Sam. At the last moment, Sam jumped to the side like a bullfighter. As Dirk passed, Sam tackled him again, this time landing on his back. Dirk squirmed to get his legs under him, and Sam fought to hold him down. Dirk's left foot found traction, and he bucked Sam off. Dirk stood waiting. Sam was still trying to decide what to do when James stepped up and pressed his gun into Dirk's back.

"You will kindly not make a sound," James said.

"Thanks, James," Sam said.

"What are friends for?" James said. "Now for the next phase of this mission. I hope David was successful, or this won't end well."

* * *

David went down the hallway the same way that he had come. He took the first set of stairs down but couldn't remember which way to turn at the bottom. He decided to go left. Almost as soon as he started he heard footsteps thundering everywhere. "Oh no!" David thought, fearing he had been discovered. Men and women started scurrying everywhere, knocking him out of the way as they passed. When he realized that they were hurrying to prepare the ship to get underway, he breathed a sigh of relief.

"I should have a while to find my way off this thing," David thought. He waited till the crowd passed, then continued walking. Thinking he should have found another stairway by now, David began to doubt himself. Finally a stairway appeared, and David took it down. When he reached the bottom, he didn't recognize the place. He turned and went back up, retracing his steps down the hall. David went past the stairway he had initially come down. He found another stairway and took it down.

After walking about a hundred feet down that hall, David decided he was lost. A crew member stepped out of a doorway.

"Excuse me, can you tell me how to get to the gangplank?" David asked.

"Are you the one responsible for getting us out of bed?" the man asked.

"Don't shoot the messenger. That was Harrison's idea."

"In that case, you're on your own, buddy!" he said and stomped away.

Panic surged in David's heart. "I have to calm down. I have time to find my way." He took three deep breaths to settle himself. David shut his eyes and tried to visualize the walk coming onto the ship. "OK, I think I'm going the right way."

* * *

"So what do we do next?" Sam asked huffing and puffing after his battle with Donegan.

"David should be back soon," James said. "I think it would be best if we deposit this guy somewhere with his feet tied and go from there."

"What is David up to?" Dirk asked.

"You don't need to know," James answered.

Sam stood there nursing his fingers and trying to come up with a plan. The thought struck him that he needed to find the gun that he had lost during the fight, and he began searching in the leaves. Then he cringed at the thought, "What if Dirk grabbed it!" Sam remembered that Dirk's hands were tied and decided he couldn't have done that. But the thought kept nagging at him.

Sam decided to trust his instincts and approached Dirk to check his hands. Dirk started to spin, and Sam jumped him, tackling him again. He grabbed at Dirk's hands and found the gun. He tugged and finally wrenched it from his hands.

"He had my gun," Sam explained. He got up and heard a familiar screech. Wingston dive bombed Dirk and took another peck at his eye.

"That bird's going to blind me," Dirk whined. "You're lucky that you're incompetent," He directed to Sam. "You'd be dead if the safety weren't on."

Sam felt sheepish, realizing he had forgotten to take off the safety. But he was also grateful.

"Let's move to the road so we're ready when David comes. We can deposit this guy in a nearby ditch," James said.

Sam fiddled with the gun till he got the safety removed and followed James as he led Dirk along.

James found a spot along the side of the road that was hidden from the pavilion by trees. "David should be along any minute."

* * *

David's panic increased as he continued down the hall. He found another stairwell and took it down. He was having difficulty remembering if he had gone up two or three flights. Everything looked the same. He kept walking. Then the ship moved, and his heart nearly stopped. "They can't be unmoored already!"

David burst into a trot. Finally he heard voices to his left. He opened the next door he came to and stepped through it. He was outside near the bow of the ship.

The same guard from whom he had asked directions passed by and laughed, "Looks like you are stuck with us."

David went to the rail at the edge of the deck. The ship was slowly pulling away from the dock. David looked over the edge. The water was a long way down. "I can't stay on this boat, I just can't," David said to himself. "I have to get back and help." He looked at the water again, summoned his courage, and catapulted over the rail.

CHAPTER 50

James kept the barrel of his pistol snug against Dirk's back while they waited at the side of the road. Sam kept checking his watch. Minutes seemed like hours.

Dirk called out, and James whipped his elbow around Dirk's neck like lightning, cutting off the airflow. Sam jerked his head around and looked out from behind the tree. He could just make out a guard looking in their direction.

Sam had to force himself to breathe. He kept watching, and the guard seemed to lose interest. Sam heard something hit the ground and looked back to see that it was Dirk.

"Is he dead?"

"No, but he should be."

"I think something went wrong with David," Sam said.

"You may be right," James said, turning on the backlight of his watch. "It's 3:11. Let's give him ten more minutes."

"OK, but it is hard just to stand here and wait," Sam said.

"That's why they say patience is a virtue," James joked.

* * *

David hit the water feet first, but it still knocked his breath out. He fought his way back to the surface and gasped for air. He realized that he had to stop panicking and fighting, so he forced himself to relax. He took in a deep breath, stopped kicking and flailing his arms, and floated. When he felt calm, he lifted his head from the cold water and located the pier.

David swam toward the hulking structure and realized it was the height of a cruise ship's deck. He thought, "OK, this is not a problem, I just have to swim to the end of it and get out on land."

He swam south along the pier. He thought he saw black lines on the side up ahead. Swimming closer, David discovered it was a ladder that could be used if a small boat docked. David tried to reach the bottom rung but missed. He regrouped, kicked as hard as he could, and caught the rung.

Pulling himself up with that one hand, he felt heavy. The air was even colder than the water. With water flowing out of his clothes and shoes, David dragged himself up and up. Finally he reached the top, lay down on his back, and huffed and puffed till he caught his breath.

Urged on by thoughts of Sam and James waiting for him, David headed for the car. "I hope that's the last time I ever have to do that!"

* * *

A rush of excitement ran through Sam when he saw the car lights. "Here he comes! At least, I hope that's David."

Sam stepped out into the road and waved his hands. David slowed to a stop and rolled down the window. Sam felt a blast of heat.

"Man, it's hot in there!" Sam said.

"It's a long story," David answered.

"Sam, give me a hand here," James called.

Sam hurried to grab underneath Dirk's other arm and helped James drag him to the car.

"Is this guy sleeping on the job?" David asked, getting out and hustling to the passenger side. He crawled in and helped pull Dirk into the back seat.

After they got him stuffed in, Sam looked back toward the pavilion. He could tell that a guard was facing them, and he thought he saw a phone up to his ear.

"Guys, I think one of the guards has spotted us."

"Let's go before we get a parking ticket," David said with a shiver in his voice.

"I don't want to cradle this guy in my lap, so I'm getting in the back," James said opening the liftgate and crawling in.

With the car rolling, Sam asked, "Why do you have the heat on so high?"

"The good news is that the cargo ship is on its way back to the frigate. The bad news is that I couldn't find my way off the ship before it pulled away from the dock," David explained.

"You jumped off the ship?" Sam asked, shocked.

"I couldn't think of any other way to get back to you guys, and I knew you would be waiting for me."

"Wow! I'm glad you aren't dead!" Sam said.

"Me, too," David responded.

"What do we do with this dirtbag? Then how do we get the others out of that pavilion before Harrison starts shipping them to the middle of nowhere?" Sam asked.

"That's what I've been thinking about," James said. "Let's leave Dirk tied up at the house and come up with a plan while we dry David's uniform. We may need it again."

"I don't want to have this guy at our house," Sam said. "That would be too comfortable."

"That's not very hospitable of you," Dirk sounded off.

"Since you're so into comfort, just stay lying down," James said as he pulled his gun out.

David pulled the car into the driveway, and James said, "Pull around behind the house in case they come looking."

When David parked the Cherokee, Sam said, "David, start drying your clothes. I'll shoot Dirk if he moves while James ties his feet."

"Very efficient," David said as he headed to the house.

James was tightening the last knot when Sam said, "I see lights coming. I think it's one of the buses."

"Shut the doors!" James said and slammed the one on the driver's side.

Sam slammed his shut, too, and watched as the bus crept by. Sam looked the other way and waited. When the bus did not appear on the other side, he said, "Uh oh," and felt his skin crawl.

James grabbed Sam's arm and dragged him so they could crouch behind the hemlock tree just beyond the car. "Let them get to the car and open the door. When they are distracted by Dirk, we'll come up behind them."

"OK."

James pointed to the east side of the house, "Watch that corner."

"OK," Sam said again, as the all too familiar stress tightened his nerves. He waited. He jumped ever so slightly when he saw the guard's shadowy face peek around the corner. The guard moved toward the car. As the guard crossed the yard, Sam lost sight of him behind the hemlock limbs. He started to inch forward to keep his eyes on him but was afraid he would step on a stick. He waited and listened.

Sam heard the car door open, and one of the guards said, "Mr. Donegan?" Sam looked back at James, who had his hand up. As soon as the guard got his question out, James motioned for Sam to come.

As Sam followed James out from behind the tree, he heard Dirk say, "Watch out, they are around here somewhere."

Before the guards could respond, James ordered, "Drop your weapons."

James was on the passenger side of the car, crouched down by the hood. Sam stepped close to the guards with his revolver drawn, and echoed James' order, "Drop your weapons."

Before Sam finished speaking, the guard closest to him launched a roundhouse kick, knocking Sam's gun away. Like lightning, the guard had Sam in his grasp with a gun pointed at his temple.

"I think it's a better idea if you drop your weapon," the guard said to James. "Or shall I put a bullet in your friend's head."

Sam cringed as James hesitated.

"You have five more seconds," the guard said.

James stood, held up his hands, and dropped the gun.

"Good boy. Now walk to the front of the car," the guard said as he shoved Sam in that direction. "Both of you, hands up with your chests on the hood."

Hopelessness weighed Sam down as he stretched out on the hood.

"I have these guys, Gary. Go ahead and untie Mr. Donegan."

"It's about time," Dirk said.

Just as Gary holstered his gun, Wingston landed on the top of the car. Gary noticed the bird and said, "That's odd. What's a bird doing out this time of night?"

While he was still speaking, Sam heard the high-pitched trill of a raptor. Then he heard the guard standing over them scream. The guard dropped his gun and grabbed at his eyes. Sam realized what was going on before James did and ran toward Gary, who was reaching for his gun. Wingston hit Gary in the eye just before Sam got there. As Gary reached for his eye with one hand and swatted at Wingston with the other, Sam grabbed his gun.

"On the ground," Sam ordered. He glanced over to see James tackling the other guard. Sam blinked and shielded his eyes when the deck light came on and David stepped out.

"What's going on out here?" David asked.

Sam spotted the gun he had dropped and grabbed it. He saw the other guard's gun gleaming in the light and ran to pick it up. He tucked one of the pistols in his waistband, aimed one at Gary and the other at the guard James had pinned to the ground.

"We had uninvited company," he finally explained to David.

James carefully got up, watching for any movement from the guard on the ground. He found his revolver and said, "What in the world!"

"Hey, look at the bird on top of the car," David said. "I have never seen one of those."

Sam moved to keep his gun trained on Gary while James covered the other guard. He looked over the rusty colored bird with blueish gray on its head and wings. It was about the size of a dove and had two vertical black stripes near its eye. "That's a pretty bird," Sam said. "I wonder what it is."

"It's an American kestrel," James said. "But why did it attack the guard?"

"I bet I know what's going on," David said. "I think you have just acquired a bird friend, James."

Wingston landed next to the kestrel, and Canto followed close behind. Sam said, "Yep, that's what it looks like."

"Well, cool!" James said. "Thank you, my friend."

"You do realize you are in your underwear," Sam pointed out to David.

"I do, and it's cold out here! If this party gets much bigger, we're going to run out of rope," David said and ducked back inside.

The kestrel called, and James looked down to see the guard getting to his knees. "I don't think so," he said, and the guard dropped back to the ground. "Go get the rope," James directed Sam.

"It's still in the car," Sam said and opened the back to pull it out.

"You'll never get away with this," Dirk said.

"Shut up, Dirk. I would hate to have to kill someone tonight," James barked. "Lie back down."

David came out in sweats, "What can I do to help?"

"Help Sam keep a gun trained on these guys while I get them tied up. If Dirk hiccups, shoot him."

James tied the hands of the two guards and stood puzzling. "How are we going to get them to the bus while keeping everyone covered?"

"I guess we'll have to hogtie them and carry them," David said.

"Maybe we can get away with just hogtying Dirk," James said.

James tied Dirk's feet and left him and Gary under the eye of David while he and Sam marched the other guard to the bus.

"Watch his feet. He likes to kick," Sam said.

James marched the guard to the back seat and tied his feet. Sam stayed on the bus. James repeated the process with Gary. Then the three of them picked up Dirk and hauled him to the bus.

"Shall we put them with our other guests?" David asked. He drove the bus while James kept guard. Sam followed in the Cherokee.

As Sam drove, the stress shifted to fatigue. He yawned and tried to focus on the road and the bus ahead. "I have to stay awake. I can't let Evie be shipped out of here," he said and shook his head. "Surely nothing else will go wrong."

CHAPTER 51

The smell of coffee greeted Sam as he opened the door and stepped back into the house. "Am I hallucinating or is that really coffee?"

"It's coffee. I put some on while I was changing," David said.

"Bless you!" Sam poured three cups and sat down at the table with David and James. "Now what?"

"I wonder how long it will take them to realize they are missing so many people?" David asked.

"At least it's the middle of the night. Most of them will be sleeping," James offered.

"We need a plan," Sam said. "I think we need to get there and get everyone out before sunrise."

"That's a definite," James said. "The sooner the better. We have two 'guards,'" he said, making air quotes. "David and I could walk up like we have a message from Harrison and attack."

"What about the other two. I think I saw four guards around the pavilion," David said.

"I could try to sneak up on one of them," Sam said.

"We will need a way to break the lock off the gate," David added.

"If we attack while they were loading people to haul them off, the gate would be open," Sam said.

"I'm afraid that would be too risky. Too many people could be caught in the gunfire," James said.

"We need more details," Sam said and went for a pen and paper. "How many security guards were there? I think I saw twelve lined up around the hall." He wrote down, "Security Guards: 12."

"Then there are the four militia guards at the pavilion," David added.

"How many did we put in the car and bus?" Sam asked, having trouble keeping track in the late hour.

"We have Donegan and five of the twelve security guards on the yacht," James said.

"If that is all there are," David added.

"OK. If my math is correct, that leaves seven security guards from the yacht and four fully armed militia guards," Sam said.

"I liked it better before you did the math," David said.

"Well, we need to know what we are up against," Sam answered.

"I think we need to go for it now while it's three against four," James said. "You know, it sure would be nice if Viviana hadn't disappeared. We could use her."

"I can't imagine what happened," David said. "I hope she is OK. In the meantime, we have to keep going. Can anyone think of a reason to send one of the guards back to the yacht?"

"That's a great idea," Sam said. "But what could it be?"

"I know!" David exclaimed. "There has been a threat that someone is going to attack the yacht, and Harrison wants two of them there and two at the pavilion. We will fill in for the missing two."

"That just might work," James said.

Sam yawned and looked at his watch. "5:41," he said and rubbed his eyes with the heels of both hands.

"What time does the sun come up?" James asked.

Sam clicked on his computer a few times. "It says twilight begins at 7:04am."

"Oh man! We have less than an hour and a half before it gets light," James said. "We'd better get moving. Let's take all the pistols. Check them to make sure they are loaded."

David and James started popping pistols open and checking. Sam finally asked, "How do you do that?"

David showed him, and Sam succeeded. "All full," he said.

"Have you ever shot a pistol?" James asked.

"A few times when I was a teenager," Sam said. "Dad took me to a firing range. I did hit the target."

"That's good news," James said. "Are we ready to roll?"

"Let Operation Freedom commence," David said, standing up and taking his last sip of coffee.

* * *

It was 6:00am when Anne Solomon and Hal Anderson stepped bleary-eyed into the conference room to find Harrison pacing. Four lattes were sitting on the table.

"Good morning!" Harrison said with a grin. "Today is the day we rid ourselves of a bunch of pests. Anderson, do you have the aircraft ready?

"Yes. I found five choppers, and they will be arriving at sunrise."

"Just helicopters?"

"They are Chinooks, and it says they can carry forty-four people, but I'm sure we can squeeze fifty in. If there are about two thousand people, I figure it will take us two days to get them all moved."

"Good grief! That's too long. See if you can get some more lined up," Harrison grumped. "I want them out of here today!"

"I'll try, sir. But these are coming from a long way off. It's not like we have a stash of them sitting nearby."

"You had better quit sitting there and get at it then!"

Harrison continued pacing, and Anne took a sip of her latte, waiting. Harrison popped a couple of Tums. "Where is Dirk? He should be here by now."

"I don't know," Anne responded.

"Call him."

Anne tapped Dirk from her favorites screen. It rang six times then went to voicemail. "He's not answering."

"The man is getting lazy!" Harrison poked his head out the conference room door. "Jones, go drag Dirk Donegan out of bed," he said to the guard standing in the hall.

"Yes, sir!" Jones said.

Harrison muttered to Anne as he walked back into the room, "I always thought I could count on him."

* * *

David slowed the Cherokee to a stop, and Sam got out about a quarter of a mile from the pavilion. He watched anxiously as David drove on. "This is going to work. It has to," he said to himself.

Sam worked his way behind a tree just across from the guard on the east side of the pavilion fence. There was an eerie silence as he waited. The hacksaw he had stuck in the back of his pants to cut the chain had shifted. He repositioned it. Waiting was hard.

It seemed like hours before he saw James and David walking up to the guard at the gate. Sam could see they were talking, then James began walking toward the guard on the west side. That guard hurried over to the gate, and he saw David hand him the keys to the Cherokee.

"They must have bought it," Sam thought, a surge of hope rising for the first time that night. As soon as the two guards were in the car, James moved toward the guard at the south end. That was Sam's cue. His muscles tensed as he watched for the right moment.

Sam saw that the guard closest to him was watching James. "This is it," he thought. As quietly as he could, walking as Viviana had taught him, Sam slipped out from behind the tree. "I hope he doesn't look this way!"

Sam stepped behind the guard at the same time James arrived at the guard on the south end. Putting his gun to the guard's back, Sam said, "Don't move. Without a word, toss your weapon away." The guard did as he was told.

Sam glanced at the people in the fence. They were huddled together on the ground, most sitting with their heads lolled over in sleep. Sam looked toward James and saw that he was marching his guard toward the gate.

"Move to the gate," Sam ordered, and the guard complied. As they walked toward the gate, Sam noticed that people had begun stirring, apparently awakened by his words. As James ordered the two guards onto the ground Sam heard Evie's voice.

"Sam, I'm so glad to see you! Are you OK?"

"Other than a couple of sore fingers and a busted lip, I'm fine. We're getting you out of there."

"Thank God! Everyone is cold and miserable," Evie said.

Sam pulled the hacksaw out and attacked the chain on the gate. Chatter spread through the imprisoned crowd as he worked. The saw cut through one side of the chain link, and Sam launched into the other.

"Drop your weapons," thundered as the first gray light touched the sky.

Sam's heart seemed to stop as he slowly turned his head. Six security guards and two militia men stood with guns aimed at them. Sam held up his hands and watched as David and James tossed their weapons away. He dropped the hacksaw.

"Drop your other weapon," one of the guards directed at Sam.

Sam fished the gun out of his waistband and dropped it to the ground. A potent silence ensued. Sam's hopes were dashed, and a wave of guilt hit hard as he realized he had failed Evie. He had failed his people.

Sam looked over to see Harrison, Solomon, and Anderson walking up.

"I should have known it was you causing all of this trouble," Harrison said to Sam. "Do you mind telling me where you deposited my head of security so you and he can resume your little talk?"

"I don't mind at all," Sam said. "Right after you release these people and sail away from here.

One of the guards punched Sam in the face.

"No, no." Harrison said. "He will get worse than that. Where is Dirk and the other people you have kidnapped. Or are they dead? In which case you will get a slow painful death yourself."

"They are alive, and you can have them when you leave and call off this madness."

Harrison started to respond but was interrupted by a thunderous roar. Sam jumped and looked to the south. On top of the hill just past the fence he saw bears, all standing tall on their hind legs and growling fiercely. A chill went down his spine till he spotted a familiar figure. Viviana was standing in the middle of them with her bow drawn.

One of the militia guards took aim with his assault rifle. Sam started to call out to Viviana when an arrow hit the guard in the shoulder. The screech of a single eagle call erupted, then eagle and crow calls resounded from everywhere.

James ducked to the ground while Sam and David stood and watched in amazement. The bears charged while eagles and crows attacked. Sam looked up and saw Harrison, Anderson, and Solomon hightailing it away. He seized the opportunity to resume cutting the chain.

Within a few seconds, a bear was standing over each guard, snarling. Sam finished cutting through the chain, opened the gate, and wrapped Evie in a tight hug. "I thought we had failed," he said.

"It looks like you were wrong!"

People flowed out of the gate. Sam saw James scanning the crowd, and finally Tamara bolted into his arms. Sam and Evie walked over to David and Viviana.

"That was quite an army you put together," Sam heard David say.

"Thank you," Viviana replied. "Are you ever going to marry me?"

David grinned and said, "As soon as we can find a preacher!"

"I'm afraid Harrison got away," Sam said.

Sam watched as Viviana looked around. He followed her eyes to where Skauty appeared to be talking to Nadashée, who was perched on top of the fence. Nadashée looked over, and Viviana pointed her bow toward the yacht. Nadashée launched into flight, and Rey followed.

"We need to get busy," James said. He and David retrieved the assault rifles. James yelled, "Pick up all the guns you can find." People from the crowd grabbed the various pistols scattered on the ground near the bears, who still held their hostages.

"Now what?" David asked.

Viviana walked up to each bear, one by one, put her hands together as in prayer, and bowed. The bears looked Viviana in the eye and made their way back into the woods. Bald eagles and crows still flew everywhere.

Sam, Viviana, David, and James herded the guards together, even the one with an arrow in his shoulder, and marched them toward the yacht.

* * *

Anderson raced Harrison and Solomon toward the yacht in their car. Harrison called Captain Swanson, "We need reinforcements from the militia immediately!"

"What do you mean you need reinforcement? We're back at the frigate."

"What in blue blazes are you doing at the frigate?" Harrison barked.

"Following the order you sent last night."

"I didn't send any such order! Get back here immediately!"

"Yes, sir. But it's going to be a while since the militia are already aboard the frigate."

"Good grief, man. Hurry! They have broken out of the fence and overtaken our guards," Harrison pleaded.

Anderson parked as close to the gangplank as he could, and the three of them rushed past the lone guard and onto the yacht. They stood at the rail, and Harrison fumed, "Do either of you have any ideas?"

"I say we leave and regroup," Solomon advised.

"I have never lost a takeover battle!" Harrison yelled.

His yell was pierced by an eagle call that chilled his blood. He looked up to see Nadashée diving with Rey on her back. He froze, not believing his eyes, until the eagle's talons were about to strike.

Trying to dodge the eagle, Harrison lurched and fell over the rail. Rey brushed Solomon and Anderson back against the wall of the yacht. Harrison finally resurfaced with arms flailing. Solomon and Anderson exchanged a chuckle.

"I can't swim!" Harrison managed to croak before going under again.

Solomon looked at Anderson, then ran for the lifebuoy. Harrison resurfaced screaming, "Help!" Solomon returned just in time to toss the ring to him before he went under again.

*　*　*

Sam and crew, with the whole village following behind, marched toward the yacht. Sam pointed as he saw Solomon and Anderson dragging Harrison toward the shore. They all laughed.

"It looks like you're all washed up," Sam said as they approached. Harrison crawled on shore and stood dripping. Sam couldn't decipher the look on his face. It was some mixture of gratitude and rage. The lone guard had already dropped his weapon and had his hands up before anyone mentioned it.

"I need about ten people to help me search the yacht for weapons," James said. Ample volunteers rushed the yacht and rummaged through every closet and drawer. Rey landed on the top of the yacht and chortled, seeming to mock Harrison.

"What about this guy," Tamara asked pointing to the man with an arrow in his shoulder.

"I'll take care of him," Dr. Woods said, stepping up. "Are there medical supplies on the yacht?" he directed toward the guard still standing with his arms raised.

"Yes," the guard replied.

"Jeffery, do you have a gun?" James called out.

"Of course," Jeffery said and stepped forward.

James turned toward the guard, "Show Dr. Woods the medical supplies. Jeffery, if this guy even looks the wrong way, shoot him."

"Gladly," Jeffery said.

"Where are the police officers?" Sam called. Four men stepped forward. "Holmes Harrison, you are under arrest for murder, kidnapping, torturing an American citizen, and attempted genocide," Sam said.

Harrison glared at Sam, "You will never get away with this."

"I'm sure you're right. I'm sure your president will deliver a pardon or someone in high places will have you released before the trial. But in the meantime, you will be in jail until you send all of your cronies home. Take him to the jail," Sam said.

Tamara whispered in Sam's ear, "He has diplomatic immunity. The officers could be prosecuted if they take him to jail."

Sam saw Harrison grin. "You should listen to your lawyer," he said.

"You don't have diplomatic immunity from me," Sam said. "Take him on board."

David aimed an assault rifle at Harrison, "You heard what he said."

They marched Harrison onto the yacht and sat him at the foot of his conference table.

"Here's the plan," Sam said. "We're going to sail your yacht out to the middle of the sound and blow a hole in it. With you onboard, of course."

"You wouldn't dare," Harrison said.

"I noticed you can't swim," Sam replied. "That would be a terrifying way to die." Sam paused for a moment. "James, have Grandpa get someone to follow us out with explosives. I don't think this guy deserves to breathe air much longer."

James left the room.

"OK. OK. What do you want?" Harrison said.

"What I really want is to watch you and your yacht sink to the bottom of the sound," Sam said. "In fact, I think we'll do it right where you killed my dad."

Sam was pleased to see fear register on Harrison's face.

"No! No! I'll do anything. Just tell me!" Harrison pleaded.

Sam's rage surged at this man for killing his dad and for all the problems he had caused. It scared him that he really wanted to watch Harrison drown. He walked out of the room to compose himself.

"I can't really do this. I can't believe I want to," Sam said.

Evie came up beside him and hugged him. "Sam, you will have to let the rage go. It will destroy you."

"I know. You are right." He paused and took three deep breaths. "OK, I'm ready."

Sam walked back into the conference room. "The ship is ready. We'll be underway in about five minutes."

"Please don't do this," Harrison begged. I'll call off the compound. I'll never bother your people again."

Hearing Harrison say, "Your people," created an earthquake in Sam's heart. "My people," he thought. "Yes, these are my people. This is where I am meant to be." Sam felt a tear start to rise but squelched it.

"I realize that you are totally untrustworthy, but we will agree to that. Pull out your phone and instruct the cargo ship to haul the frigate to a shipyard for repairs. We will deliver your other people and escort you out of here. And you will never return," Sam said.

Harrison pulled out the phone and made the call. Sam could hear obscenities blasting from Harrison's phone. "We just started loading the militia back aboard," Swanson finally said.

"I know, but plans have changed. Secure the frigate and begin towing," Harrison said.

"It will take us forever to tow that thing!"

"I suggest you get started then," Harrison said and hung up.

CHAPTER 52

Sam and Evie stood on the bow with arms around each other and watched until Harrison's yacht disappeared over the horizon. It was a beautiful crisp fall morning. The wind was chilly blowing over the boat. Sam took in a deep breath.

"I have missed the smell of the sea," he said.

Evie hugged him to her, "I'm glad to see that yacht gone."

Sam smiled as energy surged through his veins. "We did it. We actually did it! Harrison is gone!" Sam gave Evie a hug and a big kiss. He turned and saw David and Viviana locked in an embrace. Next to them, James and Tamara were hugging and grinning.

Sam hugged Evie one more time and hustled over to David, "I think this deserves a hive five!" High-fiving David and Viviana, he continued on to James and Tamara.

"We make a cracker jack team!" Sam said as joy and gratitude washed over him like a wave. Everyone high fived and hugged all around celebrating their victory. Sam stood back and savored the moment.

By the time Jeffery Troutman pulled the boat up to the pier, Tamara and James had fallen asleep leaning on each other. Sam yawned, and Evie said, "I'm tired, too."

Sam poked James, "We need to get the boat tied up."

With the boat secured, they walked the pier toward the parking lot. Sam felt the force of the long, sleepless night all the way to his bones. Evie took his arm and said, "I think a nap is in order when we get back to the house."

"The house. How are we going to get back to the house?" Sam asked.

"I have my car, but it only holds five squeezed together," Tamara said.

"I could ride in the trunk," David offered.

"Nonsense," Jeffery said. "I can take some of you in my truck."

"Thanks for the ride," Sam said as he and Evie slid out of Jeffery's truck. They walked into the house to find Skauty on the phone.

"That's right. A week from Saturday at the high school gym. We look forward to seeing you and your people," Skauty said and hung up.

"You look too chipper," Sam said noticing the gleam in Skauty's eyes and the smile on his face.

"It is time to celebrate!" Skauty said. "I have called a potlatch for a week from Saturday to celebrate our victory over Harrison and his compound. I also understand that there is a wedding that needs to happen. If the parties are agreeable, that would be the perfect time."

Viviana clapped her hands together, "That would be wonderful! Of course, if that's OK with you, David." David just grinned.

"A potlatch! That's huge, Grandpa," Sam said.

"This is a huge occasion." Skauty replied. "We were almost relocated to a desolate place with nothing, just like the Cherokees of old. But thanks to you six, we are saved. How else can we celebrate but with a potlatch?"

"What's a potlatch?' David asked.

"It's a sacred gathering of the clans in the area for special occasions," Skauty explained. "And this is definitely a special occasion."

"I've heard you talk about them, but I have never been to one," Sam said as he noticed James grab Tamara by the hand and drag her outside. "I wonder what that was about"

Evie just grinned.

"Do you know something I don't?" Sam asked.

"Probably," Evie said.

Sam looked at Evie and tried to puzzle out what she might know.

"I'm tired," Skauty announced. "But I don't fancy going back to the house yet. You don't mind if I nap here, do you Sandra?"

"Of course not. Help yourself. Don't you want some breakfast first?"

"No, thanks. I had one of your protein bars."

As Skauty started heading toward the den, the door burst open. "She said, 'Yes!'" James said with a grin.

Sam looked at Evie, "You knew that was going to happen."

"Of course," she said.

"Congratulations!" Sam said and everyone echoed the sentiment.

"Can we make that two weddings at the potlatch?" Skauty asked.

"I hope so!" James said.

"That's terribly fast," Tamara said. "But I would hate to miss the opportunity to have my wedding during a potlatch. Let's do it!"

* * *

Dawn brought a pink mantle to the mountains Saturday morning as Evie slipped out of bed to help Viviana get ready for her wedding day. Viviana had insisted on a simple white dress. When Evie got her hair fixed and stood back to take a look, she understood why. Viviana's black hair waved and flowed down the dress. Her raven eyes and brown skin made the dress come alive. For the last touch, Evie tied one of Rey's feathers into Viviana's hair. She was simply gorgeous.

With the wedding set for ten that morning, the house was a bustle of activity. David, Sam, and James sported matching blue suits. Sam was going to be David's best man, and Skauty would fill that post for James after he walked Viviana down the aisle.

Sam looked David over with approval, "I think you'll do. Now I need to go pick up Grandpa."

Skauty also sported a matching blue suit. "Would you mind carrying those?" Skauty asked, nodding toward the clan hat and blanket sitting on the table. Sam felt a deep reverence as he picked up the two items.

"It must give you a tremendous sense of responsibility to wear these," Sam said.

"Yes, it does," Skauty answered. "It is also very humbling to put them on. You realize that you carry the traditions of a people that have lived here for over ten thousand years. I feel small when I have them on. But I also feel our ancestors helping to hold me up."

"Wow. I never thought of it that way."

"It is like standing on top of a mountain and realizing it is the lives of all who came before underneath you," Skauty said.

Sam pictured the image his grandfather had just spoken and was touched.

"Let's go. We don't want to miss the weddings," Skauty said.

A large crowd had gathered by the water. Most of the village and several people from other clans had come to celebrate the occasion. Sam was excited as he took his position beside David close to the water. He was warmed with love as he watched Evie walk in beside Tamara's maid of honor. Viviana and Tamara came next and took their places beside David and James.

Pastor Watson began the service. She startled and paused when Rey, Wingston, Azul, Canto, and the kestrel landed on their friends' shoulders. Then Nadashée landed right beside Pastor Watson She looked puzzled and started to shoo her away.

Sam whispered, "It's OK. These are our friends." Pastor Watson picked up where she left off, but Sam noticed she kept glancing at the birds. The wedding concluded with two exuberant kisses.

The two wedding couples positioned themselves to greet the crowd and receive congratulations. Rey settled beside Viviana and Canto landed on David's shoulder. Viviana noticed the kestrel standing next to James. "Hey, James! Who is your new friend?" she called across the crowd.

Tamara looked down, "Oh, he's beautiful! Is he a friend of yours?"

"It appears so," James said. "He saved our lives last night."

"You will have to name him," Viviana said.

After a few handshakes and hugs, James called out, "How about Kat? Kat the kestrel."

Sam was standing nearby and heard. He looked at James with a flood of emotions. James apparently noticed Sam's reaction and said, "I'm sorry. If that is hurtful I will change it. I just thought it was fitting since they both played such a critical role in this."

"No, I think it's perfect," Sam said, touched. "Dad would be happy to have a bird named after him. Especially a beauty like this."

People made their way to the high school. The expected crowd was so large that Skauty and the council had arranged to have the potlatch at the football field. People filled the bleachers and spilled out onto the field. The council had arranged two tables near the PA system. One was for the heroes to honor them and celebrating the two weddings. The other table held the visiting clan leaders and their families.

When the crowd finally finished assembling, Skauty wrapped the clan blanket around his shoulders, donned the hat, and stepped up to the microphone. "My fellow Tlingit, thank you so much for taking your time to come and celebrate with us today. I am honored by your presence. Today is worthy of a potlach in so many ways.

"First, I want to honor the memory of my son, Katlian Hanson. He gave his life to help prevent the removal of this entire clan. He was a good man and a great son. I will miss him terribly. Please join me in a moment of silence as we remember him."

Sam's emotions surged. Viviana leaned over, "Do you remember asking me what to do next when you first came to my cave?"

"Yeah, you said that now we learn how to live."

"I think you have achieved that," Viviana said.

After a pause, Skauty went on, "Secondly, I want to celebrate with our two wedding couples. I don't believe I have ever seen two weddings happen at one time before. David and Viviana, Tamara and

James, we wish you love as deep as the ocean and joy as wide as the sky every day of your future."

Skauty waited for the applause to die down and continued, "Finally, we gather to celebrate good triumphing over greed, the force of right sending wrong running, and the tenacity of the Tlingit people in the face of termination."

Applause erupted and carried for a long time. Then Skauty continued, "I want to thank every person in this village. You held firm in the face of danger, stood together with resolve rather than taking the easy way out, and proved that a united people can withstand tyranny."

This time the applause was louder and longer than before. When it calmed down, Skauty went on, "There are seven people who went to great lengths and placed themselves in great peril to prevent a modern-day Trail of Tears. We have already mentioned my son Kat, who gave his all. I also want to recognize the six people sitting at the table to my left. Sam and Evie Hanson, David and Viviana, will it be McCutcheon now?"

Viviana nodded.

"And James and Tamara... James, I'm afraid I have forgotten your last name." The crowd laughed. "How will you and Tamara be called?"

"Carson-Woods," Tamara called out.

"These six people literally risked their lives to bring us to where we are today. I know Sam, James, and Viviana have the wounds to prove it."

The crowd burst into a standing ovation that went on and on. Finally, Skauty lifted his hands to quieten them. The roar hushed, but people remained on their feet.

"You six people have done more for this clan than we can ever adequately repay. Without you, we would be sitting in a wilderness right now, trying to figure out how to survive." Applause exploded again.

"During a potlatch it is customary to give lavish gifts. The gifts I would like to give today are beyond monetary. One of the greatest honors we can bestow upon a person is to adopt them into our clan."

The crowd erupted again. "I propose that we begin the process to adopt Viviana, David, and James into our clan." More applause.

"They have certainly earned the honor. Tamara has always been with us. She eagerly offered her services to create a ruse that freed me from Harrison's clutches. We are all grateful to you, but I am grateful in a personal way. I was glad to get off that boat!"

A mixture of laughter, cheers, and applause flooded the field. "As you know, Evie was adopted when she married Sam. She is already a part of us, so we extend our gratitude to this precious sister." Skauty waited for the crowd to quieten.

"Finally, there is my grandson, Sam. As you can see, I am getting old. I had a heart attack a few months ago and forgot James' last name today. The last gift I would like to bestow is the greatest. I would like to request that Sam Hanson be installed as the new chief of the Sitka clan."

The roar from the crowd was almost deafening, but Sam barely heard it. Everything seemed in slow motion. Sam knew he no longer wanted to get away from Sitka. He was touched by the special gift his grandfather was offering. Tears began to flow down his cheek as he looked around at the crowd. "These are my people," he thought

Evie gave him a big hug, "You will make a great chief!" His other friends at the table hugged him and clapped him on the back in congratulations.

A wave of fear washed over Sam. "I don't know if I can do this job," he said.

Evie squeezed his hand, "Oh yes you can. I will be there to help." Sam grabbed her in a bear hug. "I love you so much." Wingston landed on his shoulder as if to congratulate him, too.

Skauty waved his arms to quieten the crowd. "Sam, would you come up here, please." Sam walked to the podium and hugged Skauty tightly.

Skauty stepped up to the microphone, "Sam has proven his mettle in the way he orchestrated the overthrow of Harrison's despicable compound. Some of you may not know, but he, Evie, David, and Viviana also exposed the nuclear waste dump created by

MC2 that threatened the whole region. I think we will be in good hands with Sam as our chief!"

As the applause thundered, Skauty removed the ceremonial blanket from his shoulders and wrapped it around Sam. Then he placed the hat on his head. The loud applause muffled in Sam's ears as he felt the weight of the blanket. He touched the coarse fabric and sensed the spirits of generations of chiefs who had worn it. The gravity of the moment nearly overwhelmed him. Insignificance and empowerment mingled in his heart.

Suddenly Sam realized that Skauty was beckoning him to the microphone. He drew back from deep within himself and walked forward. "I don't know what to say," he whispered to Skauty.

"Anything will do," Skauty encouraged.

Wingston landed on the podium as Sam stepped up to it. Sam looked Wingston in the eye, and the words he needed came to him. "Thank you. Thank you," Sam said, and the crowd finally hushed.

"In his typical fashion, Grandpa failed to mention that without him we never could have succeeded in sending Harrison packing."

Sam was going to say, "Let's give him a hand," but he didn't get the chance. The loudest, most sustained ovation of the day nearly deafened him. As the crowd applauded, it dawned on Sam just how much the people loved and respected his granddad.

Sam noticed Skauty was standing there looking uncomfortable. He went over and hugged him again. Sam finally went over and got the crowd quiet enough to speak. "Skauty Hanson has been our chief for over thirty years. He has helped us stay true to our Tlingit heritage while dealing with the changes that have threatened us over that time. I know I can never fill his shoes. But I will do the best I can and will call on him for advice every day."

Sam waited for the applause to die down. "You may have wondered about the birds you see hanging around with us. As you see, Wingston, this little tufted titmouse, is right here with me at the podium. Each bird has somehow, to put it in Viviana's words, picked one of us to befriend and help. If you were at the pavilion, then you know that we would be dead were it not for the birds' intervention."

Sam had to wait again on the applause. "Then, we also owe a big thank you the army of bears. By the way Viviana, how did you get those bears to do that?"

The crowd laughed and clapped. "Finally I want to thank all of you for your tenacity in resisting Harrison. You were the ones who foiled his plans." Sam waited again.

"I have wandered far from Sitka and if the truth be known, always thought that I wanted to stay away from here. But now my heart says, 'It's good to be home.'"

A Note from the Author

Thank you so much for letting me share this story with you. Someone commented that the Dark Wings stories have a touch of magical realism in the birds. In a sense that is true, but the birds are perfectly capable of doing everything they do in the stories. They usually don't, but they could. Perhaps the real magic is that Viviana and the others were able to discern that the birds wanted to help. Sometimes I wonder what the possibilities could be if we befriended the natural world rather than trying to conquer it.

Rey wanted me to remind you that in the bible, one symbol of the Holy Spirit is a bird.

I would be grateful if you would take the time to leave a review on the site from which you purchased the book and/or Goodreads. Reviews are important for helping other people decide if the Dark Wings books are for them.

Thanks again,
Dwain